PRAISE FOR JENNIFER FULTON'S NOVELS

Katherine V. Forrest, Author of *Curious Wine* and the *Kate Delafield* mystery series.

"The name Jennifer Fulton on any novel is an ironclad guarantee of a great read. She is one of our most entertaining and richly rewarding writers."

Lambda Book Report

"Well...let's be honest, would this novel keep our interest, stimulate our...minds, and prompt us to turn the pages into the wee hours of the night if the characters played by the rules? Fulton's very readable book is... fun and well worth your time."

Bay Area Reporter

"The writing is outstanding... each woman has a secret, or several, and as we learn about them, we learn a great deal about ourselves as well. Fulton creates characters that live on in the memory and in the heart."

Midwest Book Review

"*A Guarded Heart* is a story with several themes, and it is a novel which can be interpreted on several levels. However, it is, first and foremost, an excellent example of the romance genre. Substantial and realistic characters with problematic situations create an intense and dramatic story. Fluid and believable dialogue strengthens the development of the characterization. Obstacles, both tangible and intangible, provide the necessary impetus for the characters to change, grow, and hopefully succeed. As important as the setting is in a novel, it isn't the lush tropical paradise surrounding Lauren and Pat that enthralls and satisfies the reader. It is the wondrous metamorphosis each woman experiences which this reader found often poignant and heartbreaking, but more importantly, emphatically and profoundly reaffirming."

ALSO BY JENNIFER FULTON

Moon Island Series
Passion Bay
Saving Grace
The Sacred Shore
A Guarded Heart

Other Fiction
True Love
Greener Than Grass

MYSTERIES, WRITING AS ROSE BEECHAM
Introducing Amanda Valentine
Second Guess
Fair Play
Grave Silence

Dark Dreamer

(Book I in the Heartstoppers Series)

Jennifer Fulton

Yellow Rose Books

Nederland, Texas

ISBN 1-932300-46-5

First Printing 2005

9 8 7 6 5 4 3 2 1

Cover concept and cover art by Jennifer Fulton
Cover design by Donna Pawlowski

Published by:

Yellow Rose Books
PMB 210, 8691 9th Avenue
Port Arthur, Texas 77642-8025

Find us on the World Wide Web at
http://www.regalcrest.biz

Printed in the United States of America

Acknowledgments

My family and friends, as always, have given me love and encouragement. Fel, Jan, Sue and Connie provided intelligent reading and comments, and lavished undeserved praise on me. Lori L. Lake is, as always, a supportive editor and good friend.

For F.G.C. from Your Girl

Chapter
One

"Last night I dreamed of Iris," Phoebe said. "I promised her I
would come."
Cara looked up from the morning paper. "Shall I call our friend?"
Phoebe's face fell into shadow. "Perhaps it was my imagination."
Cara took her twin's hand. "You say that every time."

WHERE TWO PATHS crossed beneath the low silvery
boughs of a huge birch tree, a woman lay on a quilt of brown and
yellow leaves. Her hands were roped behind her back. Twigs and
earth matted her honey-colored hair.

She lifted her head as Phoebe knelt. "You found me. I knew
you would."

Phoebe unfastened the rope and cradled her. Hot tears
spilled down her cheeks. "I'm so sorry. I tried to come sooner."

"It's okay. You're here now." The woman tried to smile, but
her face was contorted with bruises.

"Who did this to you?" Phoebe asked urgently.

"I don't know his name." Her head grew heavy on Phoebe's
shoulder. "I'm so tired."

"No. Wait!" Phoebe shook her.

"Tell my folks I love them." She closed her eyes.

"Iris!" Phoebe begged.

The body in her arms felt like lead. She sank down on the
leaves next to it and sobbed uncontrollably. The smell of earth
and decay invaded her nostrils. A hand touched her shoulder.

"Phoebe?" Cara's voice. "Sweetheart?"

Phoebe rolled over, blinking into the light. Her twin cupped
a cool hand to her cheek. "Is this the place?"

Phoebe nodded. Exhaustion drained the strength from her
limbs. Her legs wobbled as Cara helped her up.

Standing a few yards from them, in suit and tie as always,
Special Agent Vernell Jefferson put his cell phone away. He

looked awkward. Men like him folded their arms when their instinct was to reach out.

"Is she okay?" he asked Cara, as if Phoebe couldn't speak for herself. That was nothing unusual. Most of the world preferred talking to Cara.

The FBI agent drew a few steps closer, his keen brown eyes assessing the leafy site. A long rectangular mound of earth corrupted the contours of the forest floor. Phoebe shivered. It was not the first time she had lain on someone's shallow grave.

Cara removed some tissues from her coat pocket and placed them in Phoebe's hand. "We should get going," she said.

They walked back to the car in silence. Overhead, the sun was trying to come out. Until it did, the day would remain damp, the wind weak but biting. Within a couple of months this area would be knee deep in snow. It was lucky they had found Iris before winter set in.

"We really appreciate this," Vernell said, opening the passenger door for Phoebe.

She met his eyes and watched his pupils betray him. Vernell was much more excited than his demeanor suggested. In his line of work, the dead spoke through their physical remains. Clearly he was impatient to decipher those of Iris.

"I have a message from her," Phoebe said.

His face quickened. "About him?"

"I'm sorry." She dispelled his hopes. "She just wants someone to tell her folks she loves them."

Vernell did a good job of masking his disappointment. "I'll take care of it." His eyes moved to Cara. "If you want to wait a while, I can have someone drive you to the airport."

"No. You folks have work to do." Cara glanced up the forest road north. "And what do you know? Here come the troops."

Phoebe followed the direction of her sister's gaze. A convoy of police vehicles was closing on them, lights flashing. Hastily she retreated into the car. Law enforcement didn't know she existed. That was part of her deal with the FBI.

Vernell walked Cara to the driver's side and waited for her to get situated. "Don't forget what we talked about," he said.

"I'll be in touch." Cara started the motor.

Vernell thanked them again, then stepped back and slapped the car roof as if it were a horse's rump. Phoebe watched him in the side mirror as they accelerated away. He waved briefly before turning to face the approaching patrol cars. She wondered how he was going to explain chancing upon Iris Meicklejohn's body miles from civilization, ten minutes hike into a dense forest near Maidstone Lake in Vermont. Or did FBI men capitalize on their mystique at times like this? Vernell said local police tended to be in awe of the Bureau.

"What did he mean?" she asked Cara. "What shouldn't you forget?"

"Routine stuff. Nothing you need to worry about."

Phoebe knew she should protest. It wasn't fair that Cara always took responsibility for the practicalities. But they had been though this a hundred times. Cara said they were identical twins, not clones. There was no reason for Phoebe to struggle over things her sister could manage easily, like computers and talking to strangers.

It was Cara who had made their deal with the FBI. Phoebe would never have had the nerve to claim she was a psychic, let alone expect to be hired for her services. Besides, she wasn't psychic. She didn't read minds or look into the future. She didn't concentrate on people's clothing and get images—not often, anyway. She dreamed, that was all.

It hadn't always been that way. Before the accident, she'd had the same garbled dreams as everyone else. But head injuries and several months in a coma had changed everything. She'd returned to consciousness convinced that a woman called Samantha needed to talk with her and that she was waiting near a willow tree north of Liberty in the Catskills. Cara had indulged her and they drove to a spot on Route 47, then hiked for half an hour until Phoebe heard Samantha's voice. A few yards off the track they found clothing and a body.

Cara phoned 911 saying they were hikers who had stumbled on human remains. The whole experience had been straightforward, even rewarding. They gave statements to the authorities and received praise and gratitude. It turned out the local police had suspected Samantha Lewis's boyfriend of killing her. Finding the body led to his conviction. It was Cara who testifed in court. The prosecutor said she was better on the stand than Phoebe, who spoke too softly and came across as kind of..."dreamy" was the word he'd used. Phoebe knew he really meant "flaky," which was something no one would ever accuse Cara of being.

When she had her second dream, nobody connected the two discoveries—they were in different states. Yet again, she and Cara were hikers who had found a body.

Then came the Sally Jorgensen kidnapping. The case was all over the television. A prominent Philadelphia judge, Sally had vanished from her home and her kidnapper demanded the release of a prisoner in exchange for her life. By then Phoebe had already seen Sally in a dream and knew where her body was.

This time, since the location was in the heart of the city, they could not pose as hikers. So Cara phoned the FBI and left a tip, declining to give her name. To Phoebe's surprise and dismay, Vernell Jefferson turned up on their doorstep a few days later.

The African American agent had traced their call and connected the dots. He could accept that two grisly discoveries might be a creepy coincidence, but three? It looked suspiciously like they had information not known to the authorities. After ruling them out as suspects, he had asked point blank which one of them was the psychic. They'd been working with him ever since.

At first, the arrangement was unofficial. The FBI does not employ psychics, and according to Vernell, most people who claimed to have such powers were opportunists and attention-seekers. Only a few individuals were the real thing and, of these, Phoebe was in a league of her own. Her complete anonymity was a condition of their agreement.

She had not asked for money, but after she'd led Vernell to several bodies, Cara arranged a meeting with him and his masters, and the FBI hired Phoebe officially. Awarded the phony title of Consultant Forensic Botanist, she now earned fees that made it unnecessary for her to hold down her 9 to 5 admin job. Vernell said he wanted her free to travel anywhere, any time. Cara said Phoebe was his ticket to the top.

Iris Meicklejohn had disappeared four weeks ago. It was not Vernell's case, but it would be now. On their way to Vermont, he said Iris might be the latest victim of a serial killer now on the radar. Phoebe wished she'd been able to tell him something that would help solve the case. But her dead visitors seldom wanted to discuss their killers. They were more interested in sending messages to loved ones. That's why they wanted their remains found. So the people who grieved for them could have closure. Once they'd attained this, they no longer wanted to talk.

Maybe she would try and reach Iris again. If she concentrated on her late at night, perhaps Iris would visit. Or, if there were other women killed by the same monster, maybe one of them would invade her sleep. Phoebe wished she had some control over the process. She had questions of her own. For a start, it would be nice to know if her visitors were in heaven. And, if they were, was Jesus really God's son who died to save us all, or just a guy far too liberal for his times? Also, could anyone explain why, if God was all powerful, he stood by while good people suffered hideous fates?

ROWE DEVLIN DID not believe in ghosts. She'd said as much to the realtor standing in front of her. Not that it made any difference. Bunny Haskell ran busy fingers through her diligently corkscrewed platinum hair and continued her pitch.

"This is the ballroom." She flung open two wide decorative doors. "They say the daughter of the family can still be heard waltzing here in the dead of night." Coyly, she arched her over-plucked eyebrows. "Right up your alley, I'm sure."

The room they entered was long and paneled in black oak. Ornately carved trim decorated a high plaster ceiling. At the far end, latticed windows and French doors faced onto vast front lawns and a wide terrace. Rowe could imagine a happy throng spilling from the room on a long summers' eve, the tinkle of champagne flutes, laughter echoing into the night. Right now, drifts of red and yellow leaves swirled around the wrought iron balustrades, serving notice of the winter to come. And it looked like Dark Harbor Cottage hadn't seen a glittering party in years.

Rowe crossed the creaky hardwood floor and stood before the windows, picturing how it would be to walk her dogs in this corner of Maine. They wouldn't know what to do with themselves, having spent their entire lives in a Manhattan apartment. She could see them now, careening across the huge meadow that extended from the cottage to the woods at the boundary of the property. This remote place was as picturesque as a scene from a jigsaw puzzle. Standing sentinel on either side of a long driveway, hundred-year-old oak trees shimmered in their bronze foliage. To the east, a stand of birches glowed bright yellow against balsam and spruces, undaunted by the late October winds. Beyond these woods lay the ocean, serene and winter blue beneath a mackerel sky.

"Secluded enough for you?" Bunny enquired with the breathless confidence of an agent who could smell a sale.

"It needs some work," Rowe said, trying not to sound like she would be willing to pay full price. "The kitchen's in terrible shape."

Bunny waved a hand. "It's a Victorian. You'd never get a fully restored property in this area for what this seller is asking."

"I'm amazed it hasn't sold sooner. Is there something I should know?"

Bunny laughed that off breezily. "What can I tell you? The market's been slow. I've only shown the place to a few families and they didn't want to deal with the renovations."

Rowe thought about the turret room upstairs with its astonishing views of Penobscot Bay. It was the perfect place to write. "Tell me about the neighbors."

Bunny consulted her clipboard. "Well, you're on six acres, so they're not going to bother you. To the north, there's a cottage owned by a family from New York. It's closed up for most of the year — they're only here for a few weeks each summer. And over there is a Shingle Style house." She pointed vaguely past the birches. "I believe two sisters live there. They keep to themselves."

Rowe pictured a pair of maiden aunts in their seventies stitching quilts on their front verandah. Who could ask for more? "Sounds ideal."

"I knew you were going to love the place!" Bunny ushered her back into the hall. "Want to see upstairs again?"

"Sure. Why not?"

From the bottom of the grand cherry wood staircase, Rowe stared up, imagining how spectacular the entrance vestibule would look with the woodwork fully restored and the curved stained-glass windows sparkling clean, shafts of tinted light beaming down. She wouldn't be able to do everything at once. She didn't have unlimited money. But she could start work on the entrance and stairs right away.

The second floor needed improvements but was not in bad shape. There were six bedrooms, one of which had been converted in recent times to a master with its own half-decent bathroom. Above this, up a narrow spiral staircase, was the airy turret room Rowe had earmarked for writing. She climbed the steep wooden steps to this retreat and crossed to its grimy bowed windows.

The view was surreal, the bay a netherworld that rose from the mists at dawn and glowed like a jewel as its gossamer cloak dissolved in the sunlight. Countless islands studded the seductive waters, their rocky shores populated by black guillemots and puffins. Rowe had taken a windjammer tour of Penobscot Bay a few months earlier when she'd first thought about relocating, and had fallen under its legendary spell. The bird life amazed her. Circling squadrons of gulls and razorbills tracked the lobstermen and schooners across the chill waters. Ospreys had made a comeback in recent years, even nesting occasionally on the roofs of homes in this area.

The turret room opened onto a widow's walk that ran along the roofline. Rowe could see herself pacing its length on a tranquil summers' day, the extraordinary seascape shifting at her feet. This place was light years away from Manhattan. In other words, perfect.

Bunny chattered on about climbing values for the waterfront properties of Islesboro, about the sought-after position this one enjoyed with its cove frontage and privacy, its proximity to Camden, and the easy drive to Portland airport. All that, and a Carriage House. Rowe listened with only half an ear. She felt remarkably contented in this room perched dizzily atop the cottage. Of all the real estate she'd viewed in the past few months, this was the home that instilled a sense of belonging, and more importantly, the feeling that she could write within its walls.

"Let's talk price," she said.

"WE HAVE NEW neighbors. Make that 'neighbor' singular." Cara dropped her hat and gloves on the kitchen counter along with a couple of bags full of groceries. The pervasive aroma of Chinese food greeted her, and yet again she gave thanks that her sister loved to cook, otherwise they'd be living on Marie Callender frozen entrees. "I spoke with the movers," she continued. "You'll never guess who it is."

Phoebe glanced up from her wok. "Someone famous?"

"Rowe Devlin, the author."

"The guy who writes those horror books?" Phoebe looked mildly dismayed.

"Actually, it's a woman."

"A woman writes that stuff? I had no idea. She must be weird."

"They're fiction," Cara said. "She's probably really normal."

"Well, I can talk." Adopting a singsong tone, Phoebe proclaimed, "Hi, I'm Phoebe Temple. I see dead people."

Cara laughed at this parody, relieved that Phoebe's sense of humor was back. Her sister was always in the doldrums for a few weeks after a Dream. "Maybe stick to the forensic botanist handle," she suggested.

"One of these days someone is going to ask me about plant spores or pollen signatures."

"And you'll tell them palynology is a science so riveting you could talk about it for hours. They'll change the subject."

"I'm counting on it." Phoebe slid their stir-fry onto a serving plate and carried it to the kitchen table. Her cheeks were flushed from the heat of the wok, and she pushed her fine ebony curls away from her face as she sat down. "Do you have to go to L.A. next week?"

"Put it this way." Cara picked up her chopsticks. "If I don't, they're not going to hire me again."

Phoebe's straight dark eyebrows drew together in consternation. "Did you stay home the past two weeks because of me?"

Cara avoided her sister's moody gray eyes. "I had things to do."

"You and Vernell are up to something. What is it?" Phoebe slid the soy sauce across the table before Cara could ask for it.

Cara chewed slowly on a piece of broccoli and considered several ways she could respond. Opting for the direct approach, she said, "He wants you to work more proactively."

"What does that mean?"

"For a start, he's wondering if there's some way you could invite the process intentionally. You know, instead of waiting for the dreams to come along."

Phoebe looked alarmed. "How would I do that? I can't control what happens when I'm asleep."

Carefully, Cara said, "Vernell thinks it might be a good idea for you to spend some time at Quantico in Virginia." She steeled herself for the inevitable. Her sister wasn't going to like this idea one little bit.

"The place where Jodie Foster trained in *Silence of the Lambs*?" Phoebe's low, soft voice sounded strained.

"Yes, training is part of what they do there." Cara tried to sound reassuring as well as enthusiastic. "They also have a big forensic science research unit and you'd be working with profilers and people like that."

"They're going to think I'm a nut."

"No, they're not. Vernell says everyone is hanging out to meet you." Hearing a small, horrified gasp, she added hastily, "Everyone who knows, that is — just a handful of people really. They even have a code name for you."

Phoebe calmed down a little, releasing her chopsticks from a death grip. "Like a spy name?" She seemed slightly tickled. "What is it?"

"Golden."

Phoebe gave this some thought. "Is that a joke name?"

"No. Nothing like that," Cara hastily assured. Phoebe was hyper-sensitive about what she termed her membership of Crazies Unlimited. "Vernell says it's because you're what they always dreamed of. Back in the 1980s the CIA tried to create people like you to spy on the Russians. They had a secret training program called Star Gate."

"Did it work?"

"I don't know." Cara dripped extra soy sauce over her meal. "But some of the people they trained are still around. Every now and then the FBI hires one for a case. They're called remote viewers."

Phoebe chewed reflectively. "Remote viewers. Yes...it is

kind of like that."

Sensing she had secured her twin's interest, Cara said, "I think you should do it. You have a gift, and you can help people. It can't hurt to see if there are other ways you could make it work." The FBI was also offering an astonishing amount of money, but Cara didn't want to discuss that. It would only cause performance anxiety. Phoebe already worried that she was letting everyone down if she didn't dream often enough.

"How long will I have to stay there?" Phoebe asked.

"Maybe a week or so."

"And you'll be there too?"

Cara had known this was coming. "Of course." Hopefully, within a couple of days Phoebe would feel comfortable and she could escape and deal with the backlog of work that had piled up over the past several weeks.

Phoebe twiddled with her chopsticks. "I don't want to feel like a circus freak."

"You know I would never let that happen."

"It wasn't all that long ago they'd have burned me for being a witch, and now I'm hired by the government and I have a spy name. Funny isn't it?"

"Hilarious." Cara said without smiling. "I'll phone Vernell. We can leave as soon as I get back from L.A."

Chapter
Two

ROWE BUTTONED HER pea coat and braced herself for the rush of cold air as she hauled open her huge oak front door and unlocked the security screen. Her Labradors, Jessie and Zoe, stepped out into the morning with the disbelief of dogs who had never seen an expanse of lawn unpopulated by people, other canines, and hotdog carts.

"Come on!" Rowe called and took a couple of tennis balls from her pockets. She hurled these across the dew-drenched meadow.

It took less than ten seconds for her pals to get the picture. They lost their minds then, running and barking like a pair of inmates fresh out of the insane asylum. Rowe strode briskly toward the birches dividing her property from that of the reclusive sisters. She considered calling on her new neighbors to introduce herself, but decided to leave that for a day when she was looking presentable and did not have two unruly dogs in tow.

Jessie, the alpha female, briefly returned to Rowe's side to check in before bounding deep into the woods, her golden coat bright against the gloom. Zoe, seven years old, black, and built like a brick house, could never keep pace with her taller, sleeker sister. All the same, she gave chase, her stumpy legs propelling her at double time. Rowe trailed after them, thankful her property had some kind of fencing, at least according to the realtor. The last thing she needed was her cloddish dogs drooling all over the old ladies next door by way of announcing the new neighbor's arrival.

There was no sign of the panting pair by the time she reached the birch stand, so she whistled a few times, expecting yellow and black shapes to hurtle from the trees. Instead she heard a shrill bark, and a split second later, an odd whimpering noise filtered through the woods.

"Jessie?" Rowe broke into a jog. "Zoe!"

Through the branches, she could make out a sprawling Shingle Style house. Calling again, she headed towards it. There was a fence, just as the realtor had claimed, but it was no longer standing. On the other side of the decaying wooden remnants lay her neighbors' back yard, a carefully tended garden that would be superb in the summer. Dotted around the perimeter were mysterious shapes swathed in bright blue plastic tarpaulins. Rowe took these for a sign of impending winter in Maine. The Midcoast was littered with them.

Hunkered down in the middle of a square of lawn, Jessie and Zoe were frozen on their haunches, intently watching a woman who was standing on the back steps. Rowe found herself rooted to the spot as well, transfixed by a pale face clouded with jet black hair that fell in narrow waves almost to its owner's waist. Large, luminescent eyes dominated features that belonged to another time. Angled slightly toward the prone dogs, her head seemed almost too heavy for a neck unusually long and slender. She looked up and a mouth Rossetti might have painted inched into a remote smile.

"Hello," she said, her eyes on Rowe.

At the sound of her voice, both Labradors whimpered and rolled onto their backs. Rowe could relate. Urging herself into motion, she followed a cobblestone path through what appeared to be an herb garden.

As she neared the beautiful stranger, she said, "Good morning. I'm Rowe Devlin. I was planning on a more civilized introduction, but—"

"Your dogs had other ideas?" Eyes the bruised purple-gray of storm clouds drew hers. "I'm Phoebe Temple. I live here with my sister."

Phoebe, Rowe thought. The name suited her. So much for the two old ladies. This woman was probably in her late twenties, although her slight build made her seem even younger. She wore a somewhat old-fashioned dress in a dusty rose color. A large baroque pearl rested on her chest a little below the collar, suspended on a black ribbon. Its color was breathtaking, platinum with a hint of lavender. Rowe knew a good deal about pearls, having bought some fine examples for her mother, who loved them. This huge pear-shaped gem was natural, she decided, not cultured. It was the kind you were more likely to find in a museum than around the neck of a woman living on an isle in New England.

Phoebe bent and extended a narrow hand, patting Jessie and Zoe in turn. "Your dogs are beautiful."

Instead of leaping to lick her face, the dogs remained on

their haunches as if they were obedience trained. Unable to account for the personality transplant, Rowe said, "You seem to have a way with them."

"I'm lucky." Phoebe straightened. "Animals are always civilized around me. Even wildlife."

"Wildlife?" Rowe tried to imagine what species there could be around here. Islesboro was not exactly Madagascar.

Phoebe pointed to a long narrow barn east of the house. "We have deer. They've been in these woods for a hundred years. In the winter, they come in to shelter and feed."

"That's great." Rowe could picture a fawn feeding from this woman's hand. She moved onto the lawn and optimistically slapped a hand against her thigh to signal Jessie and Zoe to heel. To her complete shock, they obeyed as if this were second nature.

"Of course, your dogs are very well-trained," Phoebe observed. "I wish I had one of my own, but my sister and I are away too much. It wouldn't be fair."

"You travel for your jobs?"

"Yes. Cara makes music videos, the kind of thing you see on MTV. She left this morning for L.A."

"Are you in the music business as well?"

"No." A pause. "I'm with the FBI. I'm a forensic botanist." Phoebe sounded embarrassed, even slightly ashamed. No doubt hers was an occupation many people found distasteful.

Rowe hastened to take a positive line. "That must be fascinating."

"Enormously." She did not expand. Perhaps she thought Rowe was just being polite.

"I'd love to talk more about it some time," Rowe said, determined to emphasize her complete comfort with the topic.

Despite these efforts, Phoebe wrapped her slender arms around her body and changed the subject. "Forgive me for keeping you talking out here in the cold. Would you like to come in for some coffee. I'm about to light the fires."

Rowe glanced uncertainly at the dogs.

"They're invited, too."

"Coffee sounds great. Thank you."

As she followed Phoebe indoors, Rowe knew she was being reckless, maybe even insane. She had made a rule for herself when she left Manhattan. It said: *If she's a babe, run.*

"YOU'RE AN AUTHOR, aren't you?" Phoebe asked a short time later as they sat before a log fire in a shabby-chic parlor with an incredible ocean view. "My sister told me. Horror novels, isn't it?"

"That's right."

Rowe glimpsed a trace of dazed incomprehension before Phoebe lowered her eyes. It was not her genre, that much was obvious. "I'm sure you know Stephen King lives not far from here, in Bangor."

"I'm not in his league," Rowe said. That was the truth. Even more so after her last dismal effort.

Phoebe seemed to be vacillating over a question. In a rush, she asked, "Do you believe in the supernatural?"

Rowe laughed, pleased to have the opportunity to let her captivating neighbor know she wasn't crazy. "God, no! It's my market niche. That's all."

"Oh, I see." The light faded from Phoebe's remarkable eyes and she prodded the fire.

Wondering which way to jump, Rowe covered her bases. "Of course I believe there are mysteries none of us can explain. Things beyond our present understanding. But my books are your basic schlock. Crap, really."

Phoebe turned toward her once more. In a sweetly reproachful tone, she said, "I'm sure they're no such thing," then asked Rowe if she wanted more coffee.

Without waiting for a reply, she picked up their mugs and gracefully left the room. Rowe forced herself not to stare after her, instead pondering her question about the supernatural. Perhaps, given her gruesome occupation, Phoebe needed to believe in comforting fantasies like ghosts and the hereafter. If so, she was living in the right neck of the woods. From all accounts, Maine was the paranormal portal for half the country.

When Phoebe returned, she carried a tray of muffins as well as the coffee refills. Apparently she wanted Rowe to stay a little longer. The dogs seemed fine with that. Both were stretched out on their sides, sound asleep on a well-worn Persian rug behind Rowe's chair.

Rowe finished a muffin in short order. It was light and buttery, crammed with huge blueberries. She could have eaten five, but held back. Lately she'd been comforting herself with food, and it was showing in the beginnings of a spare tire. She'd also noticed more gray in her ash blonde hair. Another legacy of Manhattan—aging before her time. She was only thirty-five. Surely it was way too soon for her to be seeing silver at her temples and frown lines between her eyes. Surreptitiously, she checked herself out in a large wood-framed mirror on the nearest wall. It had been a mistake to allow her usual short cut to grow out over the last few weeks. If her hair got any longer, it would look like Ellen's.

Depressed at how she had let herself go lately, she succumbed to another muffin, thinking: *Too bad. Who cares?* "Did you make these?" she asked. "They're delicious."

Phoebe smiled shyly. It was as if a child peeped out from behind the mask of an adult. "Thank you, yes. I like to bake." She indicated a paper bag sitting next to a huge vase of flowers on the walnut sideboard nearby. "I packed some for you to take home. Since you won't be cooking much."

Rowe was a little taken aback by this observation. "That's really thoughtful of you. But actually, I'm pretty reasonable in the kitchen."

Phoebe's expression was cryptic. "Jasper—the man who owned your place before—he always came over here to make his meals."

And who could blame him? Rowe thought. Was there a middle-aged male living alone who wouldn't cut off both hands for the chance to play happy families with *this* neighbor? She wondered if Phoebe had a boyfriend. There was an untouched quality about her that suggested not, but Rowe knew that was her own wishful thinking. Unless the entire male population of Maine was gay or blind, Phoebe Temple had to be clubbing them off.

The upscale floral arrangement on the sideboard drew her attention once more. Stargazer lilies, creamy roses and pale pink dianthus—fragrant and romantic. A florist's card was propped against the vase. Someone called "Vernell" conveyed his warmest regards.

Rowe's heart sank by degrees. Phoebe was straight. Any woman who had ever made her look twice was straight. We all have our afflictions. Hers was lusting after the unattainable. Already she knew how her relationship with the neighbors would pan out: the hermit-like writer lurks in the woods hoping for a glimpse of the siren-next-door. The sister—Rowe pictured an older, hard-faced version of Phoebe with a sensible haircut and a cynical edge—eventually shows up at Dark Harbor Cottage to let Rowe know she's making a nuisance of herself. Yet again, she gets writer's block and can't meet a deadline.

It was some kind of cosmic joke. She had abandoned Manhattan to escape her futile passion for the wife of an author buddy. Now, here was another Pasternak situation in the making. The signs were horribly familiar. Rowe drained her coffee and got to her feet before Phoebe noticed her staring like the village idiot.

"I must get going," she said. "Thanks for asking me in. It was very nice to meet you."

"Likewise." Phoebe walked her to the back door, the dogs at their heels. "If you need anything, please ask. Let me give you our number."

She took a card from an art deco hall table and handed it to Rowe. Her fingertips barely brushed Rowe's hand but set off a flurry of sensory alerts. Rowe drew a sharp breath and her nostrils were flooded with Phoebe's scent, a delicious Oriental blend of sandalwood and vanilla. Hints of juicy peach. Edible. Incredibly sexy. *Run don't walk*, she advised herself, and thanked her alluring neighbor once again for the coffee.

Pocketing the card, she crossed the immaculate back yard and resolved to see as little of Phoebe Temple as possible. The last thing she needed was another distraction. She had sent two books in well past deadline over the last eighteen months. They were both real dogs. There was one novel left to write on her current contract, and it had to be a hit, otherwise she would not be getting the new seven figure deal her agent dreamed of. So far, she had no bright ideas, and she was counting on the change of scenery to get her creative juices flowing. If nothing else, moving here meant she would never need to see Marion Cargill again.

Marion. An oily nausea invaded her gut. Marion, who tossed smiles like crusts to beggars, aware she had the power to crush, starve, or tempt. Marion, who pretended not to notice she was coveted. Sexy, heartless Marion, who spoke wistfully of love between women, as if it were a fascinating foreign land, the one stamp missing from her passport. She had teased, and Rowe had foolishly conjured a future for them. For a time, she had truly believed they would share this magical tomorrow. But here she was. Alone in Maine, a place Marion scorned.

She paused and stared back at her neighbor's house. There was a movement in the window. Phoebe Temple was watching her.

THE DOORBELL SOUNDED like it came from a distant planet. Grumbling, Rowe stopped writing mid-sentence and dragged herself down three flights of stairs. She reached the front door just as the bell shrilled again.

"Give me a minute," she yelled and wrestled the dogs into the parlor. Promising treats later, she shut them in, then answered the door.

Two young men stood on the opposite side of the ornate

wrought iron security screen Rowe had installed before she moved in. They looked like escapees from a quantum mechanics symposium, both blinking rapidly behind unfashionable eyewear. They cut their own hair, she decided, and were wearing clothes their mothers gave them for Christmas five years ago. Perhaps they had received their first male cologne that same year and reserved it for special occasions such as this. Rowe tried not to inhale too deeply. They had obviously doused themselves before leaving their car.

The taller of the pair complemented his sallow complexion and carrot-red hair with an orange plaid hat tied like a bonnet beneath his chin. "Excuse me," he said with a marked stammer. "Are you Rowe Devlin, the author?"

The autograph hunters had tracked her down already. In a tone of brisk unwelcome, Rowe confirmed, "I am."

"We're really sorry to disturb you," the shorter man babbled. "We know you must be busy writing."

The dweeb in the plaid hat, cut in. "I'm Dwayne Schottenheimer and he's Earl Atherton. We came about the cottage. Uh...first, congratulations. Kick-ass decision."

"This cottage?" Rowe ventured.

Dwayne fumbled in his jacket and produced a dog-eared business card, which he pressed to the grille. Rowe read it with a sense of impending doom: *Paranormal Investigators of New England.* The day just got worse. These bozos were here to express concern about her recent vampire novels and to explain why that sub-genre was passé and she should return to more rational themes like demonic possession and undead who cannibalize.

"We were hoping you might be able to spare five minutes to talk to us, given the importance of the topic," Dwayne said.

"The topic?" Rowe could only imagine. The same species of disgruntled fan showed up at every author event, eager to provide guidance and counsel.

"The infestation." Her carrot-haired visitor pressed on. "We're available twenty-four seven. Uh...in case you need professional help."

Confused, Rowe said, "I take it you are not referring to rodents."

Like she'd made a joke, her fragrant visitors chortled.

"We used to be with the MPRA," short, dumpy Earl said. "Not any more. Ecto-mist isn't everything."

"Uh...have you by any chance spoken with the MPRA yet?" Dwayne inquired.

What the fuck was the MPRA? Rowe decided not to ask. If

this was another paranormal society turf war, she didn't want to be the entity in the sandwich. "Guys, I'm working at the moment. This really isn't convenient."

Her visitors exchanged a look of embarrassed desperation.

Earl fidgeted with a Roswell button clinging to his lapel. "Sure. We hear you, Rowe. Man, we are big fans. *Huge.*"

"How about if we leave this?" Dwayne poked a business card into a gap in the grille. "Then, at a convenient time, you can call us and we'll be on the next ferry."

"We've got the works," Earl assured her. "EMF field testers, IR thermal meters, you name it." Casting a dark look over his shoulder, he added, "And we always take the necessary precautions. These days, you can't be too careful."

"About?"

Dwayne murmured something in Earl's ear, and the two young males turned away to discuss something in urgent whispers. Eventually they faced Rowe and inched closer to the screen.

In a low mutter, Earl confided, "We've become aware of a level of surveillance. My associate believes a competing paranormal body is responsible."

But you think it's the government, Rowe decided.

Confirming her suspicion, Earl rasped, "But my money's on the fucking feds."

This attracted a glare from Dwayne, whose conspiracy theories seemed to be limited to the more mundane connivances of ghost-hunting rivals.

"The MPRA aren't the only serious players in town," he assured Rowe. "They came out here and performed a cleansing a while back. And, " he pointed toward his clapped-out car, "the bumper sticker says it all, huh?"

Rowe read *Ghot Ghosts?* and smiled weakly. "I'll certainly bear that in mind. Thanks for coming by."

"No problem," Dwayne replied. "It was a real privilege."

Earl pulled a flapped cap from his pocket and stuck it on his head. Embroidered on the front was: *Paranormal Investigators Do It In The Dark!* As the two walked back to their car, they did a high five. Rowe was certain she heard one of them say, "Suck on that, MPRA para-nerds."

She was about to escape indoors, when she caught sight of Phoebe Temple approaching the house carrying a basket. The woman looked so shamelessly beautiful that Rowe almost wept with self-pity. What chance did she have against an arsenal of attributes like these? Her neighbor's fine ebony hair floated and tangled about the crimson headscarf that secured it. Her plain wool tweed coat flapped in the wind, revealing a full-skirted midnight blue dress and sensible brown boots.

No doubt she was going for a practical, country look. Instead, Phoebe could have stepped out of a Grimm's fairy tale. Even covered from head to foot, the woman was a temptress, the kind lovelorn poets blew their brains out over after penning countless sonnets in her honor. Rowe was just a horror novelist. She had to settle for immortalizing *her* hopeless passions in mundane passages about succubi and zombie weddings.

Phoebe gave a shy wave and climbed the steps to the front landing. As if to confirm her passage from fable to real time, she lifted the checked cloth from her basket and revealed a perfect fruit pie. "I made this for you." She hit Rowe with her mesmerizing stare. "It's blueberry and apple."

"You shouldn't have," Rowe mumbled.

"Well, since you forgot to take your muffins yesterday..."

A fact Rowe had bemoaned several times the previous evening as she munched on stale pretzels. "Please. Come in." She opened the door wide. Why not stick a Post-it on her forehead announcing: Rowe Devlin, Glutton for Punishment?

"Are you sure?" Phoebe hesitated. "I don't want to disturb you. I was actually going to leave it on your doorstep. But then I saw you had callers, so I thought maybe I'd come say hello."

"You're not disturbing me."

Rowe was struck by the irony of that remark. Her neighbor *was* disturbing. Tragically disturbing. As she took Phoebe's coat, she broke out in a sweat. That perfume teased her senses again. She wished she knew what it was, so she could buy a bottle and wallow in it in private. Her dogs clawed and whined at the parlor door.

"Let them out," Phoebe insisted. "They're so well behaved."

"I'm going to give them a few minutes to calm down," Rowe said. *And I don't want to share you.* Wisely, she kept that thought to herself.

Phoebe tried to remove her scarf but there was some hair caught in the knot. With a sigh, she turned her back to Rowe and asked, "Would you mind untangling this for me?" Helpfully, she lifted the rest of her hair out of the way.

A slender ivory nape taunted Rowe. It was all she could do not to touch it, just to see if the skin felt like the lotus petals it resembled. Carefully, she eased the scarf undone, freeing a soft, dark strand. Its consistency amazed her. She had always imagined only a child's hair could be so exquisitely fine.

Phoebe glanced over her shoulder. She didn't smile, exactly. Her eyes just grew more luminous. "Thank you," she said in her low, melodic way.

Rowe was completely undone. "Coffee?"

"Wonderful."

The kitchen lay at the far end of the long hallway, a neglected room that had last been renovated in the 1930s if the cabinetry was anything to go by. The walls, however, had been repainted some time in the last twenty years when avocado was in fashion. The murky green was peeling now, revealing a layer of hideous ochre. Rowe could see why the previous resident hadn't done much cooking. The room smelled sour and musty, and the stove was a relic. She was having a new one installed in a few days time. The solution was temporary. Her plan was to build a whole new kitchen.

"It's not the finest room in the house," she said, pulling out a chair for her guest. "But make yourself at home while I fix coffee."

Instead of stepping in, Phoebe lingered at the door, leaning against the frame, eyes riveted on the concrete wall where Rowe had positioned her cherished maple refectory table. After a long moment, she dropped her gaze to the floor, apparently stricken. Her chest rose and fell quickly, as if she were drawing breath in small gulps. She made a small, choking sound, and before Rowe could take in what was happening, the color drained from her face and she fainted.

PHOEBE FELT FINGERS at her throat, unfastening the collar of her dress. She could hear Rowe talking to herself.

"Shit. Oh, my God. Fuck."

Weakly, she forced her eyes open. The room spun. "I'm sorry," she said, focusing on Rowe's worried face.

"Jesus. What happened?"

"I'm not sure." *There was blood all over your kitchen floor.*

"One minute I was talking to you, the next minute you were out cold."

"How horrible for you."

"I'm not the one who landed in dog food. Then they slobbered all over you when I brought you in here. I'll pay for your dress to be cleaned, of course."

"No you won't." Phoebe decided her mind was playing tricks. The blood was an image from a dream. Sometimes they seeped into reality. She forced a smile. "But thank you for offering."

Rowe placed a hand on Phoebe's brow. "You still feel clammy."

"I'll be fine in a few minutes."

"I think I should drive you to the doctor."

"There's no need. I find tea with milk and sugar helps."

"This happens often?" A note of alarm.

"Almost never," Phoebe said.

Rowe gave her a piercing look from beneath mousy blonde bangs. Her eyes were an unusual smoky teal blue, the color of an ocean in shadow. They looked weary, as if she didn't sleep well. Phoebe wondered what kept her awake nights.

"I'll get you that tea," Rowe said and left the room, her dogs trailing behind.

Phoebe stared up at the ceiling and thought about Jasper. He had lived here for less than two years before selling up. The house gave him the creeps, he said. He'd had big plans when he bought it, intending to convert it into an upscale B&B. Dark Harbor Cottage was listed as haunted by the Maine Paranormal Research Association, which meant visitors sometimes showed up on the Temples' doorstep by mistake, hoping for a tour. Jasper had figured the ghost would be a drawcard. A certain species of tourist came to Maine hoping for supernatural thrills.

He had never invited Phoebe and Cara over, but was a frequent guest in their home. This one-sided hospitality had annoyed Cara at times, but Jasper always acted like there was a big renovation project happening and he didn't want anyone injured. Obviously, that had not been the case.

"I've never been in your cottage before," she said when Rowe returned with the tea. "I thought the last owner had fixed the place up."

"I wish." Rowe waved a hand toward an area of collapsed ceiling.

"I wonder why he didn't." Jasper seemed to have money. He'd bought a new place in Kennebunkport long before he put the cottage up for sale.

"Maybe it was more work than he expected. You don't always realize until you start getting the quotes."

Phoebe sipped her tea. "Have you seen the ghost?" she asked impulsively.

Rowe's straight mouth puckered slightly in the corners as if she was suppressing laughter. "You mean the dancing girl in the ballroom?"

"They call her the Disappointed Dancer."

"Uh huh." A broad grin took hold, infusing her expression with wicked charm.

Phoebe couldn't help but smile back. "I suppose you don't believe in ghosts."

"Dead people who wander around carrying their own heads? What can I say?"

"We have one you know. A headless horseman. If you stand on Stephen's Field at night, they say you can hear his hoof-beats echoing across the Narrows."

"I'll give that a shot, next time I need inspiration."

Phoebe was amazed. "I can't believe you write all those supernatural stories, but you're so — "

"Boring?"

"No." Phoebe giggled. It was unlike her to giggle, and she placed a hand over her mouth wondering if the fainting episode was responsible for this sudden giddiness.

"Okay, I confess," Rowe said dryly. "I'm a shameless cynic exploiting the superstitions of the masses for profit."

In that moment it registered with Phoebe that her skeptical companion was an extremely attractive butch lesbian. She'd already figured the lesbian part from the way Rowe walked, or rather sauntered, and the way she checked Phoebe out each time they met. But the new neighbor had struck Phoebe as fairly ordinary at first glance. Five-nine. Solidly built. Her hair was somewhere between mouse-brown and blonde, streaked in a lighter shade that was now growing out along with her trendy cut. In her faded, loose-fitting jeans and black turtleneck, she looked casual but groomed. Her sleeves were pushed up to expose firmly muscled, bronzed forearms. On one of her wrists she wore a plain silver cuff-style bracelet with a fine black leather thong embedded along the center.

Phoebe checked her fingers. No rings. She lifted her eyes and found Rowe watching her intently. Something glittered in the smoky blue of her gaze. Lust. Phoebe was accustomed to seeing it in the eyes of friends and strangers alike. People had lusted after her all her life. Mostly it embarrassed her. In Rowe's case, it made her wonder how a kiss would feel. She glanced away. The last thing she needed was another lecture from Cara about boundaries and why she had to make them one hundred percent clear.

"Feeling better?" Rowe asked.

"Much better, thanks." Aware she had probably outstayed her welcome, Phoebe sat up and slid her feet to the floor. "I should go. I'm sure you must want to get back to your writing."

"Actually, I'm not in any hurry. The new book isn't exactly spilling from my Waterman." Rowe's tone was laced with irony. She sank into an armchair a couple of feet from the sofa Phoebe was on. "Is there someone at home who can keep an eye on you?"

"No, my sister's away, filming. But I'm fine."

"Are you in a rush to get back?"

Feeling awkward, Phoebe said, "No. I guess I'm embarrassed about fainting in your kitchen. And I don't want to interrupt your work."

"Well, you have nothing to be embarrassed about," Rowe said warmly. "And, like I said, all you're interrupting is my inability to work."

"You have writer's block?"

Rowe clasped her hands behind her head and stuck one foot on a small ottoman. In a reflective tone, she said, "It's worse than that. It's like something has gone. I can write, but what I write is," she searched for a word, "barren. I'm just going through the motions. I know it probably sounds ridiculous — we're only talking about horror stories. But they still have to have integrity...some kind of heart."

"You feel the heart is missing?"

For a long moment they stared at one another.

"A deadly banishment?" Phoebe prompted softly.

Dull pain moved across Rowe's face before she countered it with a rueful smile. "I deserved that. For being so damned melodramatic. Shakespeare?"

"Of course." Phoebe knew how to make angst-ridden creative people laugh. She had plenty of practice with Cara, who stopped eating when a music video didn't work.

Rowe dropped her hands to her thighs and stood up. "Let's get out of here. Want to have lunch with me in Camden?"

Phoebe smiled. "I'd like that."

Chapter
Three

"YOU HAD LUNCH," Cara said.

There was a silence at the other end of the phone, then, "She's our neighbor."

"Is she gay?"

"I haven't asked." A defensive note. "Maybe. Probably."

"So, what's she like?" Cara kept her voice even. She had already heard enough about Rowe Devlin to have a pretty clear picture. The woman was a thirty-something dyke with a crush on Phoebe. What else was new?

"She's good company. It's funny. She writes these bizarre stories, but she doesn't believe in the supernatural at all."

"Have you slept with her?"

"No!"

Cara ran a quick count. A week had passed since Phoebe had first encountered their new neighbor. They'd had lunch a few days ago. No doubt they would have dinner some evening soon, which meant by the time Cara got home they would be lovers. "Please don't do this," she said.

"I know what you think, but it's not like that."

"Okay. What is it like?"

"I'm being clear about boundaries. No mixed messages."

That would last about five minutes if she found this woman attractive. "So, are you telling me she's not your type?" Cara could hear Phoebe breathing softly into the phone. Her silence provided the answer. "Promise me something. Promise me you'll wait."

A sigh. "I wish you would trust me."

"And I wish I didn't have to get rid of your unwanted lovers."

"Please don't be angry at me." Phoebe's voice shook.

"People are not flowers. You can't just pick them because they seem beautiful, then discard them when the bloom fades."

"I don't!" Phoebe burst out. "They pick me! What am I

supposed to do? I hate disappointing them."

"Oh, please. You hate that they disappoint you. They are never perfect. They are never what you dreamed of. How many times do we have to have this conversation?"

"Alright. I won't see her!" Phoebe choked on a sob.

"Smart move. Don't see her. Don't talk to her. And for Chrissakes don't fuck her."

A loud metallic click made Cara wince. Phoebe had hung up on her. In about three minutes, she would call back, imploring forgiveness. Cara had time to make herself a whiskey sour.

PHOEBE PULLED ON her coat, tied her headscarf, and marched out into the November sleet. A snow storm bleached the early evening sky, the first of the season. Driven by the north wind, icy white flakes whipped her face as she plodded across the long meadow that led to Dark Harbor Cottage.

At the sight of the warmly lit windows, she stopped in her tracks and almost retreated. She knew she should go back home and phone Cara again. Her sister had enough to deal with. It was time Phoebe starting making some difficult decisions and taking responsibility for herself. She could begin by letting Rowe Devlin know they would only ever be friends. No flirting. No games. It was one thing to have short-lived relationships with women in Portland, most of which ended badly, quite another to mess things up with the next door neighbor. Cara was right to be cross with her.

Phoebe pawed the snow from her face with her mittens. She had to stop expecting her twin to get her out of trouble every time she backed herself into a corner, romantically speaking. If only she could stay attracted to a woman for more than a few months. At first she always expected to, but that quickly changed and she would start dreading each date and finding excuses not to go. Some women caught on right away and stopped calling. Others pursued her, and eventually she would agree to see them. But it was Cara who showed up for those uncomfortable discussions. Women simply assumed she was Phoebe with a haircut.

Lately, trying to stay out of trouble, Phoebe had stopped going to social events in southern Maine. She was getting a reputation. It was really unfair. Other women had countless flings and no one thought badly of them. Why was it different for her? Why did she get sent a dog turd in the mail? She'd only dated a handful of local women during the years they'd lived in Islesboro, and she'd tried not to hurt anyone. She hated the stricken looks and the crying and, as a consequence, she could never bring herself to say it was over like she really meant it. That's why Cara took care of the break-up process for her.

She wished she had never allowed that. It was deceitful and cowardly, and Cara was still hung up over the last woman she'd had to dump. Hence the constant lectures on boundaries. Phoebe caught a brief mental glimpse of Bev Hagen and felt queasy. Bev was a captain in the Marines. She'd wanted them to get married in Vermont before her deployment to Iraq, and Phoebe didn't have the heart to say no. So she'd gone along with the plans, told Bev what she wanted to hear and tried to be in love with her. She'd figured if she procrastinated long enough, Bev would be shipped out and they would eventually lose contact.

But Bev was a very determined woman. She'd set a date, bought Phoebe a beautiful ring and arranged a wedding breakfast for close friends and family. The week before, Phoebe knew she couldn't go through with it and begged Cara to deal with Bev. It had gone badly. When Cara gave the ring back, Bev had slapped her face. Cara had been so mad, she told Phoebe she would never do her "dirty work" again and that she considered it a low blow to break a soldier's heart a week before she was due to go fight in that miserable war in Iraq. That was almost a year ago and Cara still couldn't let it go.

With guilty trepidation, Phoebe stared up at the turret room and made out a shape—Rowe working at her computer. This time, she was not going to break anyone's heart, she promised herself. It was not like she set out to make women fall madly in love with her, in fact, she made a point of letting them know she wasn't looking for anything long term. Was it her fault if they didn't listen?

Rowe was not the type to run after a woman, she decided. In fact, women probably ran after her. She was a famous author, after all. And attractive. Maybe she had a girlfriend, although Phoebe doubted it. From their last conversation, it seemed pretty obvious that someone had played fast and loose with her heart and she was still getting over it.

Feeling a new confidence about keeping their contact on a purely neighborly footing, she started walking again, leaning into the wind. It was snowing more steadily now, and the light was dimming by the minute. Thankfully the cottage was only a hundred yards away. If the air got any colder, her lungs would freeze.

When she reached the front steps, she shook herself free of snowflakes. Before she could even ring the bell, the dogs started barking and the door swung open.

"Jesus, Phoebe," Rowe greeted her. "What the heck are you doing out in this?"

Phoebe suppressed an irrational urge to throw herself into Rowe's strong-looking arms. "I felt like company."

Rowe pulled her into the vestibule and kicked the door closed behind them. "Is everything all right? You look kind of teary."

"It must be from the wind." Chilled to the bone, she slid out of her coat and selected a hook for it.

Rowe shot her a quick, dubious glance. "Come and get in front of the fire." She opened the parlor door and a blast of warm air engulfed them.

"I'm not interrupting your work am I?" Phoebe asked.

"Nope. The cadavers aren't going anywhere."

"You're still writing that scene in the morgue?"

"Yes ma'am. And it's still blood out of a stone."

Phoebe hoisted her damp skirt so the fire could dry the heavy fabric and warm her legs. "Maybe you should try writing something totally different."

"I'm all ears," Rowe said dryly. Her eyes were on Phoebe's legs.

Out of pure mischief, Phoebe inched her skirt higher and said, "What about kids' books?"

"Yeah, I guess JK Rowling isn't going broke any time soon."

"Or, there's romance." As soon as she'd said it, Phoebe wished she hadn't. She could almost hear Cara. *No hinting. No mixed messages.*

"Do I strike you as the romantic type?"

Phoebe promptly let go of her skirt and sat down on the sofa, not wanting to answer that honestly. "Well, you write creepy books and you don't believe in any of that stuff. Why not romance?"

"You have a point." Rowe joined her on the sofa, slouching back and stretching her legs out, one foot crossed over the other.

She looked good in jeans. She had the right build. Long, well muscled legs and not too much of a butt. Phoebe wished she could curl up with her head in Rowe's lap and fall asleep. But that would be worse than a mixed message.

"Want to come back to my place for hot chocolate?" she suggested, and immediately wondered if it sounded like a come-on.

"Are you kidding? It's getting worse by the minute out there. I'd never make it back home."

Phoebe felt a rush of panic. Rowe was right. No one would be going anywhere once this weather really set in, herself included. What if Cara phoned later and found she wasn't home? Phoebe could just imagine what she would think. She would probably call Rowe's place and make some tactless comment that would embarrass the woman.

"I shouldn't have come," she mumbled. "I wasn't thinking."

"Hey, not so fast." Rowe's sensual blue-green eyes slid over her. Softly, she coaxed, "Tell me what's wrong. We both know you didn't come out in a storm because I'm irresistible company."

Phoebe stared down at her soggy boots. She didn't know this woman well enough to unburden herself. Yet she didn't want to go home and spend days snowed in by herself with no one to talk to either. "I had a fight with my sister," she said. "I should have phoned her back, but I—"

"Wanted to simmer down first?"

"Yes."

"Smart move." Rowe offered an encouraging smile. "If you want to talk about it, I'm a good listener."

Here was her opening. Phoebe tried to frame what she needed to say, but it seemed ridiculous to tell a woman who hadn't even come out to her that they could only be friends. She reminded herself that Rowe Devlin probably fended off smart, gorgeous potential girlfriends all the time. Phoebe was flattering herself if she thought her new neighbor had anything in mind other than friendship. Besides, Rowe didn't even know Phoebe was gay. Cara hadn't thought this through properly before she made assumptions. There was no basis for her paranoia.

Phoebe took a deep breath and exhaled slowly, relieved to have figured this out before she made an idiot of herself. "It was just a sister thing. But thanks."

"Well, I'll walk you back home later, whatever the weather is doing." Rowe said. "Meantime, hot chocolate sounds pretty good. Don't suppose you want to come wait in the kitchen again?"

The prospect evoked a shudder, but telling herself not to be a wimp, Phoebe said, "Sure." There was nothing to be afraid of. It was just a room. What she'd seen in there last time must have leaked from her sub-conscious. There was no other explanation.

"The dogs don't like it in there either," Rowe told her as they left the parlor.

Phoebe fixed her eyes on the back of Rowe's head and followed her down the long, poorly lit hall into the dank kitchen. The moment she crossed the threshold, her scalp started prickling, and she felt a painful constriction in her chest. She took the chair Rowe pulled out and glanced toward the dogs.

They were pacing back and forth in the doorway, tails between their legs.

Rowe placed the milk and chocolate in the microwave, then glanced quizzically at Phoebe. "Are you alright?"

"This room...it has quite an oppressive feel." Phoebe hoped she didn't sound rude. "Have you noticed?"

"It is pretty musty." Rowe glanced casually around. "I'm going to rip everything out, go for maybe a Tuscan type concept in here. What do you think?"

Phoebe clasped her shaking hands together in her lap. "Sounds wonderful."

Rowe rattled open a drawer. "I still have some of your yummy pie left. Would you like a slice?" She set a small carving knife on the counter and took the pie from the fridge.

Phoebe wanted to speak but her mouth was frozen. The knife slowly drifted along the counter, spinning slightly until the blade pointed right at her.

Rowe's hand arrested it. "There isn't a level surface in this place," she remarked. "No wonder the last owner didn't go ahead with renovations. I'll probably have to redo the foundations."

Rowe continued talking but it was as if they were underwater. Phoebe could not make out a word. She watched the knife sink into the pie. As if from a great distance, a voice broke through the muffled silence, crying, "Run!"

She lurched to her feet, vaguely aware that her chair had crashed to the floor. Frantic, she ran from the room and along the hall, hearing hideous screams behind her. She flung open the front door and bolted out into the snow, terrified to look back. The shock of the cold made her gasp and the gasps became sobs as she heard someone behind her. She ran harder, her boots accumulating heavy white globs. Hands grabbed at her shoulders. Her foot caught on something and she fell. The hands were on her, turning her over.

"No!" she screamed, punching wildly at her captor. One fist connected before her wrists were seized and she was pinned down. She struggled helplessly for a moment, then lay still, eyes closed, waiting to die.

Close to her ear, a voice said, "Phoebe. It's me. No one's going to hurt you."

The grip on her wrists eased and Phoebe was suddenly aware of warm breath on her cheek. She knew that voice. Opening her eyes, she blinked up into the unearthly half-light of the storm.

"Rowe," she whispered and burst into tears.

SOME TIME LATER, at the Temple's house, Rowe knocked on Phoebe's bathroom door and asked, "Everything okay?"

"Come in." Phoebe's voice was just audible.

Rowe vacillated. The idea of being in the same room while her neighbor took a bath would have thrilled her a day ago, but that was before the black eye. It seemed pretty obvious that Phoebe had some kind of mental health problem. Had she forgotten to medicate while her sister was away? Rowe wondered how to raise the subject without getting punched again. Cagily, she entered the room but remained close to the door in case Phoebe suddenly forgot who she was. Her assailant was lounging in a clawfoot tub, bath foam up to her armpits.

"Oh, God." She gazed up at Rowe. "Your eye. Did you find that ice pack in the freezer?"

"Yep. Just giving it a break. It's so numb it hurts, if you know what I mean."

Phoebe looked mortified. Worse still, with her hair tied up in a knot with a narrow violet ribbon, and her vulnerable neck and shoulders exposed, she was hauntingly, achingly beautiful. In a voice husky from sobs, she said, "I don't know what to say. I'm so sorry."

Rowe took a few cautious steps into the room. "Can you tell me what happened?"

"I'm not sure where to start." Head tilted back, Phoebe lifted a sponge full of hot water and slowly squeezed it over her throat.

The sensuous ritual transfixed Rowe for several long seconds, and a strangled whimper rose from her throat. For one crazy moment she saw herself walking over there, taking the sponge from Phoebe's hands and tenderly bathing her. Not one of her brightest ideas. Groping for some traction on common sense, she compelled her thoughts back to the knotty matter of her neighbor's state of mind.

It was a delicate subject and none of her business, but the least she could do was ask a few diplomatic questions so she could assess the situation and maybe call the sister if need be. What if Phoebe was a danger to herself? Like most people on medication for their mental health, she probably didn't want to make embarrassing disclosures to a stranger.

Trying to let her know it was no big deal if she was taking happy pills, Rowe said in an off-hand manner, "Some prescription drugs have pretty strange side effects, especially if they're not used exactly as directed. Could it be something like that?"

Phoebe looked at her squarely. "Is that a diplomatic way of

asking me if I missed my meds?"

"Subtle, huh?"

"Don't give up your day job to act in art-house movies."

Rowe laughed, then groaned. "Jesus, that hurts my face."

"Come closer." Phoebe stretched out a fine-boned hand. "I won't hit you."

Rowe tried not to notice that the foam was disappearing. Phoebe's long delicate fingers brushed the inside of her wrist, sparking a craving so raw that she stopped breathing for several noisy heartbeats. The last time she'd felt like this was sitting across the dinner table from Marion Cargill, watching her flirt with her food and every man in the room, and knowing she could never have her. Rowe had realized in that moment that Marion knew exactly how desperately her husband's gay friend wanted her, and she enjoyed that knowledge. She would never leave her marriage for a woman. Like a cat walking away from a dead mouse, she would abandon Rowe when the fun went out of torturing her.

"I want to tell you something and you have to promise not to laugh at me," Phoebe said.

"You got it." Rowe reminded herself that straight women like Phoebe thought nothing of a situation like this. They took saunas together and exchanged gossip, wandering naked around changing rooms. Hell, even lesbians managed to share those kinds of experiences without assuming it had to be sexual.

Two perfect breasts parted the foam as Phoebe moved up the tub a little. They were small, high and full, the nipples a surprising pale rose hue. Rowe prevented her gaze from traveling any lower. She had enough problems. It was getting late and the storm had dumped six inches of snow in short order. By morning it would probably be a foot or more. Having escorted Phoebe home, all she wanted to do now was make sure her neighbor was okay, then get herself and her dogs back to Dark Harbor Cottage before they were completely snowed in.

Her eyes found something to focus on. A star-shaped bottle of perfume sitting innocently on the tiled vanity counter, the source of that crazy-making fragrance no doubt. *Angel* by Thierry Mugler. The guy should be shot, Rowe thought and returned her gaze to Phoebe. She couldn't help herself. What right-thinking lesbian would study the décor while a gorgeous woman sitting naked in a bath held her hand?

"I don't need medication." Phoebe's fingers slid from hers and she toyed with the bath-sponge. "The thing is, I *see* things sometimes, that's all. I know you don't believe in that kind of thing. I never used to, myself. But I had a car accident a few

years ago and injured my head. Since then, I've been...like this."
Wide, pleading eyes lifted to Rowe, begging her not to mock.

"When you say you see things, what exactly are you talking
about? Do you have premonitions?"

"No. Not usually. I see things that have already happened."

"And you saw something in my kitchen?"

Emotions flitted across Phoebe's mobile features. Anxiety.
Sorrow. Resignation. "I'm certain something terrible has
happened in your house."

Rowe cast her mind back to Phoebe's frantic departure from
the kitchen, the naked terror on her face. Whatever delusions she
suffered from, they were completely real to her at the time.
"When you hit me, who did you think I was?"

"I don't know." Phoebe rested her hands on the sides of the
tub. They were shaking. "I thought I was going to be killed. I
have dreams, too, where I see things. But today was different."
She sounded winded, her breath congealed in her throat. "You
think I'm crazy."

"I'm not making any judgments. I believe you're telling me
the truth."

Tears welled in Phoebe's eyes. "You're the first person I've
told, except for my sister and...a man who helps me."

So, she was seeing a shrink. Or was she talking about a
lover — Vernell, the guy who had sent the pricey bouquet? Rowe
wondered what was really going on with her state of mind and
thought about the sister, Cara. She had formed an impression of
an over-protective older sibling who was possibly envious of her
younger sister's looks. But recent events cast Cara in a different
light. If Phoebe had a mental health problem, maybe her sister
was just trying to find a way to keep her safe. Maybe that's why
they lived way the hell out here. Islesboro was not exactly a
mecca for attractive young women who wanted a social life.

Phoebe turned on the faucet, adding more hot water to her
bath. "I didn't choose this," she said in a defeated voice.

A wave of sadness swept Rowe. Some of the most
remarkable people in history had suffered debilitating mental
illnesses. It had to be torture for those who were themselves
enough to know their condition made a moveable feast of
reality.

She touched Phoebe's arm. "I know you didn't. And we don't
need to talk about it any more."

"Do you still like me?"

"Of course."

"You're gay, aren't you?" Phoebe slid down the tub again,
submerging herself to her chin.

In the opaque water, Rowe could make out a narrow-hipped form, the stomach slightly rounded above a small dark vee. Phoebe was not voluptuous, not like Marion. She was lissome and fine-boned, almost boyish. Remembering she'd been asked a question, she dragged her eyes back to Phoebe's face. "Yes."

"Me, too."

Heat rushed from Rowe's neck to her forehead, and her newly acquired instinct for self-preservation made her step back a pace. What was she supposed to say to this frank revelation?

Phoebe spared her the task. "I thought maybe you'd guessed."

"Why?"

"Because you invited me to lunch."

"We're neighbors. I thought we could be friends, too."

A rare, full-tilt smile lit Phoebe's face. "I could use a friend. I'm not in the market for anything else."

Was this what Rowe thought it was? One of those well-meaning brush-offs beautiful women deliver ahead of time? *Don't hit on me and you won't have to suffer rejection.* She should have been relieved, but nuts or not, Phoebe was the first non-straight woman she had been attracted to in a very long time. She was so thankful for that small mercy she felt like throwing caution to the winds and kissing her.

"Okay. We'll be friends then," she said with plausible sincerity.

Only a fool would walk away because of a small matter like a psychotic episode and a black eye, she reasoned. Once Phoebe was taking the right meds, who knew what might be possible?

Chapter
Four

"IT'S OVER? IS that what you're trying to say?" Cara licked salt off her lips and watched her willowy companion founder for words.

Adrienne had a PhD in beating around the bush. "It's not your fault," she said, nervously rearranging the olives in her martini with a swizzle stick. "It's about me."

Huge surprise. "You don't need to explain. I get that the distance is an issue."

"I feel like I only exist on the periphery of your life."

"I thought you wanted it that way. No complications, remember?"

Adrienne abandoned her cocktail ministrations to slide a hand over her short blond waves. The chunky red coral ring on her thumb drew Cara's gaze. Adrienne wore gifts from her exes like trophies, and liked to recount the lessons each woman represented to her. Cara wondered how she would be described: *Cara and I got involved at a time in my life when I was working on my self-esteem. But Cara can't commit. I deserve more, so I ended it.*

"That was my protective self talking," Adrienne explained. "And I got the impression it was what you wanted to hear."

"You were right." Cara had been completely honest with Adrienne. She wasn't planning a commitment ceremony any time soon. Yet, at the same time, she wasn't completely closed to the idea. She had figured they would just wait and see what happened.

"The thing is, there's another woman I've been getting close to, and—"

"A lover?" They hadn't made any promises about not seeing other people, but they had agreed to discuss it first if either of them wanted to.

Adrienne seemed unabashed. An accusatory note entered her tone. "If you were interested in taking our relationship to the next level, you'd have moved out here or at least we'd be talking about it. Did I miss something?"

Cara did not participate in the change of subject. "How long have you been sleeping with her?"

"It just happened. She's a really nice person."

"What does she think about you having a relationship with someone else?"

"She knows there's nothing between us."

"We date when I'm in town. We sleep together and have sex. I'm not sure I'd call that nothing." Cara could hear the edge in her own voice. "You didn't answer my question. How long?"

"It's hard to say. I met her about a year ago, and we kind of hooked up after she moved to the neighborhood a few months back." Adrienne fidgeted with the cuffs of her white blouse. "I know I should have told you sooner, but it just...evolved."

"Are you in love with her?"

"I like her a lot. But the problem is, you and I are more compatible sexually."

"Oh, right. The sex is better with me, but she's here, so you thought you could have both?"

"You make it sound so calculated. It's not like that. I don't want to hurt anyone."

Cara finished her drink, uncertain what she felt. There was no anger, just a leaden disappointment. Nothing ever seemed to work out for her. "You have to do what's right for you, Adrienne."

They sat in silence for a moment, then, as if pleading for understanding, Adrienne said, "She's there for me. She makes herself completely available." The inference was unmistakable.

Cara stood and picked up her cabin bag. "I better get to the gate. My flight is boarding soon." She took Adrienne's hand and softened her tone. "I hope you'll be happy. I really do."

"So, it's fine with you if we don't see each other any more?" Adrienne sounded vaguely disappointed.

What had she expected? That Cara would suggest they carried on a sexual relationship behind the new girlfriend's back? With a small shrug, she said, "All good things come to an end."

Adrienne's smile seemed fixed. "Well, I'll be seeing you, then."

"I doubt that." Cara bent and kissed her on the mouth, just thoroughly enough to make her gasp. "Goodbye, Adrienne. Take care of yourself."

ROWE GAZED AROUND her kitchen. The room was absurdly small for such a large home. No doubt when it was built, it had been the domain of a few underpaid domestic servants, the same women who must have occupied the tiny bedrooms on the second floor of the Carriage House. Converted long ago for storage, those dusty, cobwebbed rooms were choked to their ceilings with old furniture and boxes. Rowe had not had a chance to explore them yet.

She made herself a cup of tea and sat down at the table. The dogs stared at her from the hall, their agitation obvious. "Jessie," she called. "Come on baby. Come here."

The yellow Lab promptly sank down where she was, her wise brown eyes mournful. It would take more than honeyed words to persuade her to enter the Bad Zone. The day they'd moved in, Jessie had walked into the kitchen, and the hair along her spine rose instantly. Emitting a low, fearful growl, she'd slunk out into the hall where Zoe, who never tried anything unless Jessie first proved it was safe, lay on her belly, whining softly. Since that day, neither dog had ventured beyond the threshold.

What could they sense? Was it a smell? Rowe got up and paced around the room, opening the cupboards. With the exception of some basics and her favorite dinner set, she hadn't bothered to unpack her kitchen gear into them. Every surface seemed grimy, despite the efforts of the cleaning company she'd engaged. There was no point getting worked up about it. She intended to have the cabinets ripped out soon anyway.

She stared at the doorframe and recalled Phoebe standing there the day she had fainted. Her eyes had been riveted to the opposite wall, as if she saw something. Then she'd looked down at the floor and passed out. Rowe crossed the room and stood in the same position, scanning the walls and the floor. Other than the hideous paintjob and ancient linoleum, she could see nothing scary.

Something terrible has happened in your house. Evidently Phoebe truly believed she could 'see' things and perceived this supposed sixth sense as an unwanted gift, not a sign of illness. Because she didn't think she had a problem, she hadn't spoken to a psychologist about her delusions.

Rowe wondered what it would take to make her see the truth and get some professional help. Perhaps if there was proof that nothing terrible had ever happened in the cottage, Phoebe would accept that she needed to discuss her condition with someone other than her sister and this Vernell individual. She switched off the lights and padded down the hall to the front parlor. Impulsively, she rifled through some papers on her desk and found the grubby business card she'd dropped there the other day. If she was going to investigate the history of the cottage, the local ghost-busters seemed like a good place to start.

DWAYNE SCHOTTENHEIMER AND Earl Atherton were eager to help. They met Rowe at the Time Out Bar in Rockland to discuss the situation. Again, they'd been heavy-handed with the *Brut*.

"What can you tell me about the cottage?" Rowe asked, once her companions were done bemoaning the closure of the Sea Dog and marveling that they had to show ID to get a beer in this joint.

Dwayne removed his plaid hat and set it down on the table. "You bought yourself *the* most haunted house in the Midcoast," he assured her. Don't you worry about that."

"Oh, yeah!" Earl enthused. "We are talking mondo infestation. The Disappointed Dancer is only the start. I'm thinking there's gotta be a more—" He shot a sideways glance at his colleague.

"Malevolent entity." Dwayne supplied. "Uh...which is why we made ourselves known to you. The last occupant was driven out."

"He hired a priest," Earl explained.

Dwayne shook his head in somber resignation. "Like talking about the Holy Ghost makes *them* an authority on the paranormal."

"I see." Rowe wondered how much of this supernatural saga the realtor had known and 'forgotten' to tell her. "So what do you guys know about the history of the place? Who is this Disappointed Dancer, anyway?"

"She's your typical revenant." Earl lifted a steel briefcase onto the seat next to him and opened the combination lock. Glancing furtively over his shoulder, he fished around inside and produced a folder marked: *DHC Entities*. Written in red felt pen below this entry was: *Do Not Allow to Fall Into MPRA Hands*. He pulled out a photo and slid it across to her. "Juliet Baker. Daughter of Thomas Hardcastle Baker, a rich guy who bought the house from the Widow of Dark Harbor."

"It's believed the Widow also haunts the cottage," Dwayne said. "She's been sighted on the widow's walk, and they reckon she looks out the window of that turret room waiting for her husband's boat. He drowned in a shipwreck."

Well that explained why her writing still sucked, Rowe

thought. She had a ghost reading over her shoulder. She picked up the photo and caught her breath. A beautiful young woman stared at her from a formal pose, dark hair piled on her head. She wore a pale ball gown with a wide, gathered sash and a modestly cut bodice. A simple black ribbon adorned her long, slender neck. From this hung a huge baroque pearl Rowe recognized instantly. The woman was Phoebe Temple.

"Could I get a copy of this?" she asked.

"You can have that one," said Earl. "There's plenty more. They sell it at the Camden museum."

Rowe turned the photograph over. The back bore a museum label on which was typed: *Miss Juliet Baker on the occasion of her twenty-first birthday. Dark Harbor Cottage, 1912.* Frowning, she asked, "Are you saying the museum has the original of this photo?"

Her companions didn't know for sure. They suggested she speak to Mrs. Chauncey of the Islesboro Historical Society, the brains behind various money-making schemes for the cultural preservation crowd. Rowe knew what she was destined to discover—that this enterprising lady had rustled up a few of the Midcoast's more fetching young women to pose in costume for Victorian-style portraits. They did it in Disneyland, why not Camden?

"Have you seen the Dancer yet?" Dwayne flipped open a notebook. "Most people only hear footsteps."

"I haven't had the pleasure. What's her story, anyway? How did she get the name?"

Color inched into Dwayne's wan, freckled cheeks. "She was disappointed in love."

"Hooked up with a loser that dumped her," Earl said.

"They were meant to announce their engagement at her birthday ball," Dwayne went on. "But he didn't show."

Earl jerked a thumb pointedly at the photo. "Pound for pound, the dumbest guy alive."

"After she died they say servants used to see her dancing in the ballroom by herself some nights." Gravely, Dwayne noted, "Girls aren't like that any more."

Rowe kept her face straight. "You're thinking she died of a broken heart?"

"Committed suicide, although they called it an accident back then."

"That was one disappointed chick," Earl contributed. "And ask yourself this—could she date any guy she wanted? I think so."

No question about that. Rowe downed some beer while her

companions lost themselves in their respective fantasies about the tragic young woman in the picture. "Tell you what," she said, "if you don't have anything else planned, how about you bring your equipment out to the cottage this weekend and take a look."

Dwayne immediately broke into a visible sweat and had to remove his glasses to wipe the fogged lenses. "We were supposed to be collecting data at St. Mary's, but—"

"Dude, it's a cemetery," his chubby colleague pointed out. "They're not going anywhere."

"Right." Dwayne flipped to a fresh page in his notebook. "Can you report any paranormal anomalies so far? Maybe unusual lights or drop in temperature. Animals acting nervous in areas of the house?"

"My dogs won't go in the kitchen," Rowe said. "Kind of unusual for Labradors. That's a food-focused breed."

Dwayne and Earl exchanged meaningful looks.

"EMF Detector and IR thermal meter," Earl said. "FujiFilm Fine Pix Digital and backup cameras. 800 speed film. Handycam with Nightshot. EVP seems like a strong possibility."

For Rowe's benefit, Dwayne translated, "Electronic Voice Phenomenon. Uh...maybe your dogs are hearing something you can't hear."

Earl nodded. "Hook up three external mics and run reel to reel."

"Would it be okay if we monitored overnight?" Dwayne asked tentatively. "We'll bring our own food."

"Whatever it takes," Rowe said.

BEFORE THE KAREOKE got started upstairs, Rowe escaped the waterfront bar and wandered to her car, listening to the dissonant clanks of the windjammers that crowded the harbor. In the grisly gray twilight, the schooners looked like a ghost fleet, their sleek hulls lapped by an indolent tide. Loons and ducks bobbed on the waters, seeking out the edible remains of another New England day.

She left the parking area and turned onto US 1, taking her time so she could absorb the visual feast of her surroundings. This must be one of the most beautiful drives in Maine, she decided, the Camden Hills looming to the west, the rocky shoreline stretching like twisted fingers to the east. As she neared Lincolnville Beach, a long stretch of land took shape in the bay before her. Islesboro looked misty purple against a slate sea, its pale emerald beacon flickering from the Grindel Point lighthouse.

The line for the last ferry was long, at least by local standards, which meant there were more than ten cars, and it took a while to board. Rowe made it to the passenger deck among a throng of locals griping over the new Homeland Security requirements. The price of tickets had gone up to pay for security cameras that were unstaffed anyway, and vehicle screening held everyone up while the line attendant yammered on to buddies he noticed in the queue.

Rowe got herself a cup of coffee and found a seat by the window. The sea was dark and getting choppy, promising a queasy passage. That didn't deter locals from making the crossing to Gilkey Harbor in their own small boats. Even with a squall imminent, at least six or seven craft were crawling across the bay. Lunatics, Rowe thought. But of course being eccentric was almost mandatory in these parts.

She sipped the hot, weak coffee and convinced herself that the conditions were safe. Maggie, as they called the ferry here, only operated weather permitting, and sailings were cancelled fairly regularly once winter took hold. Thankfully it would take only twenty minutes to reach the island. None of her fellow-passengers seemed alarmed by the gathering winds, and these people knew the changeable Maine weather. The tourist season was over and the visitors and summer people had returned to their city rabbit holes, taking their it's-all-about-me attitudes with them. Once more the ferry was the domain of the die-hards who lived here all year 'round.

Rowe exchanged a smile with an older woman sitting across from her and realized she had become part of an unspoken conspiracy just by being here in November. She was a local now, even if she wasn't a native Mainer.

"You from away?" The woman poked a few wispy gray hairs into the bun at her nape.

"Yes ma'am. Moved here from New York City a few weeks ago." Rowe introduced herself properly and they shook hands.

"I'm Dotty Prescott." Pointing out a man playing cards with several others a few yards away, she added, "And that's my husband, Maurice."

"Which part of the island are you from?" Rowe asked.

"Ames Cove." Dotty's eyes gleamed all of a sudden. "Oh, my word. Are you the author who bought Dark Harbor Cottage?"

"That would be me."

Rowe immediately resigned herself to having to answer silly questions about her books for the rest of the journey. But this was Maine, where people knew how to mind their own business.

Dotty simply nodded and said, "Well now, you'll be wanting

to get your firewood covered. It's brewing up a storm. You got snowshoes?"

Rowe peered out at the menacing sky. "Not yet."

"Ever been through a New England winter?" her companion inquired with cautious unease.

Rowe had noticed the same troubled air in other locals when she admitted moving here only recently. "No ma'am. Gets pretty bad, huh?"

"You better hire a man for your roof. You don't want ice dams." Dotty waved at her husband and raised her voice. "Maurie, this is the author. She needs a man for her roof."

Heads turned. A female voice a few seats over drawled softly, "You can share ours," and Rowe found herself staring at Phoebe Temple yet again. Only this time she had short, gelled hair and was wearing designer jeans and a sleek leather jacket.

"Cara!" Dotty beamed as the babe got to her feet. "Have you been away again?"

Phoebe's sister slouched over and kissed the older woman on her cheek. "Yep. Sucking butt at another L.A. phonyfest." Bold gray eyes swept Rowe. "Hi. I'm your neighbor, Cara Temple. You've met my sister, I think."

Met her, been smacked in the face by her, watched her take a bath. "Yes." Rowe summoned a casual smile. "Good to meet you at last."

"Likewise." Cara sounded unenthusiastic. She did not extend her hand.

Aware that her own hand was hovering a few inches from her body, Rowe withdrew it.

"Have my seat." Dotty got up. "I've got Sewing Circle business to discuss with Ethel Wallace. I see her over there."

For a second, it looked like Cara would take a pass, then she perched on the edge of the seat, making it plain she had no intention of settling in for the trip. "The roof guy is Ian Crocker," she told Rowe. "He has a place in Ryders Cove, so he's not far away. I'll ask him to call on you."

"What exactly for?" Rowe felt like a slow learner. "Dotty said something about ice dams, but I have no idea what she's talking about."

"The snows get heavy here." Cara gazed at a spot somewhere west of Rowe's shoulder. Her eyes were the same stormy hue as her sister's, but not as grave. "If you don't shovel your roof, ice builds up around the edge and when the snow melts off, the water can't escape, so it ends up inside your house."

"Great," Rowe muttered. "And I have a ghost as well."

The corners of Cara's mouth tugged slightly, drawing

Rowe's attention to its kissable perfection. Identical twins, each lethally gorgeous in her own way, living right next door. What had she done to deserve this refined torture?

Cara's next comment was, "Are you seeing my sister?"

Rowe had heard Mainers were direct, but the question startled her. Was Cara a lesbian as well? Odds on. The woman had been cruising her relentlessly since avoiding the handshake. "I...er, no. I've seen her, but I'm not *seeing* her."

"Okay."

Rowe detected relief in her face and figured Cara probably tried to keep her sister on a short leash. Who knew what kinds of problems a woman with a mental disorder could get herself into? She fought back an instinct to cover her healing black eye with her hand. Cara was staring at the injury with a combination of suspicion and dismay.

"I had an accident." Rowe answered the unspoken question, but did not go into detail. If Phoebe wanted to tell her twin what had happened, that was up to her. She switched topic. "I understand you're in the music business, Cara."

Phoebe's twin unzipped her leather jacket and eased back into her seat a little, apparently deciding to stay put for the moment. "I direct and produce music videos."

"That must be pretty interesting."

"If you get off on being up to your neck in coke, testosterone and egos."

Rowe grinned. "Sounds like the shine's worn off."

"It's a living. A good one."

"That's important when you have expensive taste in footwear."

Cara blinked, then smiled a broad wayward smile, and at last Rowe saw a difference between the sisters' faces. Cara's smile involved more muscles and made more creases. It was vivacious, sensual and engaging. By contrast, Phoebe's held a siren's hypnotic allure, its very remoteness a drug. Cara's smile made you feel good; Phoebe's made you crave her.

Cara extended a leg and lifted her jean hem to expose a pair of custom black alligator boots with a finish that was slightly matte.

"Lucchese?" Rowe made an educated guess. She had tried on a similar pair once but drew the line at spending five thousand bucks on them.

"I couldn't help myself. I have a couple of Stephanie Ferguson designs, too. Phoebe thinks it's my flashy side coming out."

"My mom says the same thing about my computer. As in,

what's wrong with a typewriter?"

Cara let out a husky laugh. "You write er...thrillers, don't you?"

"It's okay. You can say it. I write horror."

"You've come to the right place."

"I sure hope so. I have a deadline hanging over my head and zero happening in the ideas department. Of course, you didn't hear that from me, and I need your promise I won't read it on some fan site blog tomorrow."

"Done." Cara stood up and removed her leather jacket. Dropping it on the seat, she said, "I'm going to grab a coffee. Want another one?"

"Sure. Thanks."

Rowe tried not to let her mouth fall open as she watched her companion cross the passenger deck. Cara wore a tight cranberry sweater tucked into her jeans. These sat on her hips, emphasizing a narrow waist, compact ass and slender legs. She was hot. And smart. And probably had a girlfriend, perhaps several. Maybe she was the one who had posed for the mock-historical photo. Rowe opened her satchel, planning to ask. But before she could locate the pic, Cara returned with their coffee.

She gave a small smile as Rowe pulled the jacket away for her to sit down. "Listen, are you doing anything later?" she asked once she'd settled.

Other than gnashing her teeth in front of the computer? Rowe managed a laid back tone. "No, I've nothing planned."

"Want to come over for a drink after supper?"

"Sure. I'd like that."

"Call it a peace offering. I was kind of rude to you before, I'm sorry."

"No apology necessary, but thanks."

They held one another's stare and Rowe felt a flicker of awareness ignite between them. It was exactly the kind of flicker that had the potential to complicate her life. She looked away.

Cara touched Rowe's wrist fleetingly, reclaiming her attention. "I can see why Phoebe likes you."

Rowe stumbled over what to say. *Please don't flirt with me*, sprang to mind, and all of a sudden, she felt weary. Weary of being the safe, stoic type that women, lesbian and straight, seemed to think they could practice their charm on without consequences. She could see Cara probably had her number already. Hers was the role of obliging butch-next-door, the one who could be depended on to fix cars and rescue damsels in distress. All it took was the promise of a hot meal, a sweet smile, and the possibility that one day something romantic might transpire.

It was not enough. Rowe was sick of being used and sick of chasing the impossible. She withdrew her hand and casually sipped her coffee. She would be a friend to the Temple twins, she decided, but she would not be toyed with. Never again would she put her life on hold for a woman who wasn't going to choose her anyway. Her therapist had said we repeat the same lesson over and over. Well, this was one lesson Rowe had finally learned.

She would enjoy Phoebe and Cara on her terms, not theirs.

EASIER SAID THAN done, she thought a few hours later as she sat in an armchair in the Temple's den. The twins were at either ends of the cushy sofa opposite her, each with her feet tucked up, each gazing at Rowe like she was the only woman on earth.

"So, you never actually had that conversation?" Cara asked.

"I knew she wouldn't leave her husband. And I didn't want an affair."

Cara swirled her wine idly. "I love how straight women think they can take a walk on the wild side and run back to hubby, and no one gets hurt. Like we don't count. It's not infidelity if it's with a woman."

"She must have hated that you wouldn't play her game," Phoebe said.

"I never thought about it that way." Rowe found the twins' take on her situation refreshing. It was a relief to be able to talk about Marion openly. In Manhattan, she couldn't lower her guard with any of her friends. Their social circles were too incestuous.

"I've met her type," Cara said. "They need a lot of attention and they don't mind whether they get it from a man or a woman."

"It must be an ego trip for a straight woman," Phoebe added. "I mean, to make a lesbian desire her. Maybe she was trying to make her husband jealous."

Rowe thought about Christopher Cargill. Had he guessed? He had to know almost everyone who met his wife lusted after her. Did it made him feel good about himself to be married to the hottest woman in the room, to know every guy present wondered what he had that none of them did? Chris didn't strike Rowe as the insecure type, and if he had guessed that she was in love with Marion, he hadn't let on. She sighed. Who knew what went on in other people's relationships? She was thankful to have left it all behind her, the whole miserable mess of life in the Big Apple.

"Bummer that it affected your work so much," Cara said.

"I only have myself to blame. I let it go on far too long."

"You were in love," Phoebe said softly. "Passion and common sense make for unlikely bedfellows."

Cara shot her twin a pointed glance, and Phoebe blushed slightly.

Detecting an undercurrent between the sisters, Rowe changed the subject. "So, you'll be away all next week?"

"Yes," Cara said. "Phoebe has a series of meetings at Quantico, and I thought I'd spend a few days in Virginia while she's there — take a look around.

Rowe tried to imagine what there was to see in winter in Virginia. It would get kind of chilly wandering around the Military Park at Fredericksburg, and somehow Cara didn't seem the type to spend vacation time soaking up Civil War history. "Sounds like fun," she said dryly.

"More wine?" Phoebe offered.

"Probably not a good idea. I need a clear head tomorrow, or I'll never get that morgue scene finished."

"You're still writing it?"

"Jesus, give the woman a break," Cara said. "She's just been baring her soul about why her writing's screwed."

"It's okay," Rowe said cynically. "I only have myself to blame if I can't write these days. I'm not in Manhattan any more. I have the perfect space for writing. But I spend most of my time staring out the window fantasizing about fried chicken. It's pitiful."

Phoebe gnawed on her bottom lip, a task Rowe would cheerfully have carried out for her. "There must be some way we can help. I know!" Her eyes lit up. "When we get back home, you can come here for dinner each night. That way, you won't have to think about cooking in that awful kitchen of yours. If you want, we could even talk about what you're writing." She glanced at her sister. "Cara always has lots of ideas. She's very creative."

"That's a nice offer," Rowe said, as if her mind was fully engaged with her writing woes when, really, she was thinking about ravishing Phoebe. "But I need to solve this for myself."

"What's your new novel about?" Cara asked.

"A woman is carrying a mutant baby that can read minds and gets her to kill people."

The sisters snuck darting looks at one another.

"Yep," Rowe said. "It's derivative crap. *Rosemary's Baby*

meets *The Omen*. Pretty unsavory."

"So the mother and the baby have a psychic connection?" Phoebe seemed captivated.

Cara, on the other hand, was unable to mask an expression of pitying derision.

"Uh huh. It's the baby that has the power," Rowe explained. "The evil spawn idea. Only, in my cunning twist, the daemonic child operates from the womb."

"Don't tell me..." Cara offered one of her wayward smiles. "It's a covert campaign tool for the pro-choice movement?"

Rowe made a show of stroking her chin thoughtfully. "I wonder if my agent would buy that?"

"Instead of killing people, why don't you get the baby to save the mother's life?" Phoebe suggested. "You know, she could be in some kind of danger and the baby warns her."

Rowe's mind clicked into gear. "The husband is seeing another woman...he's planning to kill his wife before the baby is born..."

"*Rosemary's Baby* meets the Laci Peterson case," Cara said. Her tone was not entirely dismissive.

Phoebe was gazing at Rowe with shy hopefulness, as if her idea probably sucked but might at least warrant a few seconds of serious consideration. Rowe wanted to kiss her, and then some. Hoping these horny yearnings were not written all over her face, she forced herself to entertain the new story concept. Maybe it had legs. It wasn't like her serial-killer-fetus tale had a whole lot going for it.

"Not bad," she conceded. "Not bad at all."

"See," Cara slid a foot across the sofa and nudged her sister. "Haven't I told you I'm not the only creative person in our house?" The indulgence on her face spoke volumes of her relationship to her sister.

Rowe found herself intrigued by their dynamic. It was almost as if each was the flipside of the other. Cara was outgoing, Phoebe introspective. Rowe guessed that Cara spent a lot of time trying to instill confidence in her twin. Phoebe seemed to seek her sister's approval constantly.

Curious, she asked, "Why do you two live together?"

The Temple twins regarded her solemnly.

"Trust," Phoebe replied. "No matter what happens, we know we can always trust each other." She looked to Cara, as if to measure her reactions.

"I guess the truth is, we don't need anyone as much as we need each other," Cara said in a pensive tone. "That must sound kind of creepy. But it's pretty normal for twins."

"You don't have other relationships?"

"None that get in the way." Phoebe seemed completely at ease with this discouraging pronouncement.

"What Phoebe means is that relationships come and go, but our bond will never change." Cara's looked Rowe up and down in frank appraisal. "Does that mean you won't invite us to party with you now?"

Rowe didn't know whether to be charmed or shocked. Against her better judgment, she teased back. "Any time you want to find out, call me."

Phoebe giggled. "Watch out, or she will."

Cara's eyes trapped Rowe's. "Yeah, I have your number," she warned softly.

"Figures," Rowe said and did not look away.

Chapter
Five

"WHAT DO YOU think of her?" Phoebe asked.

"She seems decent," Cara said, braiding her twin's long hair to keep it from tangling during sleep.

She had done this all their lives, since the death of their parents. Sylvia and Norman Temple had been killed on PanAM flight 759 when the girls were seven years old, and their grandmother had brought them up. Elizabeth Temple was an honorable woman who had taken great care to improve the estate the girls had inherited but seemed out of her depth with the demands of mothering. She'd once told Cara that her only son, their father Norman, had been handed over to a nanny the day he was born, as if this justified her disinterest.

"Do you think she's attractive?" Phoebe persisted.

Cara avoided answering that with total honesty. She wasn't sure how Phoebe would react if she thought they might both be interested in the same woman. All she needed was for her twin to seduce their neighbor for competitive reasons.

"I suppose," she said in a bland tone.

Phoebe gave her a sharp look. "Was it my imagination or were you hitting on her?"

"Do you really think I'd hit on our next door neighbor? We were messing with each other, that's all."

Phoebe seemed reassured. "I looked her up on the Internet. She's been on the New York Times Bestseller list."

"But not recently, hmm?"

"You know, it's funny," Phoebe removed her wristwatch and rings and placed them on the dressing table. "The first time I met her, I thought she had a damaged heart."

"Sounds like that woman Marion was your typical mind-fuck." Cara recognized the symptoms from far-off days in Junior High, before she'd learned the art of damage control. "She'd probably like to flirt, but she won't let herself."

"Pity." A smile played at the corners of Phoebe's mouth.

Cara planted a kiss on her sister's head, catching a trace of honeysuckle. Phoebe had been using the same shampoo for years. Oddly, it smelled different when Cara tried it on her own hair. "You don't need any more problems in that department and, from the looks of her, neither does she."

"Hey! I could have slept with her, but I didn't."

"Did she ask you?"

Phoebe turned slightly and looked up at her. "No. But you know what I mean. She could be tempted." Eyes glinting with mischief, she said, "Maybe some harmless flirtation would help her writing."

"Somehow I doubt that." Cara yanked a little on the braid, and Phoebe faced ahead once more.

"You are such a spoilsport," she complained.

"Otherwise known as your conscience."

"I have a conscience!"

"You just don't use it all the time."

"Oh, please." A groan. "Not Bev again. Can't you let it go?"

Cara fastened the braid with a band and dropped it over Phoebe's shoulder. "I'm just reminding you where those lapses of conscience lead."

"Well, you can stop now. I've suffered enough."

"You are such a trip," Cara scoffed. "*She's* the one who suffered. You just felt ashamed of yourself. It's not the same thing."

Phoebe got to her feet, wringing her hands. "If I could take back what I did, I would." Tears seeped into her long eyelashes, enhancing the tragedy queen routine. "I know I behaved badly."

"Have you told Bev this?"

"I keep starting a letter, then I don't finish it. She won't want to hear from me anyway."

"That's not the point. The point is you owe her an apology. Even if she rips it up and throws it in the trash." Cara set the hairbrush aside. "That's the last I'm going to say about it, okay?"

"Okay." Phoebe took a step forward and sidled into an embrace. "I don't know what I would do without you—I think I'd die."

Cara rocked her gently. Phoebe had never been completely secure since their parents had been killed. She wouldn't even speak to anyone else for a year after the tragedy. Out of necessity, Cara had become the interface between her and the rest of the world. In many ways, it was still the case, especially since Phoebe's accident. She had been in a coma for three months and had awakened oddly changed, psychologically and emotionally. The doctors could offer no explanations and had no bright ideas about treatment other than therapy and Prozac, neither of which made much difference. Phoebe had stopped both in the end.

Cara tried to be firm with her, but she found it hard to stay angry with her twin for long; she was so grateful to have her alive. "I'm not going anywhere," she said, stroking Phoebe's head where the skull had been fractured.

"Can I sleep in your bed tonight?" Phoebe asked. She always wanted this when Cara got back from a trip.

"Of course you can."

Half an hour later, as Cara was drifting into sleep, Phoebe said, "I wish we weren't going to Quantico."

"It's going to be fine. You're a big deal for them."

"If I really didn't have a conscience, I'd refuse."

"I'm very proud of you. Mom and Dad would be, too."

Cara could hear Phoebe's mind ticking over. "If this works, maybe I'll be able to talk to them."

A dull ache cramped Cara's throat. "You never know."

Phoebe rolled onto her stomach and draped an arm over Cara's middle. She always fell asleep that way when they shared a bed. There were photos of them sleeping in the same position as babies.

"If I can, what do you want me to say to them?" she whispered.

Cara called her parents' faces to mind. "Tell them I wish I knew them now. I think we'd be good friends."

ROWE OPENED HER eyes and drew a quick breath. The air seemed thin, depleted of oxygen. She listened intently and heard a rushing noise as if from a great distance. Her heart was doing its job, pushing a persistent tide of blood through her body. The muffled drum in her ears grew more rapid as she heard something else, a sound that didn't belong in her night.

Footsteps. Faint laughter. She reached for the switch that would flood her room with lamp-light, then arrested herself and lay rigid in the darkness. Where was it coming from? She slid silently from beneath her bedclothes and stepped onto the cold wooden floor, avoiding the board that creaked.

For a moment she wondered if Dwayne and Earl had shown up ahead of time to carry out some kind of nocturnal investigation. Surely they would not have broken into the cottage. She dragged on her robe and quickly tied the belt. Should she call the police now? Were there any police on Islesboro?

A smart woman living alone kept a gun on hand. Not Rowe. If she wanted a weapon, she would have to use whatever she could lay her hands on, or rustle up a knife from the kitchen. She cracked open her bedroom door and listened, motionless, trying to breathe without making any noise. The dogs were asleep in the next room, which she had converted to a cozy library. She shut them in there at night because Zoe snored like an old man, and having them on the bed meant Rowe got lousy sleep and could say goodbye to writing the next day.

She crept to the top of the stairs, thankful her thick bed-socks eliminated any sound. The footsteps floated nearer, and she knew it was not laughing she could hear, but crying. Her arms crawled with gooseflesh, and her teeth began to chatter. Lowering her weight carefully, she gripped the banister and descended. Her sensible self kept insisting that the noise she could hear was wind in the trees and something banging inside the house. She would enter the ballroom and find a trapped bird making small thumps as it flew time and again into impervious windows. Or she would wake up in bed and realize this was all a dream.

She paused for a moment at the base of the stairs and pinched at the soft flesh of her wrist, hoping to open her eyes and see her bedroom wall. Instead, she sensed a brooding malevolence, the presence of something old and discordant in the house. Her mouth dried until she could barely swallow. The ballroom loomed ahead.

What if she just turned on the lights and marched in like she owned the place, *which she did*. It was crazy to stand trembling in the hall, allowing her imagination to run riot. Yet, she had to know what lay beyond the two solid timber doors. She wanted to see with her own eyes what her mind refused to accept could exist. A ghost.

A shudder played along her spine and she groped for an ornate brass latch. Chill air and whispered voices seeped from the gap between the doors as she slowly parted them. Holding her breath, she slid inside.

Moonlight from the far windows etched the room in silver. Footfalls echoed, but she could see no one. No shimmering apparition. No mist. No flickering light. Yet she was not alone.

"I know you're there," she said, trying to sound calm.

The footsteps halted.

Rowe advanced a few paces. "Juliet?"

Something stirred the air near her face, and an ice cold hand touched her cheek. She gasped and stumbled back into the hall. Panting like she'd run a marathon, she fumbled her way up the stairs and fell into her room. This couldn't possibly be real, she reasoned feverishly. Ghosts didn't exist. There was nothing in that room.

She crawled into bed and hunkered beneath the covers, her shivers coming in fits and starts. Granted, she hadn't *seen* a ghost, Rowe thought, after her heart slowed down. But she had felt one.

"IT'S SERIOUS," DWAYNE said, sitting on the parlor sofa scrawling notes.

Rowe wanted to look over her shoulder. "Seriously haunted?" She watched Earl pack up the spook-catching equipment that would have had her cracking up laughing a few days ago.

"Hot spots all over the place. Confirmed Class Three in the ballroom. Record levels of activity in your kitchen. And that problem with the knives falling off your counter—it's a level surface, so right off we're talking object levitation. But with the other phenomena and EVP evidence, and your dogs weirding out, it could be something major."

"As in Class Five major," Earl cut in. "A malevolent entity that wants you out of that room. For starters, keep your knives in the drawer."

"You think I have some kind of poltergeist in there?" Rowe could hardly believe she had just asked that question.

"No." Dwayne gave her an odd look. "Are you feeling like maybe... "

"A poltergeist isn't a ghost." Earl cut to the chase. "Dude, explain."

"It's a psychokinetic manifestation of an individual's emotional stress." Dwayne wet his lips as he spoke. "The person who causes it is called a poltergeist agent. So, if this was a poltergeist situation, then that agent would be...uh, you."

How could any self-respecting horror writer not know that? Rowe didn't want to think about her pitiful ignorance leaking out. Her fan message boards were already a sea of perturbation.

"Right. Of course," she said, making it sound like a light bulb just lit the gloomy corridors of her memory.

Dwayne didn't seem convinced. "Clients quite often blame themselves for a haunting. But this is a residual situation."

"The ghost was here first, in other words?"

"Yep. Whatever happened in this cottage..." He lowered his voice to a near whisper. "We need to find out what it was so we can deal."

"Deal? You mean an exorcism or something." Rowe found herself whispering as well. Feeling ridiculous, she reverted to a normal voice. "I thought the last resident tried that already."

Earl rolled his eyes. "Jasper was a fucking basket case after a few months here. Man, you did him a favor buying this place. No one else would."

"We told him the priest would be waste of time," Dwayne said. "But some people need to think religion has all the answers."

"It's a scary world," Rowe said.

"Even scarier when it's run by those exact same people." Dwayne put his notebook away in the steel briefcase and rolled the combination lock.

Earl got to his feet. "I'll develop those EVP tapes some more. We've got some wailing and the Type B voice calling *Run.* I'll get that onto our website as a midi file, so you can listen any time you want."

"Great," Rowe said. Just what she needed—her very own howler.

"Your identity will not be disclosed," Dwayne assured her. "We take client privacy seriously, unlike certain other paranormal organizations."

Rowe gave him the grateful nod he seemed to be waiting for. "So, what's our next step?"

"Well, see, we need to gather more data. Measure your other rooms." Dwayne stood up and swept a sober look around the parlor. His eyes fell on the photograph Rowe had propped on the desk. "It's terrible what happened to her."

"No one likes getting dumped," Rowe said.

"No, I mean how she died, frozen in the snow like that." He stared out the window. "Must have been just out there."

Rowe cast an irritated glance at him. These two knew much more than they'd been letting on. Whenever she asked them about Juliet Baker's death, all they could talk about was sightings of her ghost.

"I thought you didn't know what happened," she said.

"Uh. We do and we don't." Dwayne shifted uncomfortably. "Like, obviously, the real story never made it into the newspapers. All the reports said it was an accident."

"But you have a different theory?"

"Well, see, when a house is haunted the paranormal investigator has to figure out why the ghost is hanging around. Like maybe they're unhappy or there's something they want to say. So, you have to ask yourself why a young lady like her would have gone out into a storm in the middle of the night. It's not...uh normal behavior. If we can get to the bottom of it and find out what she wants, then we can try a banishing."

"Which is what? Some kind of an afterlife therapy session with the ghost? You tell her to get lost and she does?"

Earl muttered, "Works a whole lot better than getting a priest to throw holy water around and order Satan out. Shit like that."

It made sense, Rowe supposed. That is, if you accepted ghosts actually existed. And since she now did, despite her attempts to rationalize her experience in the ballroom, she asked, "What do you think Juliet's ghost wants?"

"That's what we need to find out," Dwayne said. "The main report in the Camden Herald says she had a fall. Her father found her body the next morning after a maid noticed she wasn't in her bed."

"And your theory is that she walked out into the snow deliberately?"

"Maybe. It's like...a suspicion. See, we visited her grave when we were photographing orbs at the Evergreen cemetery with the MPRA and—"

"Man, what a waste of time," Earl remarked, rewinding audio tapes. "It was all about the tourists. Big fat surprise."

"Her grave?" Rowe prompted the para-nerds back on track.

"We took a photo of the headstone. You gotta see this." Dwayne reached for the steel briefcase, only to freeze, his eyes glued to the front window.

A dark shape loomed through the condensation. A pale face stared from beneath a hood.

"Oh, Christ," Rowe said.

Dwayne made an odd wheezing sound. "It's her."

"Man, that's a Class Four apparition." Earl frantically unzipped a bag and pulled out a camera. "Wicked awesome!"

The apparition tapped on the glass and called, "Rowe?"

Earl lowered the camera. "Fuck. She knows your name."

"We're going to be famous." Dwayne croaked.

Grumbling to herself, Rowe opened the window. This was all she needed—the entire world knowing she'd called in the crazies to help her deal with a ghost problem.

Cara pushed back the hood of her coat and peered in at them. "Am I interrupting something?" Flicking a glance in Dwayne's direction, she asked, "Is your friend okay? Looks like he saw a ghost."

"DON'T TELL ME — paranormal investigators?" Cara asked as Dwayne's car departed.

"How did you guess?" Rowe opened the baby gate on her stairs so the dogs could humiliate her by leaping all over the visitor.

"Let me see." Cara fended off the slobbering pair. "Bumper stickers that say *Ghot Ghosts*? The telltale Friends of Casper insignia on the back window..."

"Seems like I bought a haunted house. The guys wanted to take a look around."

"Actually, you bought *the* haunted house," Cara said as the dogs lost interest in her crotch and bolted out into the meadow. "Wait 'til summer. You won't be able to walk out your door without finding a family from Wisconsin camped on your stoop waiting for the tour guide."

"You're kidding me."

Cara gave her an incredulous look. "Are you saying you didn't know? Everyone thinks you bought it for the publicity."

"The horror writer poses on the doorstep of her haunted cottage?" Rowe rolled her eyes and launched into a glib media patter. "Author, Rowe Devlin knows what she's talking about when she writes a ghost story — "

"The sacrifices we make for art," Cara's mocked gently.

"Seems like I was the last person to find out about this place and its er...inhabitants. I know what I'm going to call this year — you know, when I write my memoirs — *The Year of My Perpetual Humiliation*."

"It can't be that bad."

"Trust me. It is."

"I can't wait to hear the sordid details." Cara tucked a hand in Rowe's arm and said in a coaxing voice, "I was sent to fetch you for lunch. Phoebe's cooking crab cakes."

"Your sister is a temptress. I love crab cakes."

"Wait 'til you taste her remoulade sauce."

"It's a conspiracy. I have to stop coming to your place. Every time I do, I can feel the fat cells piling on." Rowe pulled at a small roll around her middle.

To her astonishment, Cara's hand joined hers, sliding across her midriff. "I've felt worse."

"There was a time when I was buff."

"Not that long ago." The hand lingered. "You still have muscle tone."

A small shock of awareness jarred Rowe's spine. Cara's hand fell, and they stared at one another. Rowe wanted to look away, but something in Cara's gaze prevented her. She drew a sharp breath, and a seductive, spicy perfume invaded her nostrils.

Don't, she thought.

She must have said it out loud because Cara's pupils dilated and she murmured, "Why not?"

In the same split second, they reached for one another, and Cara's mouth parted softly. A chill of desire blossomed across Rowe's chest, stifling her ability to draw breath. She slid her hands to the base of Cara's spine and kissed her.

Their bodies fit like they were meant for union. Cara was a little shorter, and built more slightly. She moved against Rowe as if they were already naked. Starved of touch, Rowe's body clamored for the hot, firm press of flesh, the wallowing pleasure of all-over caresses, the building urgency before release. She wanted to feel a woman naked in her arms, to smell and taste her arousal, to hear her small cries of pleasure. It had been too long. Did she care if her potential sex partner was until recently a virtual stranger?

She lifted a hand to Cara's face, caressing the fragile jaw, tilting her head as the kiss grew deeper. With her free hand she pulled Cara's coat from her shoulders. She felt Cara's hands at her waist, tugging her shirt from her jeans. The kiss slowed to one of passionate intensity, and a strange calm descended on Rowe. How could the sharing of a single breath so enthrall? Mesmerized, she left Cara's mouth for her throat, kissing and delicately biting. All the while, she could feel Cara's hands moving over skin untouched for more than a year, leaving trails of prickling nerves. A ringing sound invaded the moment. She tried to ignore it, but its persistence was intolerable.

They drew back from each other, breathing hard.

Cara stared down at her coat as if she wasn't sure how it had ended up on the floor. Shakily, she said, "It's probably Phoebe."

Rowe went into the parlor and picked up the phone.

"Hey, Rowe," Phoebe said happily. "Are you coming?"

Almost, Rowe thought, then said, "I can't wait," and like a coward, "Your sister's here. Want to talk to her?"

Standing in the doorway, pulling on her coat, Cara shook her head. Rowe handed the phone to her anyway.

"Hey, sweetie," Cara said with cool aplomb. "Sorry we're running late. Rowe had to get rid of some visitors and take the dogs out. But we're on our way." Face flushed, she passed the handpiece back to Rowe and they avoided looking at one another.

Rowe tucked her shirt back into her pants and ran a hand over her hair. "Well, this is awkward."

Cara touched her arm. "It doesn't have to be. Nothing

happened. We don't have to read a whole lot into it."

"Sounds like a plan." Rowe moved out into the vestibule and took her pea coat from a hook. All she could think was that she had just avoided falling off a cliff, and she might not be so lucky the second time. She buttoned the coat and held the front door for Cara.

They strolled across the meadow, mist wreathing their faces.

"We're neighbors. So...bad idea." Cara might have been talking to herself.

Rowe agreed. "It could get pretty complicated."

Cara stopped suddenly. Snowflakes clung to her straight dark eyebrows and her top lip. Rowe refrained from licking them off. "Just so you know, the kiss was excellent. I would have liked to have sex with you."

"Me, too." Rowe cursed the phone for ringing during that hormonal interlude, reminding them that they were adults with common sense. She tried not to think about Cara naked in her bed. Why torture herself?

Cara produced a dazzling smile, which Rowe took to mean that they could now pretend it had never happened. She smiled back like it hadn't. They started walking again, but Cara was not quite ready to let it go.

"It was my fault," she said as they reached the tree belt.

Rowe inhaled the smell of damp balsam and dead leaves. "It takes two."

Cara glanced sideways at her. "I find you very attractive, Rowe."

"Let's face it, neither of us has a whole lot of competition in this neck of the woods."

Cara laughed at the back-handed compliment. "Phew. All that and charm too. Hold me back."

Rowe grinned. "Well, you know where I live."

A clump of snow fell wetly from a branch, covering them in heavy slush.

"Think that was a sign?" Cara muttered as they brushed each other off with gloved hands.

"Uh huh. The Maine version of 'Raindrops Keep Falling on Our Heads.'"

"God, you're as cynical as I am."

"Kindred spirits," Rowe said with dry sarcasm. "We must be meant for one another."

Cara swatted her arm. "Stop."

"Okay. Nothing happened."

"Agreed. No games. No fantasies."

"You got it," Rowe promised. *No tempting the Fates. No asking for trouble.*

She allowed Cara to move ahead of her as they approached the back door. Phoebe was waiting on the step, her face flushed from kitchen activities. She wiped her hands on a starchy calico apron and dropped a light kiss of welcome onto Rowe's cheek.

"I hope you brought an appetite," she said.

Rowe kissed her right back and staved off a shameless fantasy of sleeping with both twins. "You have no idea."

Chapter
Six

"I THINK I could fall in love with her." Phoebe adjusted her wobbly seat tray and removed the celery stick from her Bloody Mary. "She's different. I really like her and I haven't slept with her. That's a good sign. When I'm around her I feel so...happy. Almost silly. Do you know what I mean?"

Cara stuck the Emergency Instructions in the pocket of the seat in front and got busy with the headphones. She could never stand to listen to the crap audio on airplanes. But neither did she want to have a conversation about Rowe Devlin. Somehow she'd gotten through the past twenty-four hours without Phoebe guessing what had happened between her and their neighbor, and she wanted to keep it that way. It could have been worse, she reminded herself. They could have had sex.

She glanced at her sister and faked a smile. "We'll see what happens."

Two months, she calculated. Phoebe would find the idea of having a fling with Rowe interesting for approximately two months, then she would discover the truth. *Rowe is not perfect.* But what if she didn't sit the two months out? Cara frowned. What would Rowe do if Phoebe came on to her the way Cara had? Would she bend the rules about being good neighbors? Would Phoebe prove to be more than she could resist? A small flare of jealousy ignited in her gut. She wanted to laugh it off, but she couldn't. The idea of Phoebe and Rowe together made her stomach churn. Unnerved, she finished her vodka like it was water.

"Are you okay?" Phoebe asked. "You're so quiet today."

"Sorry, sweetie. I've got stuff on my mind. Bloodwork weren't happy with their video. ManAngel thinks his hair looks green."

"That's his worst problem? Didn't their drummer kill himself halfway through filming?"

"Their manager hired Deepak Chopra to counsel them. After

that, they got a new drummer who turned out to be better, so they were like, 'hey man, it was karma.'"

"Maybe you should work with country singers."

"Exchange suicidal coke-heads for wife-beating alcoholics, you mean?"

"Are all musicians messed up?"

"Probably not. But somehow, I manage to avoid the sane ones. Just lucky, I guess."

"It's difficult for you, coming with me this week, isn't it?" Phoebe asked.

"I want to come, but yes. It means juggling priorities."

Phoebe chewed on that for a beat, then said, "I've been thinking. It's time I stopped leaning on you so much."

"Okay." Cara knew what was coming. Phoebe had these flights of fancy every so often. Her usual response involved making some lifestyle changes that lasted a few months.

"I earn enough money to get my own apartment. Maybe I should look for something in Portland."

Cara held back a sigh. The last time Phoebe had her own place, she'd allowed some big-eyed anorexic to stay there temporarily. Months had passed and her houseguest ran up huge phone bills, stole jewelry, and eventually moved her junkie girlfriend in. One day Phoebe phoned Cara after finding a huge stash of ecstasy inside a sofa pillow cover she'd removed for cleaning. Picturing the lowlife roommates busted for dealing and Phoebe dragged into jail with them, Cara had moved her out that evening.

"You don't think I can manage." Phoebe looked hurt.

Cara chose her words carefully. "I think you manage very well when you set realistic goals for yourself."

"This thing Vernell wants me to do..." Phoebe stared at her, full of determination. "I'm going to do it by myself. Then you can go back to L.A. and not worry about me."

"Let's take it one day at a time."

"I'm serious."

"I know. So how about if I stay 'til you feel ready to manage? I can always come back if you need me."

Phoebe slid a hand into Cara's. "Sometimes the truth is I don't *need* you. I just *want* you with me for selfish reasons."

"It's not all one-sided," Cara admitted. "I worry about you far too much and sometimes I hang around just so I know you're okay. But you're right. You're not a child any more. I need to let go a little."

"I'm not afraid of what's going to happen at the FBI. I mean, I'm nervous. But it's kind of exciting, too."

"Yeah, no kidding. You'll meet all kinds of interesting people and see amazing stuff. I'm totally jealous."

Phoebe tilted her head back in a rare laugh. "You? Jealous? You ride in stretch limos and hang out with famous people."

Cara pictured herself dragging yet another shit-faced rock star out of his bathroom to make it to a filming session six hours late. "Trust me, it's not all it's cracked up to be."

Phoebe lapsed into fretful silence. "I hope I can do it."

"You'll do fine." Cara recognized the mood. Phoebe was always overcome with self-doubt when she set out on a new FBI assignment.

"I hope I won't let everyone down." Phoebe chewed on her lip.

Cara took her hand. "Just do your best. No one can expect any more than that."

THE BEHAVIORAL SCIENCE Unit used to be buried sixty feet below ground under the shooting range, Vernell said. These days they had rooms with a view in one of the sprawling honey colored buildings that made up the FBI Academy at Quantico.

Phoebe stole a sideways glance at the tall, immaculately groomed man strolling next to her. She could tell he was pleased she had come. He'd met them at the airport himself, the day before, and had waited at their hotel while they checked in and changed. Then he took them out to dinner and told Cara if there was anything she would like to do or any place she wanted to go while Phoebe was otherwise engaged, he had arranged a Bureau car and driver for her.

The VIP treatment had continued that morning. Two FBI agents picked them up from their hotel and drove them through miles of trees and army vehicles to what looked like a fancy hospital in the middle of a tranquil forest. Only it wasn't as tranquil as it seemed. They had barely stepped out of the car when the sound of gunfire and explosions shattered the morning calm.

Vernell was waiting in the parking area and led them toward the main building. He didn't seem to notice when a tank rolled past them and a swarm of trainees ran by, everyone in protective suits, oxygen tanks on their backs. A couple of them glanced at Phoebe and Cara in surreptitious appreciation. Apparently, women in civilian clothing were a novelty around here.

"I feel like I'm in a movie," Cara said.

Vernell came close to a smile. "We'll get your visitors' passes sorted out first, then we have a meeting with the Assistant Director."

After passing a bronze plaque of J. Edgar Hoover's head, they entered a sunny atrium with glassed-in walkways visible a level above. Phoebe stared up at the pale walls with their FBI themed slogans about fidelity and bravery and the like.

Awed to be standing in the beating heart of a major security and intelligence organization, she said, "I suppose if the terrorists were planning to drop a bomb anywhere, this would be a good choice."

Vernell stared at her. "Are you sensing something, Phoebe?"

"No." She felt herself color. Vernell and everyone else here thought she had astounding supernatural powers. How mortifying if she turned out to be no different from anyone else.

The Assistant Director sure behaved like he expected a prompt and accurate prediction of the second coming, and if not that, the names and addresses of every serial killer operating in the country.

"For an asset such as yourself, the Bureau is willing to overlook a certain amount of red tape," he said a few minutes into their meeting. "We're issuing you a top secret security clearance. That's a blue background pass." He paused, with an air of expectancy. Clearly this announcement was momentous and required a reaction.

Phoebe glanced uncertainly at Cara, who had not said a word since the introductions were made, allowing Phoebe to occupy center stage in this important meeting. Her sister made a small prompting gesture and hoping for the right tone, Phoebe said, "Thank you, Mr. Levin. That's a real privilege."

"Of course, you'll still need to sign in for visitors' passes when you enter the building, but you'll be able to walk freely without an agent escorting you at all times."

"Thank you, sir." Vernell took the honor in stride. He had the look of a man who knew he was holding a winning hand.

"So..." The Assistant Director consulted a sheaf of notes on his desk. "You're headed out to St. Johnsbury later this afternoon, Jefferson?"

"Yes, sir. We thought if Ms. Temple canvassed the scene, she may be able to contribute additional data."

"Good luck." The Assistant Director fixed his light blue eyes on Phoebe. "If this works out, you could meet the Director."

Guessing this was a bigger deal than the blue security pass, Phoebe said, "I'll do my best not to disappoint you, sir."

"Excellent." Mr. Levin pressed something on his desk and a secretary appeared. "Maude, Ms. Temple is working with us on a priority matter. Any sign the Company's feeling around, I want to know."

"Understood, sir." The woman gestured for Phoebe, Cara and Vernell to follow her and instructed them to take a seat in a drab waiting area while she had Phoebe's new pass brought over.

"Coffee anyone?" Vernell asked.

Cara declined. She looked like she had her mind on something.

Phoebe laughed nervously and said, "Only if it has a shot of brandy in it."

"Relax. You did fine." Vernell poured himself a glass of water.

"The Company?" Cara inquired, cutting to the chase.

"The CIA," Vernell translated.

Phoebe tried not to sound squeaky. "Am I working for them, too?"

"No. And we don't want them putting out the welcome mat."

"Do they know about me?"

"Not so far, but with the new Homeland Security protocols, seepage can be a problem...information leaks."

Phoebe repressed an urge to get up and run from the building. Cara had already warned her to say nothing to anyone about what she was doing, and only to speak with the Bureau personnel Vernell introduced her to. Obviously Cara and Vernell had discussed the situation ahead of time and come to some agreement about how much they would tell her. She could almost hear Cara: *Why scare her with talk about the CIA?*

"I can't see why the CIA would be interested in me," she said. "It's not like I have dreams about terrorists."

Vernell's eyes were coolly assessing. "We don't know what you're capable of, Phoebe. And if our friends in Intelligence get wind of you..." He left the sentence hanging.

"What?" Phoebe felt a flutter of alarm. "What would they do?"

"Your life would never be the same," he said flatly.

"Then, we'll have to make sure they don't hear about me." Phoebe was partly flattered and partly appalled to realize intelligence agencies might actually fight over her. She would never look at men in trench coats and dark glasses the same way again.

Cara touched her arm. "Relax. You have nothing to worry about. Only a few people know you're here and most of them don't even know your real name."

"Promise me something, both of you," Phoebe said. "If the

CIA comes after me, I want to disappear."

"Trust me," Vernell said, grim-faced. "We won't be trading assets with the Company."

"You didn't hear me," Phoebe insisted. "Disappear. Like in witness protection."

Cara laughed softly. "Sweetie, there's no need to get worked up."

"I watch *Alias*. Those people are scary."

Cara glanced sideways at Vernell.

"We'll do whatever it takes," he said. "Put the CIA out of your mind."

VERNELL HAD ASSEMBLED several people in a nondescript meeting room. He introduced Phoebe as Ms. Golden and that's what everyone called her. A stocky, older man with a dense mop of gray hair and a pink bowtie instantly stood up and seized her hand in a firm, dry grip.

"We've been anticipating this day." His words were thickly accented. "I am honored to introduce myself. Doctor Yuri Karnovich. My colleagues and I welcome you."

Phoebe murmured something appropriate, aware all eyes were on her. She greeted a couple of thirty-something men who appeared to have been cloned from a special FBI gene pool: neat brown hair and even features, straight white teeth, conservative gray suits and shiny black shoes. Their names escaped her almost as soon as she'd heard them.

"And this is Doctor Harriet Sutton." Vernell introduced a round faced woman who looked like anyone's grandma, but was a forensic psychiatrist.

"Call me Harriet and make yourself at home," she invited after shaking Phoebe's hand. "And if there's anything you need while we work, just let me know."

Relieved that their group was so small, Phoebe occupied the chair Vernell indicated, at one end of the table, and tried to look like she was at ease.

One of the clones pushed a cup of coffee over to her, and said, "Cream and no sugar, right?"

"Right." Phoebe wondered how he knew that. Had someone spied on her at breakfast?

"So, you're a twin?" Harriet noted cheerfully.

"Yes. Identical. My sister was here earlier, but she's gone sightseeing now."

"She doesn't have the same unusual dreams you experience?"

"No. She's...normal."

"Normal is relative," Dr. Karnovich pronounced. He went on to ask Phoebe some general questions about her childhood and the accident. To her surprise, they had her medical records and seemed to know every detail of her coma and recovery.

"SAC Jefferson has briefed you about the case?" Harriet asked.

"In broad detail," Vernell replied on Phoebe's behalf. "I didn't want to influence her perceptions."

"Yes, yes." The doctor tapped his finger lightly on the table, apparently lost in thought. After a few particularly loud taps, he said, "We're going to try some techniques that may help you focus your perceptions. Are you comfortable with such experiments, Ms. Golden? Everything will be taped on video, if that's all right."

"It's fine. I want to help," Phoebe said.

Dr. Karnovich gave her an odd, almost regretful smile and signaled the men, who produced a stack of plastic bags from a trolley near the table. They opened each one and placed its contents on the table. Every item was tagged.

Phoebe fingered a delicate gold necklace. "Did these things belong to victims?"

"Some of them did," Harriet said. "We'd like you to examine each of them and give us any impressions you form. It doesn't matter what comes up — there are no wrong answers."

Phoebe picked up a distinctive black and red hairbrush. "This belonged to Iris. I saw it in one of my dreams. She was sitting in her car, brushing her hair. Then something happened. She dropped it. That was the end of the dream."

"It was found in her car. We were never sure if it had been there a while, or not." Vernell slid a torn sweater toward her, "Can you tell us anything about this?"

Phoebe ran her hands over the soft, knitted garment. It was pale pink and bore faint traces of its owner's perfume. "I haven't seen it before." Detecting a flicker of disappointment in Vernell's eyes, she continued to hold the garment, trying to clear her mind. How did real psychics do this? Did they think about a white empty room or a grassy meadow or something? She stared down at the fine pink weave, seeing nothing, feeling nothing. "I'm sorry," she said, dismayed.

None of the other items brought any clear images to mind and she could sense a palpable disappointment in the people around her by the time she was done. Glancing at Vernell, she felt bad for embarrassing him in front of colleagues he no doubt hoped to impress.

"I wish I could tell you things," she said. "It just doesn't seem to work that way for me."

Dr. Karnovich instantly offered a reassuring smile. "Do not worry yourself, Ms. Golden. We are right now exploring. It is a process of elimination, you understand? So we learn that the handling of articles draws the blank—that's okay. The gift is different for everyone."

They spent the rest of the morning showing her photographs, handwriting, and home movies. Then they put her into a glassed-in room and had her choose flash cards of different shapes to see if she was telepathic. Phoebe flunked everything.

"I guess I won't be meeting the Director, after all," she said over lunch.

"We've only started our tests," Vernell said. "Tonight you'll sleep here. Doctor K wants to measure your brain activity."

Phoebe shuddered at the thought of sleeping in a laboratory hooked up to electronic machines, with strangers watching her. "Does Cara know?"

"She offered to sleep nearby if that would make you more comfortable. We could set something up in one of the observation rooms."

Phoebe shook her head, determined to not to be a baby. "No, I'm fine by myself. But I'm not sure if I'll be able to dream in that kind of situation."

"No one expects you to," Vernell said in same tone she'd heard him use when he spoke to his young son over the phone.

"Where are we going this afternoon?" she asked.

"St. Johnsbury, Vermont. I want you to take a look around a house there. It's owned by a woman we think may have been abducted by the man we're looking for."

The moment he said it, a memory flashed into her mind, a tiny fragment of a dream from the night before. "Is her name June?"

Vernell's dark brown eyes lifted to hers. "June Feldstein."

"She's hurt." Phoebe touched the back of her head. "Here. He must have hit her."

Vernell's voice took on an urgency. "She's alive?"

"They're always alive in my dreams," she said sadly.

"THE PHOTO IS authentic." Mrs. Chauncey flipped through a folder of carefully preserved images, each encased in its own plastic envelope. "Ah, here it is."

Juliet Baker's original portrait was larger than the

reproduction sold in the museum stores, and Rowe stared down at the sepia image, trying to make sense of her neighbors' uncanny resemblance to this long dead woman. Obviously the two families must share some common ancestry.

Now that she really focused on Juliet's face, she could see her nose was a little wider and shorter than the Temples' and her chin was slightly less pronounced, the shape of her face more rounded. She was beautiful, but hers was an adolescent beauty. She was not quite as finely chiseled in her bone structure, her jaw line was less pronounced. The differences were subtle, but Rowe could pick them out. Having her face only inches from Cara's had branded the Temples' features into her memory.

She was struck again by the pearl at Juliet's throat. How had it ended up in Phoebe's possession? "Do you know the Temple sisters, Mrs. Chauncey?" she asked.

"Not personally. But we wave."

"Have you ever noticed that they look rather like this Juliet Baker."

"I can't say I have." Mrs. Chauncey's penciled eyebrows inched together. "But now you mention it, I see what you mean. Fascinating."

"Maybe they're related in some way."

Mrs. Chauncey's nondescript blue eyes took on a coy glitter. "I guess old man Baker spread his seed a little more widely than anyone knows. Perhaps Juliet had a half brother or sister born on the wrong side of the blanket."

"So, if we want to find out who that is, we'd have to research the Temple family tree," Rowe concluded.

"Which is exactly what we can do thanks to the Harry Stewart genealogy records bequest." With an air of satisfaction, Mrs. Chauncey smoothed her long beige sweater over her broad hips and scanned a shelf full of tall leather bound volumes.

The head of the Islesboro Historical Society, this woman made it her business to know everything worth knowing about the families who had lived on the island since the first cottages were built. She was thrilled by Rowe's project and said she would like to feature any findings in the next Society Bulletin. Everyone knew about the Disappointed Dancer, of course. She was almost as famous Lilian Nordica, whose ghost could be heard singing opera in the Farmington auditorium.

With a ladylike grunt, she hauled a hefty volume onto a ruthlessly polished table and opened it. "The Temples are Mainers through the maternal line," she said, reverently turning the thick pages. "Early last century a Verity Adams lived in the Temple's house. She had a daughter Anne, whose daughter Elizabeth married a Temple. Elizabeth is the twin's grandmother."

Rowe crossed the room to stand at her hostess's elbow, inwardly repeating this potted genealogy so she could grasp who was who. "The twins' parents are dead?" she asked, deciphering a small entry on the family tree.

"Plane crash," Mrs. Chauncey confirmed. "Elizabeth Temple brought the girls up after the accident. She still owns the house, as far as I know. But she lives in Miami these days...so much easier to hire help there."

"So, if Mr. Baker fathered a child, who would it be?" Rowe scanned the birthdates.

"There's only one possibility." Mrs. Chauncey sounded intrigued. "And this is very odd...Anne Adams was born in December 1912—"

"To Verity Adams, who happened to be widowed fourteen months earlier," Rowe completed, noting the date of decease for Henry, the husband. "Longest pregnancy in history."

"The Bakers were summer people," Mrs. Chauncey mused. "Normally they would have arrived in April and departed in September. But in 1912 they extended their visit, it seems."

Rowe did some mental calculations. If Thomas Baker wasn't on the island until April, Anne must have been born prematurely if she was his child. She wondered if the twins knew of their possible connection to Dark Harbor Cottage and its ghost.

"Do you know when the Baker family sold the cottage?"

"Your attorney can tell you that. It will be on your property title." Mrs. Chauncey closed the genealogy volume, her face thoughtful. "There's something else that may interest you. For the longest time, an old lady who lived here wrote letters to the Editor of the Camden Herald seeking information about her daughter. The girl was once a maid for the Bakers. It sounds like she ran off with some young man, never to be heard from again."

"When was that?"

"Around the time Juliet Baker died. The girl's name was Becky O'Halloran. Her mother was in service, too. She was Verity Adams' housekeeper for many years."

Rowe's head spun. The more she learned, the more tangled the cottage's past became. And she'd discovered virtually nothing about Juliet Baker herself, other than the intriguing possibility that she may have had a half-sister. Could that information hold the key to laying her ghost to rest? Rowe was dubious. She thought about a cemetery picture Dwayne and Earl had shown her and the strange inscription on Juliet's headstone: *Pray you now, forget and forgive.* She sensed a clue in those words, the same words spoken by King Lear to his daughter Cordelia.

Had Juliet discovered her father's infidelity with their neighbor and been so distressed that she had done something stupid? Was that why her ghost roamed the house? And where was Juliet's mother in all of this?

Rowe thanked Mrs. Chauncey, wrote a donation check for the Historical Society, and strolled outdoors. Immediately she felt like a stranger in a strange land. It seemed every pickup truck on the street had a snowplow mounted on it, and every driver was wearing peculiar head gear. She and her shiny Lexus SUV looked like they'd beamed down from the Mothership.

A guy driving a dog sled waved at her and slowed his team. "Hey Rowe," he called like he knew her. "How's that book coming?"

"Great," she lied.

"Well, things can only get better." With a nod of dour encouragement, the stranger yelled a command to his dogs, and they hurtled off down the road.

Rowe got into the Lexus and rested her head on the steering wheel. She was a washed up writer living in a haunted house in Maine in the middle of winter. She had now exchanged a hopeless passion for someone's wife for a doomed crush on her neighbors. Plural. And instead of finishing the piece of crap novel her agent was hounding her for, she was on some wild ghost chase with two young males who thought the government was spying on them.

The dog sled driver was right. Things could only get better.

JUNE FELDSTEIN'S HOME was a graceful butter yellow Victorian on the hilltop of St. Johnsbury, a picturesque town in Vermont. A portrait artist in her thirties, Feldstein lived there alone. Phoebe felt like a burglar standing in the missing woman's bedroom, handling items that belonged to her.

Vernell and Harriet were having a muffled conversation out in the hall, waiting for her to make some kind of pronouncement. Hoping to spark a paranormal revelation, she entered the closet and ran her hands over coats, dresses, pants and shirts. June was a tidy person. Her clothes were divided by season and organized into color groups. Although there were some good quality pumps on a rack of their own, it looked like she wore sensible shoes most of the time. She had small feet, Phoebe noted, and her tastes were more conservative than one might expect of a creative person. Even her underwear was unadventurous— drawers full of plain white cotton panties and bras, and unsexy pajamas. If June had a boyfriend, he obviously didn't expect her to be anything but a lady at all times.

How did a woman like her, living in a town like this, get abducted by a serial killer? Phoebe wondered what common thread linked the victims this monster chose. She thought about Iris. She'd been in Vermont on vacation, staying in a bed & breakfast place not far from St. Johnsbury. So it seemed as if the killer was probably a local man or someone who had once lived here. According to Vernell, he had to know the area. Iris's grave had been well off the beaten track in the heart of the Northeast Kingdom, a location a stranger would not have stumbled on.

Phoebe wandered over to the bed and lifted a framed photograph from the bedside cabinet. June was an attractive woman with a high smooth forehead and straight light brown hair to her shoulders. Her smile was warm and open. She looked like the kind of woman you would choose for a friend.

"Where are you?" Phoebe asked the picture. All she could hear was the muted tick of the grandfather clock in one corner and the sound of Vernell and Harriet moving around elsewhere in the house.

On an impulse, she lay down on June's bed and stared around the room, seeing what June would see every morning when she awakened. Rose-hued wallpaper and dark wood. A simple white plaster ceiling studded with wood beams. Floor length brocade drapes in dark green. Mellow antique furniture. A large bowl and pitcher stood on a marble-topped wash stand in one corner. Numerous paintings occupied the walls. Faces. Landscapes.

Phoebe's eyes were drawn to one of these, a scene of a lake. She pictured June sitting at her easel in this tranquil setting, painting what she saw. An image flashed into her mind, glimmering, edges ragged as if reflected on moving waters. A snow-capped mountain. Naked spruce trees. She closed her eyes and felt strangely light, as if she were floating. A slender brush occupied her hand, paint heavy on it's bristles. A gray jay foraged near her feet.

A shadow moved and she had a brief sense of something not quite right, then the bird took flight, and she was thrown suddenly from her chair. In front of her lay tubes of paint, ejected from their box. Someone wrenched her palette from her hand. She tried to get up, but her head spun, and she realized she had been struck a blow to the back of her skull. Sinking onto her stomach, she saw a pair of big feet in tan-colored boots, black pants tucked into them. As she turned her head to look up at her assailant, she fell into a pitch dark void and could not stop falling.

She cried out, but her voice seemed disembodied. Phoebe opened her eyes. Vernell and Harriet were staring down at her, alarm vying with poorly disguised eagerness.

"I saw his feet," she said. "June was painting a picture." She tried to call the scene to mind. Mountains and trees. Like most of Vermont. Very helpful.

"Did you fall asleep?" Harriet asked.

"Kind of. I was looking at those paintings on the wall and listening to the clock, and the next minute I was there. It was like I was her. I was seeing what she saw."

Harriet took out a small cassette recorder. "So, it was more like a trance than being asleep?"

"Yes. It was like being hypnotized."

"Have you ever been hypnotized, Ms. Golden?"

"No. It seems creepy."

Harriet's bright blue eyes shot sideways to Vernell and he gave a nod that was almost imperceptible. Taking a few paces away, he spoke quietly into a lapel mic, and within seconds, Phoebe heard running feet and two FBI agents entered the room.

Vernell indicated June's paintings. "Get these packed up."

"This is wonderful." Harriet took Phoebe's arm and led her out of the room while the men worked. "I think you've found a way to enter a meditative state outside of sleep. It's almost like self-hypnosis, and if this experience is any indication, you can access the unconscious."

"So, I am a real psychic then?"

Harriet gave her a funny look. "Of course."

"Do you work with a lot of other people like me?"

"There is no one like you." Harriet escorted her downstairs to a formal living room and told her to sit down.

"I'm fine." Even as she said it, Phoebe felt light-headed.

"You're extremely pale, and you're hyperventilating."

"I faint sometimes." She perched on a sofa and made an effort to slow her breathing.

Harriet signaled one of the agents who was humping paintings out to the cars parked in front of the house. "Tell the SAC I'll drive Ms. Golden back to the Bubird."

"Really, I'm fine," Phoebe protested, not wanting to be coddled like she was some kind of mental case.

But Harriet ignored her, and after they'd sat for a few minutes, she took Phoebe's elbow and escorted her out of the house. As they walked down the narrow cobblestone path to the curb, the doctor lowered her voice and said, "I'm going to tell you something. This is just between you and me."

"Okay."

"The Bureau will want to own you round the clock. Don't allow it."

Surprised to hear this from one of the people assigned to wring information from her, Phoebe said, "I have no plans to sign my life away. I don't want to do this full time."

Harriet sighed. "We can be very persuasive."

"Are you saying I would be coerced?"

"I'm saying you are the one with the power. You have what we want, and no one else does. Whatever happens, remember that. You might need a lever one day."

Chapter
Seven

ROWE CHISELLED OFF the final rusted hinge and lifted the door from its frame. It was not as large as the doors in the cottage, but solid hardwood, and her back strained as she tried to hold it steady. Grunting with exertion, she shimmied it along the grit-laden floor and propped it against the wall, dislodging clumps of dust that rained down on her head.

"Lovely," she said, brushing herself off as best she could. Obviously no one had set foot in the Carriage House for years, maybe even decades.

Wielding a flashlight, she fought her way into the servants' cramped quarters, fending off the cobwebs that festooned the contents. Where to start? Boxes were piled high atop old furniture covered in dust sheets. The electricity wasn't working, and the sole window on the opposite wall was completely screened by clutter, blocking any natural light.

She should have hired an odd job man from the village, Rowe decided, as she lifted a heavy stack of boxes. These she lugged down the rickety stairs to the empty garaging space below. The floor was damp, so she'd laid plastic sheeting. Her plan was to empty each of the small servants' rooms and systematically search the contents for information dating back to the Bakers.

On some level, she was aware that the task was a huge distraction from her work. There was no reason why she needed to do this now. The sane option was to wait until summer and invite Mrs. Chauncey and her volunteers in. This was exactly the kind of assignment that would get their motors running. But no. She had to freeze her ass off in a dark, dank building looking for who knew what to prove a half-baked theory about people who had lived here a hundred years ago. *Why?*

With flimsy conviction, she answered her own question: "Because I have a ghost."

The real reason was much more prosaic. She was at an

impasse. Her new book was crap, worse crap than the last two, such turgid crap that she would be lucky if her publisher refused it. Only they wouldn't. Instead they would trumpet a new bestseller that would cement her demise into the ranks of those authors-in-decline who cash their fat advance checks only to foist underwhelming garbage on the public. She would get the promotional push denied to better novels written by authors down the pecking order. Then, when her patient fans eventually started jumping ship and her book sales no longer covered her advances, the gravy train would creak to a halt. Hers was not a big enough name to nourish the indefinite hope that one day she would return to form and publish something good with all forgiven.

If she wrote a decent book now, she could arrest the downward spiral before it gathered momentum. But, so far, that wasn't happening. Just hours ago, she had printed her manuscript, read it, then consigned it to the fire. The book richly deserved a rejection slip—if an unknown author submitted it, that would be its fate. She was almost tempted to send it in under cover of another name, just to prove her point. But it was not exactly earth-shattering news that countless over-hyped novels by big name writers stocked the shelves of airport bookstores while excellent works by those less known came and went without a ripple.

Tomorrow she would call her agent and tell the truth—that she needed to take a year off, and maybe then she would write something worth the paper it was printed on. If her publisher would not grant an extension on her contract, so be it. She would have to return a chunk of change and walk.

Fortunately most of her last big advance was unspent. Her publicist thought it was time she started acting like a celebrity, so the public would believe she was one. But Rowe had been reluctant to throw money away on a fancy fortress of a house with elaborate security and round-the-clock bodyguards, and even more reluctant to initiate gossip about her private life, then give indignant interviews when it showed up in the media. She had enough problems

Gloomily, she ferried and stacked boxes until she had cleared a broad path to the filthy little window that the housemaids of yesteryear must have wished they could gaze out of during daylight hours. She dragged a tall dresser away from it, rubbed the panes with a wet cloth, and stared out into a galaxy of snow. The flurries of a few hours earlier had become a blizzard. She contemplated returning to the house and camping out in front of the parlor fire with some reheated pizza and a good book. But she'd come this far and she was filled with anticipation, wondering what she would discover here amidst the detritus of lives long forgotten.

Weak winter light threw the room into vapid monochrome, revealing shrouded shapes crammed against moldering walls. Dragging a protective mask over her nose and mouth, she drew off some of the dust sheets. Incredibly, the furniture she unveiled was not junk, but fine quality Victorian pieces. A piano. Dining chairs. A mahogany chiffonier. She pulled a stack of boxes away from the front of a roll-top writing desk and tried the middle drawer. As her commonsense self had expected, it was locked. So were all the others, and the roll top itself.

She groped beneath the desktop, hoping to locate a key. Her fingers connected with a small metal box screwed in to the wood, and she got down on her hands and knees to inspect her discovery.

"Genius!" she congratulated herself, withdrawing not one but two keys from the concealed receptacle.

Just as she hoped, one of them unlocked the desk drawers, the other the roll top. This slid back with surprising ease and Rowe found herself staring at the motherlode. Rolls of letters, stacks of ledger books, cards, receipts. She opened an inlaid wooden box and gasped. An antique Waterman fountain pen complete with eye dropper and ink would thrill her any time, but this one told her she was looking at the Baker's domestic workstation. Before World War One, most fountain pens were dropper-filled.

She positioned her flashlight to one side and reached for a roll of letters. As she caught sight of her grubby hand, she groaned. Did she really want to cover all these old documents with black grime? There was probably historical stuff here Mrs. Chauncey would kill for. Besides, if there was one thing that turned Rowe's stomach, it was having filthy hands and nails. Now that she'd seen hers, all she could think about was a hot shower.

Shivering with cold, she emptied a box and filled it with the contents of the desk. Halfway through this task, something caught her eye and she reached into the cavity behind the small upper drawers and extracted a thin, rectangular fabric purse.

Her pulse leapt. Someone had hidden this—obviously a woman. The purse was pretty and seemed to be made of silk. Elated, she unfastened the ribbon ties and withdrew a half-finished letter. It was written in a refined hand and dated July, 1912:

Dearest James,

My heart is miserable. I know some accident must have befallen you en route to Dark Harbor. I can tolerate any embarrassment, the whispers and vindictive gossip, if I can but be assured that you are safe and we shall soon be married.

In your silence, my thoughts prey upon its cause. Surely my father's ill-timed bombast could not have discouraged a true heart such as yours. If it is indeed his honest desire not to settle upon me the promised sum, it is my most fervent belief that this is of no consequence to you and could not in any way pertain to your absence upon the occasion of my birthday ball.

Although I feel most dreadfully alone, it is of some faint consolation to have shared the burden of my fears and secrets with my dear Becky. A more loyal and faithful confidante to her mistress could not be found. It is upon her counsel that I write this urgent plea...

Rowe searched every crevice of the desk for the next page of the letter and any other correspondence, but came up empty handed. She read the unhappy words once more, then folded the page and returned it to the purse. Clearly there had been some shit going down between Juliet's father and the prospective husband and threats that her marriage settlement would not be paid. Reading between the lines, it looked like Juliet believed this could be the reason she had been dumped. She was unhappy and hurt, but Rowe didn't get the sense that she was suicidal.

She was intrigued by the reference to "Becky." This had to be the maid Mrs. Chauncey had mentioned. Had Becky's elopement with her own young man pushed the jilted Juliet over the edge?

Rowe tucked the purse deep inside the box to protect it from the snow. Feeling thoroughly satisfied with her afternoon, she fastened her jacket, dragged on her wooly hat, and braved the bruising cold.

"COME WITH ME." Iris took Phoebe's hand and they floated out of the white room with its blinking equipment and tinny blipping sounds, and up toward the star-coated sky. Far below, the world glimmered as if the mantle of night were crawling with fireflies.

"You look better," Phoebe said, noticing Iris's bruises had gone. "Are you in heaven, now?"

"I'm not sure," Iris answered. "You're here and you're not dead, so how can I be?"

The lights became streams of golden lava so bright that Phoebe closed her eyes. She and Iris fell to earth without touching the ground. A willow tree loomed above them.

"This must be what it's like to walk on the moon," Phoebe said as they waded through air toward a pale, wooden house.

Iris pointed to a ventilation grill in the concrete basement wall, and Phoebe lay down to peer inside. In the black interior, all she could make out was a metallic gleam.

"Call her," Iris said.

"Who?"

"You know."

Phoebe tried to call June's name but it was like talking under water. Her voice bubbled out in a dull hiss. A shock of lightning drenched the basement interior and Phoebe saw her then, inside a cage like the kind they store oversized baggage in at airports. She was sitting huddled in one corner with a blanket around her, her legs drawn up, her head resting on her knees.

"June," Phoebe wheezed, helpless to inject the cry with power. Frustrated, she told Iris, "We have to get her out."

"He'll be back soon."

"We can smash this wall. Help me." Phoebe beat the concrete with her hands, making no impression.

"I can't. I have to go now." Iris drifted away.

"No. Wait!" Phoebe followed her, trying to run on legs that felt weak and heavy.

The front of the house looked out on a road lined with tall trees. A dark van with tinted windows rolled to a stop at the curb, and a man got out and glanced around. Phoebe dropped to the ground, terrified. The man stopped at his mailbox. Those boots. Phoebe could see them in the streetlight. Heavy, light colored, with reinforced heels and pale soles.

The man stared directly at her. He had a small beard, and his hair was cut short and flat across the top. His eyes were narrow and his face and shoulders so fleshy he seemed neckless. Phoebe crawled frantically toward the nearest tree. He started to walk toward her, a strange sick smile on his face. She screamed and this time the sound burst from her lungs, piercing the starry night and opening the earth beneath her. Through the chasm she fell until a hand caught hers and Cara's voice summoned her.

"Sweetie. Wake up."

Phoebe opened her eyes. Her body shook violently. She clasped her hands, trying to still them. "I saw him. I saw his face."

Cara held her close and stroked her hair. "You're safe now. He can't hurt you."

"She's in a cage in the basement under his house. We have to get her out."

Dr. Karnovich bustled through the door and approached the bed. Speaking like he had a hairball lodged in his throat, he said, "This is very good. Very good." He took a sweet from his pocket, opened the wrapper, and offered it to Phoebe in the palm of his hand as if rewarding a child who had just taken nasty medicine.

Phoebe took the candy automatically and put it in her mouth, surprised that she felt less shaky almost immediately.

Dr. K took her pulse, listened to her heart through his stethoscope, then asked, "Can you remember your dream?"

"Most of it. I saw the man. Please tell Vernell."

"He's on his way."

"Now?" Cara looked astonished.

"We have to hurry," Phoebe said. "June's alive. I saw her."

Cara took her hand. "Remember the other dreams. They're always—"

"No. This is different. I know she's alive."

Sounding like a priest in the confessional, Dr. K asked, "What makes you feel that, dear child?"

Phoebe struggled for a moment, trying to understand why this was not the same as every other dream. It dawned on her the reason she'd been able to converse with the others was that she was a visitor in their realm, the realm of the dead.

"June couldn't hear me," she said. "That means she's not dead yet."

ROWE STOOD IN the vestibule and told herself it was mind over matter. She was sleepless. For hours her mind had been churning with stressful ruminations on her career, and countless questions about the people who had lived in her house a century ago. Now she wanted a cup of tea. All she had to do was walk into the kitchen and boil the kettle. She turned on the lights and took a few paces, watching her shadow swell across the wall ahead of her.

The hallway seemed longer than usual, the kitchen lying in wait like a dozing beast. Rowe reminded herself that the only truly sinister presence in her house was a fax she'd received from her publisher late that afternoon outlining some unattractive legal options. Her feet, in fleece-lined moccasins, followed orders and led her to the kitchen threshold. She stood there, inhaling air of a different character—musty, torpid air.

Walking into the kitchen was like entering a cell. You could feel the resentment of past occupants seeping from the walls. Rowe's hands felt sweaty and her heart began pounding like it needed to escape from her chest and head for the door. Stubbornly, she filled the kettle and sat it on the stove, telling herself that stress was the real problem tonight. There were no footsteps in the ballroom, the Widow was not tapping on the turret room door. She rinsed her favorite teapot, an antique black basalt Wedgewood she'd splurged on after she got her first ever royalty check. Refusing to look over her shoulder, she spooned tea leaves into the tea-ball and wished the water would boil.

As the seconds slithered by, she distracted herself by exploring the fridge. Phoebe had baked a pecan pie just before she and Cara left for Quantico, and they'd dropped off the leftovers for Rowe on their way to their airport. She wiggled the knife drawer open, irritated that she kept forgetting to wax the edges to stop it from sticking. From the quivering knives, she selected a small carver and placed it on the counter. As usual, it tried to move. Irritated to find herself unnerved by this, Rowe slapped her hand down on it.

Dwayne and Earl had claimed the counter surface was level and there was some kind of malevolent presence guarding the room; clearly nonsense. Rowe had renovated an old house once before. There was no such thing as a straight line or a plumb wall. As for an evil presence — they wished.

The kettle whistled, and she switched her attention to making the tea and putting away dishes she had washed earlier. As she lifted crockery into the cabinet next to the sink, a shiver twitched her spine, and she felt certain she was being stared at. To turn or not to turn? Telling herself she was being ridiculous, she did not look back at the counter where the pie waited, but instead took her time stirring the tea. When finally she turned, mug in hand, she froze.

The carving knife was no longer on the counter. Instead it was several inches above the chipped tile surface, the blade pointing directly at her. Rowe dropped her tea in fright and took a swift sideways step toward the door. The knife catapulted after her, and she plunged out of it's path, diving for the floor. The lethal blade struck the wall behind her and embedded itself.

"Fuck. Damn." Rowe was soaked with wet tea, and a shard of ceramic jutted from her right palm. Above her the half open knife drawer began rattling violently. Horrified, she scrambled to her feet and shoved it closed, leaning back against it, breathing hard. "Who the fuck are you and what do you want?"

she yelled. "Come on chickenshit. Show yourself."

She stared around the dingy room. Was this a dream? Her hand throbbed with pain and she pulled out the long shard. Blood dripped from the wound to the floor, blending with the liquid already there to form a reddish pool. Rowe found a kitchen towel and wrapped it around the injury. It wasn't serious, just painful. At least she was alive.

With trepidation, she yanked the knife from the wall and returned it to the drawer, hurriedly shoving it closed.

"This is my house and you're not getting rid of me that easily," she informed the peeling walls.

Fuck this. She was going to bring a team of workmen in here as soon as the worst of winter was over. They could demolish the goddamned room. There were plenty of better locations for a kitchen anyway. Maybe she would convert the huge formal dining room she never used. There was enough space for a state-of-the-art kitchen and then some. Rowe picked up the pie and crossed the room. Her hand was so sore she was whining. Screw the mess on the floor. She would clean it up tomorrow.

"Your days are numbered, pal," she announced from the safety of the threshold. "I'm going to take this place apart brick by brick."

The kitchen gave her the silent treatment. Rowe felt self-conscious all of a sudden, seeing herself as someone else would: a well-known author holding a pie, standing in the doorway of an empty room, talking to herself. And she had thought Phoebe needed professional help.

Chapter
Eight

"LET'S START WITH the eyes, Ms. Golden." A rangy forensic sketch artist named Colby Boone pinned several computer-generated composites to a whiteboard. They looked like androids.

Phoebe picked out an image. "This one. But his eyes are set deeper and his eyebrows are thicker. It was dark so I'm not sure about his eye color."

"And a flat top hair cut, you were saying?" Colby's accent was distinctively Texan. It suited his dark tan and his cowboy shirt and boots.

He wasn't FBI, Phoebe decided. You didn't have to be telepathic to figure that out. "Yes, like they have in the army."

The artist worked quickly, his sun-bleached blond head bent, his pencil darting and weaving over a sketching block. "Compare those beards now, would you, ma'am."

Phoebe compared the android pictures with her mental snapshot. The computer-generated faces were even-featured on both sides, unlike real people. She plumbed her memory for the tiny details and irregularities that would make the image more true to life.

"The beard is a shade darker than the hair. And something else. His ears are quite small compared with his face and the left one sticks out a lot more than the right."

"Probably sleeps on that side," Colby said. "You have a good eye for detail."

"I'm motivated."

They worked on the forehead, the nose, the shape of this face. The picture Colby finally placed in front of her was remarkably close to her recollection of the man, and he looked much more like a real person than the computer image.

"Wow." She examined the sketch carefully. "That's amazing."

"Machines still can't replace the human eye."

"I guess artists like you are being phased out these days."

"It depends how good you are." Eyes the same color as his jeans glinted with humor. "You don't have to be able to draw a straight line to make one of these computer pictures, and that's a good thing for small police departments. On a big case, they usually bring in a real artist to work with important witnesses like yourself."

Phoebe felt a pang of guilt. She didn't like having to deceive people about who she was. Vernell had told Colby she was a key witness who had seen the suspect in the vicinity of an abduction. It was the truth, in a roundabout way, she supposed.

"You made this very easy for me," she said. "I think what you do is incredible."

The Texan gave her a broad smile. "Mighty nice of you to say so, ma'am."

The door swung open, and Vernell entered the room with a well-scrubbed young agent Phoebe had never seen. Aware that Vernell had been working since Dr. K called him in the middle of the night, Phoebe was amazed at how fresh he looked. His white shirt was crisp, his conservative maroon tie perfectly pressed, and his suit pristine. He smelled faintly of high quality aftershave and hair product. Phoebe tried to imagine him in casual clothing and failed.

He picked up the sketch and studied it closely. "This our guy?" he asked her.

"Definitely."

Vernell handed the sketch to the young agent and told him to scan it and make copies. There was the same leashed excitement about him that Phoebe noticed whenever they found a grave. Today it brimmed closer to the surface, making his dark eyes more intense and his speech rapid. He had mentioned this was his first big case as an SAC, Special Agent in Charge. The possibility that June could still be alive had him chomping at the bit to catch the killer red-handed.

"Looks like we're done here," he said, thanking Colby and collecting up the other sketches they'd done of the van and the house. "If you'd like to come with me, Ms. Golden."

Phoebe got to her feet and said farewell to the artist. She'd enjoyed their session and appreciated how he had made her comfortable, chatting between times about his ranch and animals. He had even suggested a couple of breeders when she said she wanted a puppy. Phoebe checked the back pocket of her jeans as she accompanied Vernell and his colleague along the drab corridors of the Behavioral Science Unit. She'd made a note of the kennels' names, just in case Cara suddenly decided they could have a dog after all.

"There's something we'd like to try," Vernell said.

Phoebe had known this was coming, having sensed his frustration during the debriefing session after her dream. She had failed to seek out important details like the van registration, the street name, the number on the letterbox.

"You want me to go back?" she asked.

"We can't wait until you sleep again. If June's alive, the clock is ticking." He met her eyes. "We'd like to try hypnosis."

Phoebe frowned. "I don't know how I feel about that. I mean, I'll do it, but it makes me nervous. What if I can't wake up or something?"

They turned a corner. Dr. K was standing outside his office, fidgeting like a man who needed to smoke. At the sight of them, he beamed at Phoebe, whom he now treated like a cross between a movie star and his favorite laboratory dog. Apparently he'd heard her last question.

"Don't worry, my dear Ms. Golden. Nobody leaves my couch thinking they are a frog." He waved them into his lair. "And when you wake from your trance, I have something for you." He took a box from his desk top and lifted the lid. "Jeff de Bruges on rue Mouffetard. Who can leave Paris without visiting the markets, hmn?"

The smell of rich chocolate made Phoebe's mouth water, and she thought instantly of Pavlov's dogs. Now she knew why Dr. K had asked about her favorite foods during their first interview — evidently, he thought she would work for treats, too.

"They look delicious," she said, pondering which one to take.

He closed the box before she could decide and placed it on a shelf. "They are all yours whether or not we enjoy success." He tweaked his bowtie in a self-congratulatory manner. "See. The FBI pays you in chocolate. That is something to tell the grandchildren, no?"

He ushered her into a comfortable armchair, reclined it until she was semi-prone, then clapped his hands. Vernell rolled out a veiled board and parked it opposite her chair. Dr. K angled this so that Phoebe would have to keep her head up to see it, then whipped the cloth away like a magician revealing a dove.

"It's one of her paintings." Phoebe smiled. A lake in winter, the water iced over. "It looks so cold."

"Cold as the Urals," Dr. K noted in a murky undertone. "Look at that ice. Imagine yourself there. Touch it. Imagine running your hand across it. And listen to this." He turned on a small cassette.

Phoebe recognized the sound immediately. It was the

grandfather clock she'd heard while she lay on June's bed.

"Yes. You know that clock, don't you? It's making you sleepy. Very sleepy." Dr. K picked up a small brass bell. "Listen carefully. When I ring this bell," he rang it to illustrate, "you will wake up, and you will remember everything, but it will feel to you like a dream. At all times you will be able to hear me and you will be completely safe. Do you understand?"

"Yes." Phoebe listened to the clock and stared at the lake. Already she could feel her limbs getting heavy.

Part of her wanted to stop right now, get off the chair and go back home to Dark Harbor. But how would that help June? If there was a chance that she was alive and Phoebe could do something to save her, she had no choice. She tuned in to Dr. K's voice and allowed herself to relax completely. Her eyes felt heavy and she closed them, then found she could not open them again. She was drifting. Colors swirled against her eyelids. The ticking of the clock seemed louder.

"You know where Iris took you," Dr. K said. "You can remember everything. You can see everything."

Phoebe gazed down at the world below. Instead of shimmering lights there were cars, buildings, a vast city. Water.

"What do you see?"

"The Capitol. Buildings. Highways."

"You're traveling north?"

"Yes." Ceaseless blue. The sky, the ocean. Phoebe felt vividly content. Floating. Lost. Suspended in a beautiful nowhere. She tried to keep herself on track, but she was drifting farther and farther from the shore. "Iris," she called. "Iris, please come."

She could hear the soft, regular march of time. Yet she could feel nothing. Her flesh was no longer flesh. She was made of cloud, prey to the wind, recklessly, terribly alone in a world unraveled into skeins of color spread endlessly across a canvas she could not escape. She called Iris again.

This time her dead friend answered. "What are you doing here?"

"Take me to his house," Phoebe requested.

Iris's honey blonde hair swirled around her face. She looked sad. "I don't want to go there any more."

"Please." Phoebe took her hand. "Just once more. It's very important."

The colors on the canvas changed, running together, and Phoebe felt her stomach plummet. She released Iris's hand and cradled her head in her arms, bracing for a sudden crunch. Instead, like sails when the wind drops suddenly, she sagged into inertia.

"We're here," Iris said. "You should have brought them with you."

"I will. But they have to travel the normal way." Phoebe stared along a quiet road. The houses were on large blocks of land.

"I saw it all," Iris said. "The blindfold came off in the van, and I looked out the windows. A sign said New Hampshire. I don't know which town."

"What is the name of the street?" A man's voice came from nowhere, the accent heavy and foreign.

Phoebe repeated the question to Iris, who said, "Pennysdale."

"Look at the mailbox," Dr. K ordered.

"There are no numbers on it," Phoebe hovered before it, trying to make out the dusty outline of numbers that had once been there. "It's Pennysdale Street. Somewhere in New Hampshire."

"Is the van there?"

"No."

"Who are you talking to?" Iris asked.

"The FBI."

"Tell them to drive fast," Iris said forlornly.

Phoebe kissed her on the cheek. "I wish I could have done this for you."

"It's okay. My parents talk to me more now...my ashes at least. They say things they never used to say."

"Can they hear you if you talk to them?"

"Sometimes my mother looks up as if she does. But I think she feels silly. She always starts doing housework."

"I want to find my parents." Phoebe became aware of a bell. The sound grew louder and louder. "I have to go," she blurted as colors cascaded around her and a blinding sterile sea washed everything white.

She stared up into a beam of bright light. Dr. K placed his index finger a few inches before her eyes.

Phoebe knew the drill from her head injury days. Tracking the fingertip right and left, she asked, "Am I really awake?"

The doctor placed the box of chocolates in her lap. "Completely. And you remember everything, do you not?"

Grieving for Iris, Phoebe said, "Yes. Everything."

"WE HAVE TO hurry," Phoebe urged, appalled that Vernell hadn't sent people immediately to smash down the doors and rescue June.

He had explained that they'd had to use her pictures to locate the right house in the right Pennysdale Street and find out if the occupant resembled the man she and Colby had drawn. Then they had to stake out his place of work. He assured her that nothing could happen while their man was not at home. Now she and Cara were in a Bubird, on their way to New Hampshire so she could make a final positive identification of the house before they sent in the SWAT team.

Vernell checked his watch. He did that constantly, when he wasn't leaving his seat to talk on the phone out of earshot. He said, "We'll be landing in twenty minutes."

An agent approached and spoke to him in an undertone. Phoebe could just make out what he said. "The residence is staked out. No sign of the van. According to neighbors, the suspect leaves early in the morning and gets back around five."

"Place of work?" Vernell asked.

"The static team is in position. Twenty rent-a-goons."

"I don't want this rabbit spooked. Floating box until he enters the target location."

"Yes, sir." The agent straightened and returned to the rear of the plane, his eyes straying to Phoebe as he passed her seat. Like everyone, he looked curious.

"Feeling okay?" Cara placed her hand over Phoebe's.

"I just want her to be alive." Phoebe wished she'd had time to check on June before Dr. K rang that bell.

"I know. Me, too." Cara stared out the window for a moment, then shot a look at Phoebe. "Whatever happens, you did good, sweetie."

Phoebe glanced around the cabin. It was full of men, some in suits, others in black body armor. Despite their calm outward demeanor, they were restless, and a palpable excitement pervaded the cabin. Occasionally she caught one of them looking at her and Cara. She wasn't there under cover of her fake forensic science ID. Instead, to explain Cara's presence, Vernell had given everyone the same story he told the forensic artist, that she was a key witness and that her sister was there to provide emotional support. People accepted this with identical twins.

A circus of cars and vans were waiting at the airport. As everyone disembarked, several agents from the plane immediately ringed Phoebe and Cara like they were about to be fired on, and guided them to a dark red Chrysler sedan with tinted windows.

One of their escorts slid into the front passenger seat and twisted around to talk to them. "When we get there, we'll park a short distance from the house. The SAC will walk you past the place. If it's the right house, just say the word, then return immediately to the car and stay put."

"Who are all those people?" Phoebe gestured at the crowd gathered around Vernell. "Are they the FBI agents?"

"Yeah, mostly. Agents out of Boston. And some local cops."

Phoebe's stomach rolled. What if she had it all wrong? What if she was actually losing it and none of this was real. She had seen *A Beautiful Mind*. People who were going crazy usually had no idea.

"Okay, ladies. I'm out of here," the agent said. He left them alone in the new-smelling interior.

Cara adjusted her jeans over her boots. "Well, this is a whole lot more exciting than a day at the studio. And the good news is, if they nail this guy, you just made a hundred thousand bucks."

"What do you mean?" The Bureau already paid her a salary of eighty thousand dollars. No one had said anything about a raise.

"That's the deal I made with them," Cara said. "I didn't say anything because I didn't want you getting all stressed about having to deliver."

"It's too much." Phoebe was mortified, imagining how she would feel if someone close to her was the one imprisoned in a madman's basement. "This is a woman's life. I don't expect money."

"Of course you don't, but we won't mention that fact." Cara looked at her seriously. "You work for these people, and you deserve to be rewarded properly for the impact this has on your life. Who knows how long you'll be able to do this. I'm thinking about your future. Anyway, a hundred grand is peanuts to them."

Cara had always been the one who was responsible about money. What had Phoebe expected—that her twin would allow the FBI to exploit her for nothing? If she'd been the one negotiating with Vernell she wouldn't even have a salary.

"You're right," she said. "I guess I got stuck on the ethics."

"You're not doing anything unethical accepting money for your services," Cara reiterated. "Imagine how much it costs for all the man-hours on a case like this. If you can shorten the investigation, you're saving them a fortune. That's the way Vernell sees it. Trust me, you're a real bargain."

"A hundred thousand dollars," Phoebe murmured.

"After tax," Cara said with satisfaction.

"I'll be able to get you that sports car for your birthday." Irrationally, she thought of Rowe and wondered what kind of gift would thrill her.

Cara grinned. "No, that money is going away, so if anything ever happens to me, you'll be okay."

Phoebe gulped a breath, her thoughts instantly back on track. "Don't say things like that. Nothing is going to happen to you."

Cara embraced her. "Silly, of course it's not. And it's your money. You can spend it on anything you want. You've earned it."

Phoebe leaned into her twin's shoulder, inhaling the comforting scent of her. Cara smelled faintly of the outdoors and of *Coco*, the distinctive spicy fragrance she always wore. "Maybe I'll get myself that new stove," she said. "You can invest the rest or whatever."

Cara laughed softly. "You and your stove fetish."

The car's front doors swung open and two men got in. Vernell was on the passenger side. Phoebe didn't recognize the driver. All FBI men were starting to look the same to her.

Vernell introduced the agent, a guy called Farrell, and said, "Ms. Golden is our witness."

"Thank you for assisting the Bureau," the agent said, and started the motor.

Vernell got on his cell phone. The agent talked into a radio. Most of what they said was incomprehensible, a scramble of numbers and mysterious acronyms. At one point, the agent turned to Vernell and said, "Rabbit tracks, sir."

Vernell responded with, "Get a bird dog on it. Not too close." And they accelerated into the traffic.

Phoebe's watch said 4:10 pm when they arrived at Pennysdale Street. The scene was not remotely similar to anything she had imagined. There were no police cars with lights blinking, no signs of life other than a man shoveling snow from his driveway a few doors from where they parked.

Alarmed, she said, "He'll be home soon. Where is everybody?"

No one replied.

"Wait for me to open your door, then step out of the car and take my arm," Vernell instructed. "We're looking around the neighborhood because we're thinking about buying real estate here."

"Okay." Phoebe buttoned her coat, pulled on her gloves and tried to look casual as she stepped out onto the pavement.

Walking along the quiet suburban street with Vernell she felt safe knowing he probably carried a gun beneath his charcoal gray overcoat. But it was all she could do not to break into a run and drag him along behind her to rescue June. Tall trees and a curve in the road obscured the houses they were approaching, and she could almost feel the dark blue van creeping along the street behind them.

"Everything's fine," Vernell said. "You're doing great. Look up at me and say something, then we'll laugh."

"Why?" She gazed up at his nutmeg brown face. "He's not here to see us."

"For all we know he doesn't work alone. There may be someone in the house, watching." He laughed as if he didn't have a care in the world.

They rounded the curve, and Phoebe instantly recognized the trees she'd hidden behind and the broad sweep of the yard. She wanted to scream, to run behind the house and yell through the grille to June to hang on a little longer. Help was on the way.

"That's the place," she said, laughing as he'd told her to.

"Good." Vernell's eyes swung left and right. "We're going to cross the road here and you're going to walk back toward the car. Don't run."

"Where will you be?"

"In this SUV." He stopped next to a forest green Ford Explorer parked at the curb and opened the driver's door. Bending, he kissed her lightly on the cheek. "We're saying goodbye. Go back to the car and wait with your sister."

Phoebe forced a phony smile. "She's in the basement, 'round the back of the house."

"I know. Thank you."

Phoebe walked away, forcing herself not to increase her pace. Out of the corner of her eye, she saw something move. Several shadowy figures ran from behind one house to the next. They were carrying assault weapons. Another dark form was just visible against the roofline of the house she was passing. She lowered her head, breathing deeply, understanding that she was seeing a highly organized plan in operation. The place was surrounded. Every innocently parked car, every shadow on every rooftop, every man shoveling snow or changing tires was part of a team about to swarm into the white house and rescue June from the hell of her captivity.

Phoebe prevented herself stopping and yelling: *You're safe. We're coming!* Instead, flooded with relief, she reached the red Chrysler and opened the door like she was in no big hurry to get in the car.

"Well?" Cara asked.

Phoebe dropped into the back seat and exhaled long and hard. "It's the house."

Agent Farrell spoke into his radio, then opened his door and instructed, "Remain with the vehicle please ladies." With that he left them.

"We can't see anything from here," Cara complained. "And the windows are all fogged up." She bailed out and climbed into the driver's seat. "If we're going to have to sit here for God knows how long, at least I want to know what's happening."

Before Phoebe could protest, Cara started the car and moved out onto the road, driving twenty or so yards then making a U-turn. "There," she said, parking not far from the Explorer. "Now we'll see everything."

"We're going to be in a lot of trouble," Phoebe said.

"Who cares?" Cara climbed over the seat and settled next to her once more. "Anyway, you're the golden girl. You can do no wrong."

Phoebe cringed. Whenever Cara took that tone, it usually spelled trouble. It had been that way all through their childhood. Cara always imagined she could get away with disobedience and most often she did. Grandma Temple was never one for spanking or punishment.

"Where's Vernell?" Cara knelt on the seat and wiped the fog from the rear window.

Phoebe contemplated going all vague on her, but Cara could tell when she was lying, "In that SUV." She pointed to the Explorer.

Cara looked satisfied. "Good. This is exactly the right place to be then."

"Whatever." Phoebe knew better than to argue when Cara's stubborn streak took over. Secretly, she was pleased. She wanted to see what happened, too. *Just hold on, June.* She hurled the thought into the ether, hoping it would find the woman trapped in the cage. "I hope they shoot him dead," she said.

Cara cast a startled look her way. "Unusually bloodthirsty for you, sweetie."

"He doesn't deserve to live."

"I couldn't agree more." Cara stiffened. "Oh shit, Vernell's getting out of the car. He's probably coming to give us an earful."

"No. He's going over there."

Phoebe scrambled onto her knees and peered out the back window with Cara. As Vernell crossed the road, five men in body armor ran around the front of the house. He pressed the door bell and waited, then pressed it a couple more times. The seconds crawled by, then he made some kind of signal, and heavily armed men with shields converged from all directions, running, crouching, guns at the ready. Vernell stepped back from the door, stood to one side, and took a gun from beneath his coat. At his command, a group of agents jogged up the front steps and flattened the door inward with a battering ram. Phoebe heard shouts of "FBI," and the agents stormed the house.

"God, I wish I could get footage of this," Cara said. Heedless of the danger, she wound down the side window and stuck her head out.

Phoebe looked at her watch. It was now 4:30 pm. The guy they were after would be here any minute. She gazed at the house, astonished to see armed FBI agents materializing from nowhere. About ten of them with enormous guns ran past the car and took up firing positions behind several cars grouped in front of the house on the other side of the road. Where were all the residents?

"I guess everyone's been told to stay indoors." Cara answered the question as if she'd had exactly the same thought.

"Get your head in the car," Phoebe urged. "What if there's shooting?"

As if to support her plea, a sharp knocking sound shook the Chrysler, and Cara dived back inside, yelping, "What was that?"

They both craned around. A black-clad agent opened the driver's door and stuck his head in. "Ms. Golden. The SAC wants you."

"Now?"

"Right away. Put this on." He thrust a bulletproof vest over the seat as if Phoebe would know what to do with it.

Cara took the vest and tugged it down over Phoebe's head. It was amazingly light.

"Are you sure this stops bullets?" Phoebe asked.

The agent gave her a patient look. "Let's go, ma'am.

They ran across the road and into the tree belt, then up to the house. Phoebe steeled herself, expecting to be sent away from the scene in disgrace. There was probably a little old lady living there who had now dropped dead of a heart attack. The basement probably had nothing in it but a few mice hiding from the cold and some dusty old walking frames. Countless FBI personnel had traveled here on taxpayers dollars. What if it was all for nothing?

Vernell was waiting inside the front door. As soon as she got inside, several agents propped the door back into it's frame. Vernell took Phoebe's elbow and guided her through a group of his colleagues. To her surprise some of them were women, and she felt a little silly, having assumed everyone carrying a gun must be male.

Someone shouted, "Upper level secure."

Another shout. "Take up positions."

"Did you find her?" Phoebe asked.

"The cage is empty." Vernell sounded strained.

"Empty?"

The full meaning of that simple answer loomed like a fogbank before her. They were too late. June had been alive, unlike the others, and Phoebe had failed her. Tears blurred her vision. Had he killed her last night, after she and Iris visited? Had he sensed something, smelled impending danger like an animal?

"She has to be here somewhere," Vernell said bleakly. "You saw him last night and so did the next door neighbor. He went to work as usual this morning. He hasn't had an opportunity to dump the body yet."

"That's why you want me here. To speak to her now that she's dead—to find her?" Phoebe felt a crushing sadness.

"Do you need your sister?"

She didn't, but the thought of Cara out there in a car if there was some kind of gun fight made her nervous. "Yes, if she could be here afterwards."

Vernell said something to one of his team and led Phoebe to a door at the rear of the house. "I'm sorry you have to see this," he told her.

The room was lit by a single fluorescent tube dangling from a low ceiling. An ozone layer of terror and despair hung in the air, mingling with the stench of urine and feces. Phoebe covered her mouth and nose. Her flesh crawled as they approached the cage. She took in chains, bloody bedding, empty plastic water bottles.

"He'll be coming home soon," she said, sickened.

"You've nothing to fear. We'll have him as soon as he steps out of his van."

"We could do this later, if you want."

Vernell shook his head. "Once the forensics team is in here, we won't have access for some time." There was unmistakable urgency in his tone.

Responding to it, Phoebe entered the cage and felt her breath cramp in her lungs. Her legs folded and she sank onto the filthy blanket. She was freezing cold. Hunching into a corner, she pulled the blanket around her and stared at a small grille high on the opposite wall. Through it she could see the sky fading as dusk approached. She stared at this tiny slice of the outside world until exhaustion made her lie down. Her eyelids drooped and merciful darkness claimed her. She would refuse to wake, she thought. To be awake was to know, and to know was unbearable.

Powerful hands gripped her shoulders. She lay limp, refusing to be present in her body. She could hear a male voice, but it seemed far away. Her head jerked to one side and a searing pain made her gasp.

"Yeah." The voice grew closer. "That's right bitch. You don't get to choose when you get lucky."

Pain radiated from her center, sucking at her like a rip tide, and she imploded into an agony so intense, all she could do was surrender to its terrible power. Then she was aware of being dragged, her bare heels moving across cold steel wire before scraping on concrete.

"You're going to spend some time thinking about how you're gonna make this up to me tomorrow, or it's over. If there's one thing I don't have to put up with, it's a boring bitch who can't talk nice when the man of the house gets home from work. Understand?"

She was lifted then and dumped into a cold hard box. A loud metallic bang made her open her eyes. There was no light. She wanted to move but she couldn't. All she could do was breathe. In some strange way the darkness and the silence, and the metal walls around her, felt safe. Safer than the cage. Tears filled her eyes, and she thought of her mother.

Warm arms held her suddenly. A hand stroked her hair. Phoebe opened her eyes and stared up at Vernell. She summoned her voice from deep within the prison of her chest. "I know where she is."

Vernell helped her out of the cage and Phoebe led him across the concrete floor to a shadowy corner of the room. He scanned the area with his flashlight, finally training the beam on a long steel rifle box.

"Jesus," he choked out.

Leaving Phoebe standing in the shadows, he ran to the bottom of the stairs and bellowed, "Get some bolt cutters down here."

Within seconds a powerfully built agent appeared. Vernell shone the flashlight down onto a padlock, and the agent snapped this off effortlessly. Thrusting his flashlight at Phoebe, Vernell wrenched open the lid and frantically placed a hand on the neck of the naked woman inside.

"She's alive!" His cry was almost shrill. "Paramedics!"

Disbelieving, Phoebe stared at the motionless woman, then reached inside and took an icy hand in her own. "You're safe now, June," she said.

June's eyes opened, blinking against the light. She didn't say a word but the fingers inside Phoebe's fluttered.

Chapter
Nine

ROWE DROPPED A servants' pay book on the coffee table in front of her and adjusted up the sound on her TV so she could watch the evening news. As always, she wondered why she bothered. She could have written the items ahead of time herself—the daily insurgent car bombs in Iraq, the Michael Jackson saga, the latest football celebrity rape accusations and Hollywood couple splits.

She shared some nachos with Jessie and Zoe and stared gloomily at the photo of Juliet Baker. The Disappointed Dancer was a poor substitute for Phoebe and Cara. It had only been a few days, but Rowe missed her neighbors. Trying not to fall in love with either of them sure as hell made life interesting.

A sound bite called her attention back to the screen and she cranked up the volume. The caption read: *FBI Arrests Alleged Serial Killer.* A reporter at the scene breathlessly recounted how a New Hampshire house was stormed and a woman rescued alive. An African American FBI agent in a fine tailored suit gave a brief interview. The camera panned around milling feds in body armor and showed a big guy with a crew-cut being led off in handcuffs.

Some kind of scuffle ensued when the suspect kicked one of the feds. The camera man rushed in for a closer shot. As the camera jerked its way toward the action, Rowe was startled to see Phoebe and Cara standing on the sidelines next to the tailored agent who gave the interview. The camera was only on them for a moment, but there was no mistaking the Temple twins.

Suddenly the name she had seen flashed on the screen minutes earlier registered fully. Special Agent In Charge, Vernell Jefferson. Was this the same Vernell who sent flowers to Phoebe? It had to be. So the gesture was work-related, a thank you from her boss. Rowe cast her mind back to a conversation she'd had with her neighbors before they left for Quantico. They'd made it sound like Phoebe had a few boring meetings to attend and Cara was going sightseeing. Obviously Phoebe had downplayed her involvement in a big investigation.

Rowe was impressed. Her neighbor could not be entirely flaky if she was at the scene when an arrest was made in a high profile case. But what was Cara doing there? Rowe could not imagine that the FBI allowed friends and family of staff to tag along for the ride. Intrigued, she thought about calling Cara on her cell phone. The day they left, Cara had given Rowe a set of house keys and her cell phone number in case of an emergency. At the time, Rowe had sensed an unspoken invitation.

Did she want to hook up with Cara? How would Phoebe react if her sister and Rowe got involved? She depended on Cara a great deal. Would she see a lover as some kind of threat? Were the twins single because introducing third parties into their dynamic was a nightmare? Entirely possible. And Rowe could live without that kind of drama, thank you.

Steering her mind away from temptation, she picked up the servant's pay book once more and returned to the pages that had caught her eye earlier. Becky O'Halloran had started work for the Bakers in 1910. One of several servants, she was paid $5.50 a week plus food and accommodation, good money for the time, according to the comments written in the front of the book, presumably by Mrs. Baker. Servants' wages had gone up because employers suddenly had to compete for staff with hundreds of new factories. The cook earned more than twice as much, Rowe noted. The Bakers didn't have a large staff at their summer home — no housekeeper or butler. They appeared to employ the cook's husband for odd jobs, and there were two other maids, both paid even less than Becky.

The last time Becky had signed the pay book was on December 7, 1912, just two days before Juliet was found dead in the snow. In the first entry for 1913, someone had written "O'Halloran no longer in service."

What was the significance of the maid's disappearance and what, if anything, did it have to do with Juliet's death? Had Becky run off with Juliet's lover? Rowe doubted it — if the guy had planned to marry Juliet in the hopes of money, he certainly wouldn't elope with a servant. Maybe she'd left for the reason many housemaids did back then – dismissal when they fell pregnant to their master. If old man Baker had fathered a child with the widow next door, maybe he was also unfaithful to his wife with the servants. Had the lady of the house found out and sacked Becky? That was also the norm in those days.

Perhaps Becky had disappeared to the nearest big city in the hopes of getting rid of the 'problem.' Had she suffered a backstreet abortion and died, as thousands in her situation did? If so, that would explain why her mother had never heard from her again. Rowe pictured a frightened young woman collecting a month's pay and leaving Islesboro on her way to an unknown fate. How did she get where she was going? Had she walked in the snow to the village? Surely not. Someone must have picked her up. That's why people had assumed a young man was involved.

So, on December 8, finding her maid had vanished, Juliet wandered from the house. Was she looking for her? Did she play some kind of role in Becky's departure? Were the two youngest women in the household allies across the barriers of class? Had they come up with a plan together only to have it go wrong? Was Juliet actually trying to run away when she crept out into the merciless winter that night?

Rowe toyed with the bandage on her hand. The cut she'd incurred in the kitchen was painful this evening, the flesh tugging where it was trying to heal. She turned to the photocopies she'd made of some of Mrs. O'Halloran's letters to the editor of the Camden Herald. She was convinced that if Becky had been planning to run off, she would have said goodbye the last time they spoke, which was December 7. They were close.

Many of her letters to the editor referred to Mr. Baker as a "gentleman with secrets to hide" or "a gentleman unfitting of that title," and Mrs. Baker as "his unhappy invalid wife." Mrs. O'Halloran seemed convinced Baker knew something about her daughter's disappearance. Rowe was struck by a sentence in one of the last letters: "Out of my great respect for another, I have not revealed facts in my possession. But, almighty God knows all and Mr. Baker will one day be judged for his sins."

Mary O'Halloran had been Verity Adams' housekeeper for many years. If her mistress had been pregnant by Baker, she must have known about this "sin." Others probably suspected the truth, but in those days an elaborate social conspiracy existed whereby a community could choose to turn a blind eye to problematic facts. Birth dates that called a child's paternity into question, for example. Appearances had to be preserved.

Rowe dragged out a telephone directory and flipped through the listings. Even if Mrs. O'Halloran had not disclosed Baker's "secrets" in the local newspaper she must have told someone. The old lady had died in her eighties in 1952. Any other children she'd had were probably dead or senile, so Rowe was looking for grandchildren. She picked up the phone and dialed the first O'Halloran she found. Giving some story about research for the Historical Society, she asked the man who picked up if his grandmother was Mary O'Halloran.

He said no, but he knew which O'Hallorans she was after. They were all related. Mary had twelve children. Rowe phoned the woman he identified as Mary's oldest granddaughter, hoping she might know of a deathbed disclosure about Thomas Baker.

The granddaughter, now sixty-five, said Thomas Baker was a villain who had wronged her family but no one could prove as much. It was a long time ago, but the O'Hallorans never forgot an ill turn. She said her grandmother had prayed regularly to St. Jude and lit candles for several other holy martyrs, hoping for news of her lost daughter.

"The rumor was he did something to Becky," she told Rowe. "He made threats, too."

"What kind of threats?"

"He said Becky stole some Baker family jewelry and if he ever found my grandmother had it, he'd make her wish she was never born."

"Any idea what it was?"

"Grandma wouldn't say."

"I wonder why not," Rowe thought out loud.

"No one crossed Thomas Baker. That's what she always said. He was not a nice man."

"SO I'D BE living at Quantico during the week and going home on weekends." Phoebe stared down at the written offer. A salary of $150,000 plus a car. She was flabbergasted.

"The Bureau would provide a house or condo for you in the town — whatever you want. Free of charge." Vernell looked at Cara as if he expected her to make the decision.

"It's a very good offer." Cara touched Phoebe's arm. "What do you think?"

"I don't want to live here. I don't know anyone."

"You'd be part of our community," Vernell said. "The Bureau is a big family. You'd make friends."

"I'm not an agent. What would I say about my job?"

"You'd be an Intelligence staffer. No one will expect you to disclose specifics about your work. People will assume you're something to do with Homeland Security. Everyone is confused these days about who's doing what."

"That's encouraging," Cara said sarcastically.

"I need to think about this." Phoebe put the contract back into its envelope. She would have some time to herself at home over the next few days while Cara was in L.A. This was not a decision she could make until her head was clear.

Vernell looked on edge. "Is there something you want that we're not offering?"

Phoebe shook her head. "No. It's a fantastic offer. The thing is, I'm not sure about living away from home. Why can't I just come down here and stay for a few days whenever you need me for a special case?"

"It isn't that simple. If you're on site, we have immediate access, and we can take rapid action. That's what the big salary increase is about. We know it will be tough, so we're willing to compensate you fairly."

"It's very generous." Phoebe felt like a fool. How many people would think twice about an offer like this? She had never earned more than 30K in her admin job.

"You saw what happened with the June Feldstein case," Vernell said. "The clock was ticking. If you'd been in Maine, Dr. K would not have been able to hypnotize you and we wouldn't have gotten to her in time. There's a bunch of high priority cases the Director wants you working on right away."

Phoebe felt bad. She could see his point. All the resources were here at Quantico. But she knew if she were living on site, she would be stuck in Dr. K's office non-stop. He'd probably have her spending more time hypnotized than awake. She thought about Harriet's warning. The Bureau would own her. Was that what she wanted for herself?

"Maybe we could reach a compromise," she said, catching a look from Cara that seemed almost startled. Apparently her sister didn't think she was capable of sticking up for herself.

"We can be flexible," Vernell said cautiously.

"I want to work from home. You can pay me less, and I'll spend one week each month here. The rest of the time we could use one of those computer hook-ups...you know, so we can see each other while we talk. Maybe Dr. K will be able to hypnotize me over the screen. Or, you could send him to Maine."

"Let me see what I can do." Vernell stood and took a poster tube from the bookshelf behind him. Handing it to Phoebe, he said, "Colby left this for you, by the way."

Expecting to find memento copies of the mugshot and the other sketches, Phoebe popped off the cap and withdrew a single rolled leaf of heavy paper.

"Oh, my God." Cara stared at the image unfurled on the table. It was a pastel drawing of Phoebe holding a puppy. "That's sensational."

"When he's not working for us, he's a professional portrait

artist," Vernell said. " Mostly for wealthy clients."

"I've heard of him." Cara sounded amazed. "He turned down a couple of rappers last year. Says he doesn't paint misogynists."

As she and Vernell chatted about Colby's talent and how he didn't need the lousy money the FBI paid, but had a conscience, Phoebe read the note that had fluttered from the tube. *You said you wanted a puppy. Maybe this little guy will do in the meantime.* How sweet of him.

"God, we'd have to pay a fortune for this." Cara held the picture up. "We'll get it framed right away. I can't believe we'll have a Colby Boone portrait in the living room." She glanced at Vernell. "Did you guys arrange this?"

"No. I guess Mr. Boone just took a liking to your sister."

"Well, any artist in his right mind would want to paint her." Cara returned the picture to the tube and handed it to Phoebe.

Touched by Colby's gesture, Phoebe followed Cara and Vernell through the building to the car waiting outside. She could tell from the sketch that he had seen right through her cover story about being a witness, and she was unnerved. Had she accidentally revealed something? Had she sounded implausible? How was she ever going to convince anyone she was an Intelligence agent?

She wondered if anyone else saw what she saw in the picture, the sorrow that haunted her eyes. Embarrassed that she had failed to hide her true feelings from the artist, she slid the tube along the backseat of the car and stood at the door while Vernell exchanged a few words with the driver, then shook hands with Cara.

"Agent Young will wait," he said. "He can drive you to the airport whenever you're ready."

"I could get used to a car service like this." Cara grinned and got into the passenger seat.

Vernell closed her door courteously, then faced Phoebe. "Once I've spoken with the Director, I'll give you a call. I can't guarantee he'll go for it."

"That's fine." Phoebe shook his hand. "Thank you for not pushing me."

Vernell acknowledged her with a faint smile. "You can thank my wife. She says you get more bees with honey."

INTO THE HUSH of winter, Rowe hurled a tennis ball and watched Jessie and Zoe churn a hail of snow as they ran across the meadow after it. Staring down at her feet, she tramped slowly after them. The light was fading. They had maybe a half hour left before the purple trees turned black and the moon began to glow like a fog-light through the heavy cloud cover. There was more snow on the way. By tomorrow, she and the dogs would be housebound, sheltering from the freezing peril just outside their door.

She had never felt this way in Manhattan—so keenly aware of her vulnerability to the elements, her isolation. The feeling was energizing yet at the same time strangely claustrophobic. This was how she imagined she might feel stranded on a desert island, hoping for a boat to appear on the horizon, and dreading that when it finally did, she would be forced to return to the real world.

The crack of a branch pierced the heavy silence like a gunshot, and Rowe jerked her head up. A familiar figure emerged from the naked birches a few yards ahead. Rowe's heart leapt and an irrational joy seized her.

"Hey!" Phoebe closed the gap between them with several long strides. "Guess what? I'm home."

"I thought you weren't coming back 'til next week."

"We got finished early. I was coming over to see if you want to have dinner with me." She brushed snow from her coat. A dusting of white powdered her coal black hair. One of the trees must have showered her as she walked through the woods. "It won't be exciting. Just soup."

Rowe kept her immediate thought to herself—that a dry crust and stagnant water would be exciting if her neighbors were sitting around the table.

"Come over now if you want. Bring the dogs." Phoebe stooped to pat the two canines lying prostrate at her feet. "We could watch a video or something. I'd like the company—Cara's gone back to L.A."

"Sounds great."

Cara was away. Rowe waited for a pang of disappointment that didn't eventuate. She fell into step beside Phoebe, and they labored through the trees. Every wooden limb seemed to have been dipped in an icy glaze. There was almost no smell, and the only sound she could hear was that of breathing. Her own, loud and hollow in her ears. Phoebe's, a soft rush next to her. The panting staccato of her dogs.

"You could break a leg in this...step on something." She ducked beneath a low branch. "You have to be an idiot to go outside once winter really sets in up here. I can see that."

Phoebe looked at her sideways, perhaps reading these pronouncements as relocation remorse. "That's why a lot of people keep their homes here, but only come in the summer."

"Yes, well." Rowe hoped her tone made it clear she had no plans to join that confederacy of the faint-hearted.

"How's your book coming along?" Phoebe asked, as they reached the house.

"I burned it in effigy." Rowe kicked her snow boots against the back steps. "Printed the file and stuck it on the fire."

"Did that feel good?" Phoebe hung their coats. Her eyes swept Rowe from top to toe in a guarded foray.

Perfect, Rowe thought. She'd walked out the door in jeans that needed to go in the laundry yesterday, and a heavy shapeless cable sweater over a checked shirt. The bottoms of her jeans were now soaked and she figured she probably didn't smell that great, either. She hadn't showered that morning. Her bathroom was too damned cold.

"I felt completely at peace for several minutes," she answered Phoebe's question, following her neighbor's slender figure through the kitchen to the den, where the twins' old-fashioned wood stove radiated heat. The dogs caught on immediately and threw themselves down onto the nearest rug to bask.

"Let's get warmed up," Phoebe invited. "Want to take off your boots?"

Trying not to notice that her neighbor was casually stripping off an outer layer of damp clothes, Rowe unlaced her boots and stuck her hands out toward the heater. "I need one of these wood burners," she said. "The cottage is an ice box."

"They heat the whole house." Phoebe stretched out a hand. "Give me your jeans. I'll put them in the drier."

"It's okay. They'll dry off pretty fast if I pull up a chair."

Phoebe regarded Rowe with a delicately contained smile. "I wasn't planning to have you sitting around in your boxer shorts. I'll go get a robe."

As soon as she left the room, Rowe pulled off the soggy jeans and joined the dogs on the rug close to the heater. She was oddly pleased that Phoebe had made the correct assumption about her underwear. Her mind instantly changed gear, generating an image of Phoebe in matching bra and panties. Oyster colored. Lacy. Sexy, but also a little modest. Phoebe wasn't the type to wear a hot pink thong and see through bra. Not that there was anything wrong with showgirl lingerie if that's what got your motor running. But Rowe preferred her lovers in something classier.

Lovers. As soon as the thought crossed her mind, she groaned out loud. When the snow melted, she would go find the local lesbian watering holes and zone in on someone who also had sex on the brain. A short fling was exactly what she needed. No hassles. No complications.

A pair of feet in fluffy pink slippers halted in front of her and Phoebe held out a robe. She was wearing a cream chenille gown, not remotely seductive. Bundled into its sensible coziness, she looked adorable. "Want to take a bath with me?" she offered in a matter-of-fact tone. "There's only enough hot water for one. I don't mind sharing. Cara and I do it all the time."

"Cara's your sister." Rowe's voice came out in a croak despite her best efforts.

Phoebe shrugged. "It's up to you. We can use Cara's tub. It's bigger than mine. Come see."

Ignoring warning qualms, Rowe got to her feet, removed her sweater and pulled the robe on over her shirt. A bigger tub might work out okay, she rationalized as she followed Phoebe upstairs. She had already seen Phoebe take a bath. What was the big deal about being in the water with her, naked limbs slithering? In Sweden no one worried about that kind of thing. They didn't read sexual meaning into every nudity situation.

Cara's bathroom belonged in magazine, with its slate floor and huge, sunken oval tub set below a picture window. The room was very modern. Blown glass art objects were backlit in recesses around the walls and an amazing opaque glass hand basin perched on a black cast iron stand.

Phoebe turned on the faucets. She had a dreamy expression in her eyes, as if anticipating something that was to be. "Choose some music," she said, pointing at the opposite wall.

Cara had not only decorated her bathroom like it belonged in a state-of-the-art loft apartment, she had also installed a high-end sound system. Rowe was almost afraid to touch the sensitive equipment. Feeling like a klutz, she slid the new Joss Stone DVD into the player and adjusted the volume.

Phoebe glanced across her shoulder approvingly. "I like her. Can you believe she's a white girl?" She twisted her hair into a knot and secured it on top of her head.

Rowe smiled. Nerves rolled through her gut. Phoebe seemed so calm, not a trace of ambivalence. No coyness. Her manner was warm but not flirtatious. This would be a very different story if it were Cara sitting on that step. Thank God it wasn't, Rowe thought, and was instantly startled at herself. Hadn't she been pondering the merits of a fling with Cara? If anything, she should be feeling let down that she was in these promising circumstances with the wrong twin.

She met Phoebe's eyes, and for the first time noticed they were pink-rimmed, as if she'd been crying recently. Phoebe looked away and reached into the tub, trailing a testing hand through the water.

Watching the graceful motion of her arm and the arch of her neck, Rowe had a sense that Phoebe had invited her into this private world because she needed a distraction. She had not ventured out on a freezing day just for the hell of it. She had not asked Rowe over on an impulse, just because they met by chance on a walk. She had been coming to get her. She wanted company, but there was more to it than that. This bath was some kind of comfort ritual, something Phoebe would normally do with her sister, but Cara wasn't here.

Rowe was not sure how she felt about being seen as a safe substitute. She was flattered that Phoebe trusted her enough to do this, but it was kind of dispiriting to be seen in such a sisterly light. Guilty that she couldn't view Phoebe quite the same way, she said, "I'll finish getting undressed in your sister's room if that's okay."

"Of course. It's directly across the hall." Phoebe smiled that far-away smile of hers. "Do you like bubble bath?"

Rowe hesitated in the doorway. The additional concealment of a foam layer versus the flowery scent?

"You don't," Phoebe concluded. "That's okay. We have fragrance-free soaking salts."

"Now, you're talking."

As she left the room, Rowe noticed Phoebe hit a switch on the wall near the tub. The lights promptly dimmed to a level that would make getting naked into the bath less of an ordeal. Thankful, she crossed the hall to Cara's bedroom. Also a designer statement, the room was an expensive blend of Japanese and modernist design. Cara had done her best to convert her part of the house into the kind of apartment she wanted to live in. The décor didn't really suit the place, but it was striking all the same.

Rowe folded her clothes and sat them on a black lacquered chair. The piece was astounding, a subtle pattern of cranes in translucent jade tones visible only when you drew close. She lifted her clothing back off the gleaming surface, uneasy about littering a costly work of art with her laundry. Instead she dropped everything on the floor just inside the door.

Tying her robe tightly, she crossed the hall and found Phoebe standing naked at the tub, one foot extended into the water. She looked like a nymph. Rowe stepped back and knocked like she hadn't seen anything, giving her time to reach for a towel.

"Come on in," Phoebe turned slightly. She made no attempt

to cover herself. "I left the shower running for you."

Rowe closed the door behind her, throwing the room into merciful near darkness. She knew her face was bright red. Avoiding the thin pools of light seeping from behind the glass objects around the walls, she removed her robe, hung it on a hook, and quickly entered the glassed-in shower. It was lined with slate, the same as the floor, and had the kind of luxurious European fittings Rowe wanted to use when she got around to renovating her bathroom at the cottage.

She soaped and scrubbed herself methodically, almost unable to believe she was doing this. Again she contemplated Phoebe's invitation, finding it difficult to accept at face value. Surely her neighbor was not so naïve she thought bathing with a woman who was not her sister fell into the same innocent category as taking a sauna with strangers at the gym. Was this a seduction minus the flirtatious overtures? Was Phoebe playing it cool and expecting Rowe to make the first move? No, that would pre-suppose she had been overwhelmed by Rowe's stoic charm and wanted her. Highly unlikely.

For a split second she contemplated getting out of the shower, getting dressed and going home. Then she decided to act like a grown up. She had no plans to go to bed with Phoebe, and she was perfectly capable of leaving if things got uncomfortable. Resolutely, she turned off the jets and stepped out onto a toweling mat.

Phoebe had lit a candle and placed it on the window ledge above the bathtub. A pale gold halo shimmered on the misted glass behind. She was sitting on the edge of the tub, candlelight dancing across the graceful arch of her back, her small pale breasts and slender thighs. She rose and extended a hand. Rowe took it.

They climbed into the tub together and, facing one another, sank down into the hot water. This was bizarre, Rowe decided. In fact, it was completely surreal. She slid her legs to one side, angling herself slightly away from Phoebe to face the door. For a long moment they sat stiff and unmoving. Rowe could smell a sweet, musky fragrance. The scent was faint, probably coming from one of several bottles of oil lined up next to a burner on the ledge below the window. She closed her eyes and tuned in to the Aretha-like voice of the British soul singer.

An odd sadness assailed her then, a sense that this was all wrong. She was sharing a bath with a woman who was not her lover, in a home that was not hers, on an island she'd run away to. Her work was shit, her personal life a disaster. Her days drifted by, carrying her like a disinterested passenger to a future that seemed more and more like an accident of fate, not the tomorrow she had planned for herself.

She sifted through memories trying to find one that would serve as an anchor, confirming that she had once known certainty and contentment, and would know it again. There was a time when everything had seemed perfect, when she'd thought she was on the fast track to permanent happiness. She had just made the New York Times Bestseller List and had found herself living in her own garden apartment in the West Village, dating women who claimed to adore her. It was her first summer in her new home. She had just sent her parents on an expensive cruise and given her brother a new car.

She woke up one magical morning after making love all night with an intelligent, charming woman who wanted her to give up horror novels and write poetry. Out in her tiny walled-off garden, surrounded by jasmine and roses, she'd written a couple of stanzas, just to see if she could. They were so ridiculous, so dismally trite, she had laughed at herself, her pleasure completely unburdened by doubt. In that moment, she had known exactly who she was, and she had liked that person. How could she have lost her confidence so completely?

"What are you thinking about?" Phoebe asked.

"I was having angst."

"About your book?"

"Not exactly. My book is more of a consequence than a cause."

"A consequence of what?"

Rowe hesitated, wondering how she would sound if she told the truth. Like an idiot, no doubt. "I'm not really sure," she said, chancing it. "I feel like I took a wrong turn somewhere and ended up in the wrong future."

Phoebe lifted a sponge from the water and slowly squeezed its contents over her back and shoulders. "What was the right future?"

"Good question. I thought I knew. For a while, I felt like I was on the right path and all I had to do was stick to it."

"Maybe you did. Maybe you're still on it."

"You're suggesting everything is just part of a bigger plan?"

"Perhaps. I mean, we can only ever know that in hindsight."

Rowe relaxed back against the tub, finally getting used to the idea that she was naked with Phoebe. "I saw you and Cara on television," she said, steering the conversation away from her sense of failure.

"What do you mean?"

"A couple of nights ago. Some serial killer was arrested by

the FBI and there you were."

Silence. In the wavering shadows, Phoebe's face looked rigid.

"Is everything okay?" Rowe asked.

"Yes. I'm just...surprised. I had no idea."

"You guys must be pretty pleased with yourselves getting that woman out alive. Amazing."

"Yes." Phoebe's voice sounded thin.

"I was wondering. How did you persuade them to let Cara come along?"

A long pause. "It wasn't like that. I asked Cara to meet me at the location afterward. I get kind of stressed sometimes, and it helps if she's there."

Rowe could tell there was much more to it than that. "What was your role? I mean, you were obviously right in the middle of the action. What does a forensic botanist do in that kind of case?"

Phoebe toyed with the sponge. "Well, I'm not usually there when an arrest is made. This case was a bit different. My boss invited me along because my work really helped lead us to the killer."

"I'm impressed. So plants revealed stuff about this guy? Fascinating. What was the biggest clue?"

"I really can't discuss it. You know...before the case goes to trial."

She sounded so jumpy, Rowe dropped the subject. "Sure. Understood."

Phoebe swirled water absently with one hand, then heaved a sigh. "I'm sorry. It's all bullshit," she blurted. "I'm not a botanist. That's just a cover. I'm an analyst...in the Intelligence field."

Rowe wanted to act cool, but it was hard with her mouth hanging open. "You're some kind of secret agent?" she managed eventually.

"No. Nothing like that," Phoebe mumbled. "I can't discuss my work. You know...homeland security."

"Jesus." Rowe could hardly get her head around it. Never in her wildest dreams would she have guessed Phoebe was a member of the intelligence community. "What about Cara? Is she in your line of work as well?"

"No. The MTV stuff is her real job."

"So this nutjob serial killer — was he a terrorist as well? Or is that something you can't talk about?"

With another sigh, Phoebe drew her knees up and rested her head on them. "I wish I could tell you everything, but I can't."

"Understood." Rowe made it sound like she didn't care. "I don't want you saying anything you'll regret later."

"Thank you."

"I guess it must be kind of a fine line, trying to figure out what you can and can't talk about." She tried to put Phoebe at ease. "You have the trial to consider, too. Do you have to appear?"

"I'm not sure. Probably not. My work is more behind the scenes." Phoebe seemed to get impatient with herself all of a sudden. She slid her feet back along the tub toward Rowe and submerged her shoulders. "Want to run some more hot water?" she asked over-brightly.

"Maybe in a while. Give your water cylinder a chance to heat up again." Rowe wondered what Phoebe really wanted to say. Trying not to press her, she said in a neutral tone, "If you ever need someone to talk to, I'm here. I mean, I know you have your sister, but..."

Phoebe's movements slowed. She gazed at Rowe, her eyes dark as midnight. "It gets lonely. Even with Cara."

"Keeping secrets?"

"I don't want to lie to you."

Rowe grinned, hoping to lighten up the mood. "I'll let you off, in the interests of national security."

A foot nudged her thigh and, in a playful tone, Phoebe asked, "Are you mocking the FBI?"

"God forbid."

"You should see it there. At Quantico. Talk about a paranoia zone."

"You just went for the women in uniform, didn't you?"

"I am *so* transparent." Phoebe's tiny smile gave way to cautious laughter.

She held so much back, Rowe thought. It was if she stored most of herself away, along with her FBI secrets. Impulsively, she asked, "Why do you live here, so far from...everything? Why not L.A. or something? Wouldn't that be easier for Cara?"

"We've talked about it on and off. But this is where we grew up. The house is actually our grandmother's. She brought us up." A slight pause. "Our parents were killed in a plane crash when we were children."

"I'm sorry." Rowe made like she didn't know. This didn't seem like the right time to explain that she'd been researching the Temple family tree. "That must have been hard."

"Grandma looked after us well. But she's not the motherly type. We did that for each other."

"You're very close, aren't you?"

"I think most twins are."

Rowe made a noise of agreement. Who was she to comment

on their obvious co-dependency? Identical twins seemed to have a different bond from other groups of siblings.

"And I like it here, too," Phoebe said, in a reflective tone. "I'm not sure if I could ever feel truly at home anywhere else. This place feels...safe, somehow."

"That's because you don't live in a haunted house."

The comment was supposed to be light-hearted, but Phoebe took it seriously. In an earnest tone, she said, "If I were you, I'd demolish that kitchen."

"Why?"

"Just a feeling." She shifted a little, sending a tremor through the warm water. "I think it would change the energy in the house if you did."

Rowe sensed a deliberate evasiveness. She was certain there was something Phoebe hadn't told her about the cottage. Was it any wonder? Having more or less implied that she thought her neighbor was mentally ill, Rowe was probably the last person Phoebe would confide in. She tried her luck anyway. "Tell me what you saw in there. Please. I'll listen with an open mind."

Phoebe hesitated, no doubt weighing up the risks of being completely frank. "Blood," she said after a moment. "There was blood all over the floor. And someone—I think it was a woman— told me to run. I felt like I was being chased and my life was in danger. Out in the snow I was sure I was about to be killed."

"Who did you think was chasing you?"

"I have no idea."

Rowe turned on the hot water and held her uninjured hand beneath the faucet testing the temperature. Juliet Baker had died in the meadow, just a few hundred yards from the cottage. No one could explain what she was doing outdoors. Had she run from the house, terrified for her life? Had Phoebe somehow tuned in to what Juliet had gone through? If so, could she do it again?

Wondering how she could arrange such an experiment, Rowe said, "I've been researching the history of the cottage. You said something happened in the kitchen. I've been trying to find out what that might have been." She moved the fresh hot water with one hand, stirring it through the bath.

"Any luck?" Phoebe seemed interested.

"I've learned some things. There was a young woman who lived in the cottage early last century. She died in mysterious circumstances. Her name was Juliet Baker."

"Juliet," Phoebe whispered.

"You've heard of her?" Rowe turned off the faucet.

Phoebe slid up the tub into a sitting position. She looked

uneasy. "Is she the Disappointed Dancer?"

"Yes, and I found out something very interesting," Rowe said carefully. "She may be related to you. It seems her father might have had an affair with your great-great-grandmother."

"Verity Adams?" Phoebe gave her a sharp look. "How does that make us related to the Bakers?"

"I think Verity's daughter might have been his child." Certain a clue was staring her in the face, she asked, "Phoebe, that pearl of yours. Where did it come from?"

"My mother left it to me. It was handed down in my family."

Verity, Rowe thought. Somehow Verity had ended up with Juliet's pearl. Did Thomas Baker bestow it upon his mistress after his daughter's tragic death? Was it one of those costly gifts given where money would be considered crass. It was more proof of Rowe's theory.

Treading carefully, she said, "I have a photograph of Juliet Baker wearing the pearl. I've also discovered something interesting about your great-grandmother's date of birth." She explained that Anne was conceived after her mother was widowed.

Phoebe looked shocked. "Well, this is a skeleton in the closet if it's true. I wonder if my grandmother knows anything about it."

"She may not. It's the kind of thing families cover up."

"I'm not so sure. She's always been kind of weird about the past. When you lose your parents, you need for someone to tell you those stories...you know, family legends. Grandma will talk about my father, but that's it."

"I hope you don't mind me bringing this up," Rowe said. "I wasn't prying. It's just that I've been trying to figure out what really happened to Juliet. My ghost hunters think we can lay her to rest if we figure out what's keeping her in the house."

"What are you planning to do? An exorcism?" Phoebe's voice overflowed with disapproval.

"No, nothing like that. More of a conversation. I think the general idea is that the ghost needs something done so she can be at peace. If we can find out what that is we'll be able to release her."

Phoebe set the sponge on the ledge. "So, you've changed your mind."

"About?"

"Ghosts."

"What can I say? It's easy to be a smartass about things you've never experienced for yourself."

Phoebe was silent for a short time, then said, "I may be able to help you."

"Really?"

"If you promise not to treat me like I'm insane."

"You're one of the sanest people I know," Rowe said and realized she meant it. The more she learned about Phoebe the more fascinated she was by her. "I promise. No idiot comments about medication."

"It's a deal." Phoebe smiled faintly. "Now, I'm going to get out of this tub before everything wrinkles."

"Good idea. Let's do it." Keeping her eyes averted, Rowe got up immediately after Phoebe stood, and they both reached for their towels and climbed out.

"I'm going to my room to dress," Phoebe said tactfully. She opened a cabinet door. "There's some guest supplies in there, if you need them. Toothbrush, comb, hair dryer, and so on. I'll bring up your dry clothes and put them in Cara's room."

"Thanks." Making an effort, Rowe said, "This was a nice idea."

"I liked it, too." Phoebe lifted her robe from the door. Indicating the candle on the window sill, she said, "When you're done, would you mind blowing that out?"

"Sure. See you downstairs."

As soon as her ravishing neighbor had departed, Rowe closed the door and leaned back against it, releasing a long pent up breath. She wished she could feel as calm and detached about this impersonal intimacy as she should. Instead, she felt exhausted from the strain of trying to act normal during their soak. Worse still, all she could think about was running after Phoebe and throwing her onto the nearest bed like a Neanderthal. Evidently her sex starved body had its own agenda, one completely out of step with the girlish bonding ritual Phoebe seemed to envision. And, a bad case of lust was not the only problem. Phoebe's pull was much more than physical.

Rowe had spent the past few weeks trying to ignore this depressing fact, focusing on anything else, including Cara. The truth was, she longed for Phoebe. Hardly an hour passed without the thought of her. Rowe could not believe her bad luck. Once more, she had led herself down the garden path toward inevitable despair. She had escaped one futile crush, only to exchange it for another that seemed even worse. Was this some kind of writers' disease—a twisted version of having a Muse? Was she doomed to a lifetime of unrequited yearnings for women who didn't want her?

Morosely, she toweled herself and crossed the hall to Cara's bedroom. Her freshly dried clothes were laid out on the bed, and she caught a trace of Phoebe's seductive perfume in the air. The smell went straight to her groin, reminding her yet again that she was a slave to her libido and she should flee before she did something she would regret.

It struck her then that she was making all kinds of assumptions. For a start, she was kidding herself that Phoebe was like all the rest—the sultry, narcissistic sex-goddesses she invariably fell for. Yet, she wasn't. There was something almost virginal about her, in fact. And she was a lesbian. Most of Rowe's crushes were not.

Angry with herself, she dressed mechanically and examined her bad hair in a bamboo-framed mirror. Coward that she was, she had side-stepped the biggest assumption of them all—that Phoebe wasn't interested. She realized she had no idea what Phoebe felt for her. Maybe it was time to find out.

Chapter
Ten

CARA CUT A path through the usual crush of hotties on the dance floor at Girlbar and joined the meat market at the bar. For a change it only took ten minutes to get served, and she came away with two drinks — one for her and one for whoever she was about to pick up.

She'd been dancing by herself for the past hour, brushing bare skin with countless women in the hot, hazy anonymity beneath the pulsating lights. Now everything ached — her mouth, her nipples, her clit. She wanted sex. It had been too long. While she'd been seeing Adrienne, she hadn't partied with anyone else. Instead, she'd kidded herself that the relationship might be going somewhere. What an idiot. And all the time Adrienne had been seeing someone else.

She cast a quick look around the groups and pairs, seeking out parties of three. In past experience, she'd found these often consisted of a happy couple with a friend who wanted to get hooked up. That was how she'd met Adrienne; in fact, how she met most of her flings.

A sporty type in a sleeveless white T-shirt caught her eye. She was standing with a pair of chapstick lesbians and looked as jaded as Cara felt, a fact each of them seemed to recognize. They exchanged an appraising stare, then discreet, empathetic smiles, and Cara sauntered over to the group.

"Thirsty?" She offered the sporty woman her spare martini, introduced herself to everyone and said she was from Maine.

The chapstickers, Liz and Jadeene, were a couple and their friend was called Fran. They were from Northampton and were in L.A. for a week staying at La Montrose, a hotel Cara knew well from flings-gone-by. She suggested they find a table.

Once they were seated, she asked, "So what's everyone's dysfunction?"

As usual, the icebreaker generated some laughs. Liz and Jadeene confessed to being compulsive home renovators who only took time out from grouting and sanding floors to have sex and write their term papers. Fran, who was a few years older and had almost finished her PhD in criminal justice, had a thing for tattooed babes who loved her and left her. Her pals had dragged her to Girlbar so she could stare all she wanted at her nemeses, then return safely to Northampton, heart intact.

"In that case, we should dance," Cara said. "I'm not tattooed and I won't love you."

"Are you picking me up?" Fran asked as they headed for the dance floor.

"Would that be a problem?"

Fran shot her a direct look. "Hell, no. But why me?"

"My dysfunction is having one night stands with brainy chicks. Of course if I discover you can't discuss anything except your dog and your favorite beer, we're in trouble."

Fran laughed. She was cute. Her dark brown hair was cut short and spiky and had a copper tint in it. She was about the same height as Cara, but a little heavier built. She wore Diesel jeans and some cool jewelry, and her T-shirt revealed well-worked muscles and an intricate knotwork tattoo on one shoulder. She seemed more at ease in the club scene than her friends, a little bored even.

The music made conversation impossible, and once they started dancing, Fran was content to get up close and personal without knowing Cara's last name. The pounding beat, the smell of sweaty bodies, booze and stale cigarettes, the feel of Fran's hands, worked the usual magic. Cara felt free, entirely her own person.

They danced for a while, edging hotter by degrees, until their breasts were crushed together, hard nipples teasing through thin cotton. Fran slid a knee between Cara's thighs, softly grinding against her swollen center. The pressure was unbearable, not enough to get her off, too much to endure without release. She slid a hand beneath Fran's T-shirt and trailed her nails lightly over the slick arch of her back.

Near her ear, she shouted, "Want to get out of here?"

Fran answered with her hands, squeezing Cara's ass and forcing her down so her thighs spread wider over the knee between them. Desire crawled from her belly to her throat. She tucked a hand over Fran's waistband and slowly tugged, then reached for the belt and opened the buckle a few notches. Watching the play of expressions on Fran's face, she unfastened the top few buttons of the Diesel jeans and slid her hand inside, over a firm belly and cotton briefs.

Fran's hand closed on hers, easing it from its damp burrow.

"Let's go," she said hoarsely.

They straightened up their clothes and found Liz and Jaydeene, who had to be convinced that Cara was fit to drive and would bring Fran back to the hotel later. They weren't charmed that their pal was bailing, but Cara was fine with that—she wasn't shopping for a foursome.

As they drove out of the parking lot a few minutes later, Fran asked, "Where are we going?"

"Just a few blocks. I rent a short-term apartment when I'm in town."

"What kind of work do you do?"

"I make music videos."

"That must get old."

Cara glanced sideways, mildly surprised. In L.A. any mention of her work was usually greeted with envious gasps and questions about the bands she worked with. "Yeah, it does." She turned onto North La Cienega. "I think about writing a lesbian flick sometimes. You know, some low budget thing I could film myself."

"We could use a new lesbian movie." Fran combed her dark hair with her fingers. "If I have to sit through *Claire of the Moon* at another potluck, I'll probably kill myself."

Cara grinned. "Congratulations on sitting through it the first time. I needed drugs." She made a right onto Fountain.

As the car climbed, her passenger stared out the window at the lights glittering across the Hollywood Hills. "I've never been up here," she said. "It's beautiful."

"Yeah, you don't see the seedy side at night." Cara halted in front of her apartment building and waited for the gates to open. The Isola Bella was her favorite place to stay in West Hollywood. She loved the old Spanish feel of the architecture and beautiful gardens, and the apartments were large and very private. She led Fran up the terracotta tiled steps and let them in to her place.

"This is great." Fran swept a look around the softly lit downstairs living area.

"Beats staying in a hotel." Cara dropped her jacket over the back of an armchair. "Can I get you a drink?"

"Sure, if you're having one."

"Actually, I'm not. But I can fix you anything you want." Cara lifted a hand to Fran's cheek, trailing her fingertips over the smooth skin. "Or we could run with plan B. Take a shower and pick up where we left off."

Fran's sleepy hazel eyes grew warm. "My dates usually make me work a bit harder."

"My dates are usually begging for it by now." Cara slid her

hand to the back of Fran's head and caressed her mouth with the ghost of a kiss.

She tasted of mint and alcohol. They experimented as strangers did, finding a fit. Then their mouths relaxed and joined in a kiss that was hot and hungry. As if by tacit agreement they drew back and checked in with each other.

Fran's gaze fell from Cara's lips to her breasts. A split second later her hand took possession of Cara's crotch, working her through the dense fabric of her jeans. "You feel good," she groaned.

Cara smiled. She was wet with anticipation, her clit a throbbing reminder of her needs. The pumping sexual microclimate of the club always had that effect on her. It also helped that she found this woman sexy. "Let's get naked," she said.

PHOEBE STARED OUT the kitchen window into a sea of white and felt guilty that she had convinced Rowe to come over. The snow was now a blizzard, and although it was only a ten minute walk to Dark Harbor Cottage, Rowe would freeze going home in this weather.

She heated the butternut soup she'd made earlier and carried it into the den, setting it on top of the wood stove. The bath had been a mistake. She could see that now. She had expected to feel comforted. Instead she felt disoriented, trapped between longing and isolation, acutely aware of what was missing in the life she'd chosen to lead. The truth was, she wanted more than cozy female camaraderie with Rowe, and much more than a stand-in for Cara.

She was suddenly demoralized. If Rowe were interested in her, they would have had a very different experience naked, alone, with candles and music. But Phoebe had done her best to make sure their bath was congenial and non-sexual, and it seemed Rowe had been perfectly content with that. She reminded herself that Rowe was still lovesick over that married woman in Manhattan and probably not ready to move on.

But even if things were different, was that really what Phoebe wanted—her next door neighbor for a lover? Or was she simply missing making love? It had been months. Yet, oddly she had no desire to go out and find short-term company. She was searching for something else, but hadn't recognized until this moment what it was. With a jolt of clarity, she knew she wanted a mate. Not a fling. Not a lover who'd be content to be relegated to the sidelines of Phoebe's real life with her sister. She wanted someone she could belong to.

Phoebe pictured Rowe standing naked in the bathroom, solid torso and thighs, strong shoulders, the kind that were good to bite. It was impossible not to imagine Rowe's weight on her, the feel of her mouth, her caresses. Phoebe warned herself yet again not to go there, but her resolve was waning. She didn't care what Cara thought. She was attracted to their neighbor and she also really liked the woman. She liked being with her. Rowe made her feel safe and didn't treat her like a second-rate carbon copy of Cara.

Phoebe wished she had changed into something more alluring than a white shirt and a pair of loose-fitting olive corduroy pants. She hadn't even put on lipstick, such was her determination to send no mixed messages.

"Guess I'm spending the night." Rowe's voice floated across the room.

With a guilty start, Phoebe turned to face her. "I'm sorry. I should have thought about the weather before I tempted you with food." Lifting the saucepan lid, she made a show of stirring the soup. "We have plenty of room, and I can give the dogs some leftovers for their dinner." She knew her voice sounded strained, but she couldn't relax.

Rowe studied her face and something changed. The air seemed heavier. She took a few steps closer and said, "Phoebe, there's something I need to say."

Phoebe replaced the lid on the saucepan with a nervous clatter and set the spoon aside. "Sure," she replied with trepidation.

Rowe was probably going to tell her, just in case it wasn't clear, that they would only ever be friends. It was ironic, Phoebe thought—she had given Rowe the very same message just a few weeks ago. She met her neighbor's sensual blue eyes and had the impression she was embarrassed about something.

"Phoebe, I know you only want a friendship with me, but I have to tell you I'm very attracted to you." Rowe's mouth formed a small, wry grimace. "I'm sure you've probably noticed. I guess I was wondering if it's mutual, or if I'm just doing what I always do, which is get hopeless crushes on women who aren't interested."

Heat seared Phoebe's cheeks and her heart pounded in her ears, out of step with her breathing. She took a step toward Rowe and said, "It's definitely mutual." Their hands met. Rowe's were larger and stronger than her own.

Rowe said, "Hell, I wish you'd told me this before we got in that bathtub. I was a wreck."

Phoebe laughed. She felt like crying. Her mouth was trembling before Rowe caressed it tenderly apart. The kiss was so sweetly yearning, so honest and naked, Phoebe felt like they were new to this, somehow untarnished by past disappointments. Long fingers threaded through her hair, shaking it free of its ribbon. As their kiss deepened, Phoebe tilted her head back into Rowe's cradling hand and opened her eyes to find she was being watched intently.

They stared at one another, and Phoebe took Rowe's tongue deeper, at the same time moving against her, blatantly communicating her desire. Rowe's mouth left hers and moved over her throat, teasing with tongue and teeth. Her chest rose and fell unevenly as she unbuttoned Phoebe's shirt.

Gazing down at the ash blonde head, Phoebe had a moment of anxiety. She'd always felt her breasts were too small. Even with the help of her get-cleavage bra, they would barely fill a hand.

Rowe did not seem discouraged by this lack of voluptuousness. Between kisses and bites, she looked up, face flushed, and said, "I want you so badly."

"I want you, too," Phoebe told her.

Rowe took her hand. "Where's your bedroom?"

THE ROOM THEY entered was pale and furnished in dark Mission-style oak, the bed high and old-fashioned. In the fireplace to one side of the bed, several large logs burned slowly, spilling shadows and light. Bathed in the soft glow of the fire, Phoebe lit a scented candle and drew back the plain white bedcovers. Watching her, Rowe felt sick with desire. She was reminded of a woman she saw in a recurring dream, a dark-haired wraith whose features were always blurred. Rowe could never quite reach her. The closer she came, the farther the woman would retreat, until Rowe was running, arms stretched out like a small child. She always awoke from that dream just as it seemed the woman was within reach.

Without a trace of coyness, Phoebe removed her blouse and stepped out of her corduroy pants. Underneath she wore only bra and panties, the pretty kind, ivory satin and lace. She came closer, unfastened Rowe's belt and eased her shirt from her jeans. Where she pulled clothing aside, the fire warmed Rowe's naked flesh, but she goose-bumped anyway at the brush of Phoebe's fingertips. Feeling as inept as a high school kid, she lifted a hand to Phoebe's breast. Through the filmy satin, the nipple hardened against Rowe's palm, moving with the shallow rise and fall of each breath.

Rowe stared at the delicate flesh and waited for time to stop. For it seemed, in this moment of all moments, that she could choose her fate. Was this the path to happiness or the road to nowhere? She had no idea. All she knew was that in this brief eternity, trapped between doubt and yearning, she could not escape the journey. With shaking hands, she unfastened Phoebe's bra. Her breasts were beautiful, the skin tightly puckered around each rosy nipple.

Phoebe slid her panties down and stepped out of them. Naked, she presented herself before Rowe with perfect candor. "I hope I please you," she said, her dark steady gaze free of guile.

Rowe touched her cheek, moved in a way she had not thought possible since the first time she'd made love with a woman. "How could you not?"

She shed the rest of her own clothing, and they moved to the bed and slipped between the fine cotton sheets. For a moment, they lay on their backs, not looking at one another. It seemed to Rowe then that Phoebe must be just as overwhelmed as she was. The distance between them was closing so fast it made her head spin. She was breathing too rapidly, she thought, almost hyperventilating. Heat rose from her groin to her belly.

She rolled onto her side to face Phoebe, and asked, "Are you sure about this?"

Phoebe moved into her arms. In a husky voice, she said, "Kiss me."

Her eyelids descended and her mouth met Rowe's as if imprinting itself, closed at first, lips giving slightly but not enough. This hint of reserve unleashed a hunger in Rowe that stampeded through her body. She shifted her weight, pinning Phoebe on her back, leaning over her, one bracing hand on the pillow next to her head. This time she made sure Phoebe could not hold anything back, kissing her hard, refusing to be shut out. She tasted sweet. Hot. Slippery. Urgent. Their tongues communed in the silent accord of desire. Rowe lost herself in the ebb and flow of mouth on mouth, the feast of craving this invoked. When she could no longer stand the exquisite torment, she lifted her lips from Phoebe's and dragged the sheet back to uncover every inch of her.

Phoebe's arms drifted up and her hands dropped onto the pillow above her head. She opened eyes glazed with desire. Watching Rowe watch her, she tilted her hips just enough so that her legs parted slightly, exposing a modest thatch of dark hair. The invitation made Rowe's chest constrict. Phoebe was provocative, but there was innocence, too, in the shallow rise and fall of her breasts, the girlish belly, the delicate curve of her mouth.

Losing herself, Rowe explored the body offered, stroking, kissing, tasting. With every caress, with every breath, she was strangely aware that she was peeling away the layers that divided friends from lovers. Phoebe was familiar yet foreign. Rowe wanted to touch her everywhere, to know her inside and out. She wanted to dissolve into her, to pleasure her, to invent a bright new world that was theirs alone. It was not just sex, she thought. It was something more primal. What she'd always expected to happen, but never had, was happening now. She was making love with her soul engaged. For the very first time she made sense to herself. A strange joy surged through her and she wondered if Phoebe felt as she did.

Leaning on an elbow, she stretched out alongside her and brushed a hand over her pale throat and down to the bony fortress of sternum and ribs. The heart imprisoned there beat against her palm as if it wanted to be held. Rowe continued down, moving over firm flesh and soft silken hairs matted with fluids. Longing to see and feel what she could smell, she changed position, spreading Phoebe's legs and kneeling on an angle next to her.

Resting one hand on the swell of that dark mound, she urged the swollen flesh back enough to expose Phoebe's clit, pink and rigid between glistening folds. Slowly, she smothered it between two fingers, drawing the hood down before releasing it, increasing and decreasing pressure until she felt the shaft stiffen completely.

Phoebe's small whimpers aroused her unspeakably, luring her fingers down through the slick kiss of flesh to the parting in between. She entered with more restraint than she felt. The cry this evoked made her hesitate for a moment and she looked up, seeking Phoebe's eyes.

"Don't stop."

A plea Rowe answered with a gentle thrust. Working her way deeper inside, she bent low and took Phoebe's clit in her mouth, rolling the hood back with her tongue and sucking and tugging until she could feel Phoebe flexing and contracting around her fingers. She heard ragged gasps. Fingers dug into her shoulders. Shivering, Rowe moved in and out faster and harder, responding to the tempo of Phoebe cries, the kneading clench of her hands, and compulsion of her hips.

She was so close to coming herself that she moved her free hand between her legs and almost lost it instantly. Clamping her thighs over her knuckles, wanting to wait, she curled her fingers a little inside the hot sheath of Phoebe's body and bore down harder with her tongue. Phoebe's breathing grew ragged and one of her hands moved to Rowe's head, the fingers twisting in her hair. Her body stilled against Rowe, her hips exerting relentless pressure.

Rowe slowed her thrusts, eased the tension of her mouth and heard a low, animal cry as Phoebe let go. A gush of fluid surged around her fingers and filled her palm. Astounded, unbearably turned on, she released the fist clenched between her own legs and worked her fingers along her clit with just enough pressure to make herself explode. Coming hard and fast, she gave herself over to sensation, her head resting on Phoebe's stomach.

When the spasms finally subsided, she forced herself up just enough to gently kiss Phoebe's saturated core then fell back against the cool sheets. Sapped, her heart pounding wildly, she stared across at her new lover. Phoebe stared back and for the first time in her life, Rowe felt she was truly seen. The experience was as disconcerting as it was thrilling. She had no idea what to say, how to express what it meant.

Phoebe reached out and took her hand. "Happy?" she whispered.

Tears flooded Rowe's eyes. "Incredibly."

CARA DROPPED HER car keys on the table and quickly undressed. Briefly, she considered getting back into bed without showering, but she smelled of sex, and who wanted to wake up with a stranger's juices on their hands and face? She strolled into the bathroom and turned on the shower. In the mirror she checked out the few blotches on her throat and breasts. Even soft bites always showed up later on her fine pale almond skin. She didn't mind. In fact, she was always turned on by the evidence of a good fuck. Some of her encounters left more emphatic marks, but Fran was the gentle type.

They'd had fun and Cara felt a pang of regret that she'd insisted on taking her one-night-stand back to La Montrose. But having casual partners sleep over was not a good idea. It was awkward the next morning. They would suggest breakfast and Cara would feel bad if she said no. Then came the inevitable conversation about seeing one another again. Sometimes they both understood this polite lie was just a way of saying goodbye, but there were always women who didn't get it and insisted on exchanging phone numbers.

Cara stepped into the shower and stood beneath the hot jets, methodically soaping herself. Women like Fran were the exception not the rule. She'd been completely open about her agenda, or lack of it, and they'd agreed on their intentions like mature adults. They were both looking for the same thing. No strings. At one time, Cara had assumed that she and whoever she picked up would be on the same page. But this was not always the case, so she'd evolved a few rules to avoid feelings getting hurt. She was always honest about where she stood. No one spent the night. They treated one another with respect. And no meant no.

She turned off the shower, dried herself, cleaned her teeth, applied face cream, and got into bed. She still didn't understand why she had broken her rules with Adrienne. Look where it had gotten her. She'd spent a year seeing no one else and feeling pretty good about having a steady girlfriend, even if they were on opposite coasts. She'd actually started thinking about buying an apartment in Westwood, figuring Adrienne could live there and Cara would divide her time between her two homes. She couldn't move out of the Islesboro house—Phoebe would never cope with the idea of her "leaving."

Cara rolled onto her side and stared into the darkness, trying to identify the feeling that came over her at these times. It was an odd hopelessness, a sense of something restless within, as if a part of her was tethered to some deeply buried stake and was gnawing at its ropes. Puzzled, she slid a pillow beneath the bedclothes and curled into it. It wasn't like she was unhappy. She had a great job, a nice home and people who loved her. She could buy most things she wanted and was free to do pretty much anything she liked.

Of course most people would claim that being single was the problem, like you weren't complete unless you were in a long-term relationship. Cara had never felt that way. As far as she was concerned, being single had a lot going for it. For a start, no girlfriend meant no drama. Who had time for that shit? Besides, she didn't need another person to make her feel complete. And she couldn't possibly be lonely. When you had an identical twin you were never really alone.

The thought preyed on her. Sometimes she wondered if she was controlled by her own unique urges or if her mind was somehow colonized by her twin's. It was almost as if she couldn't trust her most private thoughts to be untainted. Over the years she had grown accustomed to the sense that she and Phoebe shared a strange unconscious dance. There was no escaping it. Even in sleep, the music played on, and they moved in step.

Now, as she closed her eyes and allowed her mind to drift, a profound contentment advanced on her, evicting her nagging anxiety. She knew the feeling was not her own, but she surrendered to it anyway, and closed her eyes. The pillow she was hugging smelled of Fran, she realized an instant before sleep. Funny how the scent of another human being could be so comforting.

Chapter
Eleven

PHOEBE HUNG THE final red glass apple on the Christmas tree and hit the power. Zoe instantly leapt up from the rug and barked at the blinking lights. She was one of those dogs who reacted to change, losing her mind if a houseplant was moved six inches. Rowe had installed a new chandelier in her vestibule and Zoe got hysterical every time she saw it.

"Come here, silly." Phoebe gave her a reassuring cuddle and, once the Lab had calmed down, guiltily fed her a treat.

Rowe insisted on rationing these because Zoe tended to put on weight and she'd snuck off to the deer barn recently and stuffed herself on apples. Phoebe wasn't meant to give the dogs table scraps either, but they knew a sucker when they saw one.

She surveyed her decorations with satisfaction. The room smelled of pine and the cookies she'd baked that morning, and with the garlands and Christmas stockings, it felt homey and festive. Cara drew the line at angels and nativity scenes, pointing out that Christmas was nothing but a pagan feast hijacked by an upstart new religion trying to make conversion painless for the heathen. Officially, in the Temple home, they celebrated the solstice festival of Yule.

Phoebe was dismayed that she hadn't made it to Boston to shop this year. Her work for the FBI had been a huge distraction. Next year she would organize things better. Meantime, thank goodness for the Internet. Yesterday's mail delivery had to be dragged by handcart to the door. Phoebe went over to the table where her gifts for Cara and Rowe were piled up waiting to be wrapped. She wanted to have everything done by the time Rowe got back from her last minute shopping expedition to Portland. Cara wouldn't be home until Christmas Eve, and she would bring all her presents with her, professionally wrapped by those glamorous sales clerks in the ritzy boutiques where she shopped.

This year, for once, Phoebe was going to give her sister something just as fabulous as anything Cara might choose from

Tiffany or Louis Vuitton. Sliding a square red leather box from its shiny white outer, she opened it carefully and inspected the contents. Cara had coveted a Cartier Pasha watch for many years and had even pinned a picture of the model she wanted on the refrigerator a few months back. Phoebe had taken this as permission to splash out, something she and her twin seldom did. When you grew up making your own soap and wearing second hand clothing, frugal habits were hard to shake.

Grandma Temple had ingrained in them her views on extravagance and waste—the elderly lady still insisted on driving a twenty-year old Ford rather than squandering money on a new car. Over time, Phoebe and Cara had recognized that her ideas were extreme, but Phoebe still practiced many of the home economies they were reared with. She grew most of their vegetables, canning and freezing through the summer so they would have enough to last through the winter. And despite Cara's insistence that there was no need, she made their soft furnishings and sewed many of her own clothes.

Phoebe knew she should be enjoying her glamorous FBI salary, but she couldn't assume it was going to last. Her second sight had arrived out of the blue, and it could vanish just as quickly. Meantime, she was thrilled that she could donate extra money to WSPA and other causes she supported and buy some special things for the people she cared about. Humming to herself, she wrapped Cara's watch in a sheet of beautiful embossed paper that would horrify her grandmother, who always presented their gifts in recycled tissue, decorated with dried flowers she had pressed herself.

After tying Cara's box to a high branch, she wrapped a few of the more mundane gifts she'd bought. Books, DVDs, perfume, clothing. She'd also had the Colby Boone pastel framed. This was now hanging on the wall near the tree. While she was in the gallery, she'd purchased a couple of other paintings, one of them for Rowe. She still couldn't believe her luck at the find. It was an oil painting of Dark Harbor Cottage by an unknown artist, painted about a hundred years ago. The moment she saw it she knew it belonged in Rowe's front parlor in the gap above the rolltop desk they'd dragged in from the Carriage House.

Ignoring an urge to take it from its protective crate, she contented herself with wrapping it beautifully. Rowe was going to be delighted, and the painting wasn't the only special gift. Phoebe opened a small box and studied the ring she had chosen for her lover. She supposed some women would be frightened off receiving this less than a week into a new relationship. But it wasn't a wedding band, and Rowe had mentioned one day that she'd lost a signet ring she was fond of. Phoebe had found a heavy handmade replacement she could imagine Rowe wearing. She hoped it would fit.

Picturing her pleasure, she felt her body react as it always did to the mere thought of Rowe. Her breathing shortened, her nipples grew taut and she got wet. Weak kneed, she pulled out a chair and sank down into it. She still couldn't believe they were lovers. More amazing still was that, for the first time ever, she felt certain she was in a relationship that had a future. The conviction was instantly tempered with unease. She hadn't told Cara. She knew she was putting it off out of cowardice, trying to avoid a shadow being cast on her happiness.

She didn't want her sister's steely perception slicing through her own, wounding her with doubt. It was so often that way between them. Sometimes it seemed they shared a mind, thinking each other's thoughts, feeling each other's fears, living each other's lives in countless tiny ways. They often wore the same colors unintentionally, injured the same limbs on the same days, made the same impulse purchases when they weren't shopping together. It was as if they inhabited an invisible womb, each seeking space to grow yet held captive by their dependence on the same blood supply. They were eternally trapped by their togetherness, Phoebe thought. They were one another's first and most enduring passion, each the soul mate none other could be.

That was why she needed to tell Cara face to face, not over the phone. Being with Rowe did not mean rejecting her twin. But she had a feeling Cara might take it that way.

"WHY DIDN'T YOU tell me before?" Cara spooned cranberry sauce into a crystal bowl.

Phoebe closed the oven door and wiped her hands awkwardly on her apron. Her eyes pleaded and her mouth was set in the small mutinous line that always spelled trouble. "Because I didn't want us having one of *those* conversations over the phone."

"So instead you wait until Christmas Day to explain she's joining us because you're now fucking her."

Phoebe flinched. "Don't say it like that. I'm in love with her."

"How can you possibly say that? You only met the woman a few weeks ago."

Cara carried the cranberry sauce into the dining room. The table was set for three, and Rowe was going to show up pretty soon. Swallowing her anger, she found a place for the sauce and refolded the napkins to give herself time to control her breathing. Damn Phoebe. Why couldn't she behave like a responsible adult just once? And Rowe. Cara supposed she couldn't blame her. The woman was obviously lonely and had let herself be charmed. So much for her reluctance to get it on with Cara because they were neighbors. Apparently her reservations had not extended to Phoebe.

She plunked down the napkin rings harder than she intended, stalked over to the bar and hauled out the champagne glasses. When she turned toward the table again, Phoebe was standing in front of her, tears rolling down her cheeks.

"Please don't spoil this," she begged. "Please be happy for me. I really think she's the one."

"I don't spoil things for you, Phoebe. You do that for yourself."

"This is different. You have to believe me. I've never felt this way about anyone. "

"I wish you could hear yourself." Cara moved past her to set the glasses on the table. "I wish I had a tape recording of the times you've told me you were in love and it was going to be different."

"I know I've done some stupid things in the past," Phoebe said with shaky dignity. "When I think about those other women now, I can see that I never loved any of them. I just hoped I did."

"You think that's changed?" Cara softened her tone. "Honestly, sweetie. I'm not saying this to hurt you. I know you want to believe someone is going to walk into your life and sweep you off your feet. But that's just a fairy tale."

Phoebe stared at her. "Why are you being like this? Is it because I invited her for Christmas?"

"No. I don't give a damn if you invite ten people without discussing it with me. You're the one doing the cooking."

"Then what? Please tell me."

"I have told you."

Phoebe shook her head, wispy curls drooping from the Grecian knot she wore while cooking. In a voice thick with tears, she said, "Can't you feel how different this is? You have to know."

Cara did sense a more profound emotion in Phoebe, but she refused to validate her twin's happy delusion that this time she'd found true love. "All I know is that I asked you not to do this, and we now have a situation. Sooner or later it's going to end up in my lap."

"Don't you have any faith in me at all?" Phoebe grew pale. "For God's sake, Cara. I don't understand why you're so angry. If it doesn't work out, I promise you I will deal with it. So please...at least act like you're happy for us while she's here."

Cara felt a burn of frustration. Phoebe seemed unable to move beyond her need for someone's blind adoration. Apparently it wasn't enough that she had a twin who loved her and shielded her from harsh reality. Cara supposed it had something to do with the loss of their parents. Ever since she could remember, Phoebe had repeated an almost childlike quest for approval and attention over and over with women who seemed like authority figures. They were usually much older— Bev had been in her mid-forties. And they were the type who put her on a pedestal and treated her like she was made of porcelain.

Rowe didn't exactly fit the profile. On the other hand, Phoebe's choices were limited right now and their attractive, single neighbor was right next-door. Cara swallowed a sigh. She wouldn't have minded playing around with Rowe herself, and it would have been a whole lot less complicated for all concerned. Rowe had been interested. Maybe she could still be tempted. Cara seriously doubted the woman was kidding herself about the nature of her liaison with Phoebe. She had obviously been down that road too many times to harbor naïve illusions. No doubt she was enjoying having a beautiful woman in her bed. Did it really matter which twin it was?

Cara smiled. Rowe could be handled, of that she was confident. "You win," she told Phoebe with a sigh. "I'll be nice to her."

BEFORE ROWE WAS halfway along the path, the back door flew open and Phoebe stood there. It had been a slow slog to the Temple's house, dragging a covered handcart, with Zoe and Jessie cavorting out of shouting range like they were seeing snow for the first time. They would have to go straight to the laundry and get dried off. Rowe could imagine them leaping all over Cara, smearing mud and slobber down her expensive designer clothing.

"Hey, baby!" She waved to Phoebe. "The dogs are filthy, sorry."

Phoebe called them, and as usual, they hurtled toward her then flopped down at her feet, models of good behavior. Looking past them, Phoebe asked, "Need a hand?"

"No. I'm fine, thanks. But we should probably make sure they don't jump up on Cara." Rowe studied her lover with a smile she knew was probably sappy.

Phoebe's cheeks were stained crimson, a paler shade of the skirt she was wearing. In her simple white blouse, with her ebony hair drawn up into a careless knot, the wild color in her face and her eyes shy and bright with passion, she looked so stunning Rowe was rooted to the spot, hardly able to breathe.

The strength of her reactions shocked her. It had been much easier to long for women she couldn't have, she understood suddenly. With the Marions of her past, she had felt powerless and frustrated, but somehow safe. Sustained by fantasy and hope, her romantic feelings had never had to withstand the acid test of real life. There was nothing to prove when you didn't have to be a partner. You couldn't fail in a relationship that didn't exist. It was like having a great idea for a book, but never writing it.

By contrast, being with Phoebe was thrilling and terrifying in equal parts. Rowe felt more exposed than she had at any time with any woman. In the past she had been disappointed, even imagined herself heartbroken over the women who failed to return her feelings. She could see now that she had been wandering in a maze of her own making, taking countless dead-end paths to avoid the prize her soul sought but her heart feared.

Why had she been afraid? It was as if she had courted profound desire, but only in one-sided situations. The women who actually became her lovers were those she defaulted into having sex with — good women, women she liked. The relationships were...bland. Rowe had drifted in and out of them. None had lasted more than a couple of years. She gazed at Phoebe and knew by some magic she could not explain that she wanted to be with this woman for the rest of her life, that she would never have enough of her. That if she could not be with Phoebe, she wanted no one else, least of all another Marion.

"Go inside, my darling," she said. "You're getting cold."

Instead, Phoebe walked through the snow toward her, arms outstretched. "I'm so happy you came. I missed you yesterday."

"I missed you, too."

Rowe wanted to swing her off her feet and carry her upstairs to bed. She didn't care about Christmas dinner. She would rather devour Phoebe. The craving was so powerful, she had to remind herself to breathe. By contrast, the feelings she'd had for Marion seemed tepid, even banal. Shocked, she stared down at the fine icy crystals clinging to her jacket, each a tiny masterpiece of nature, unique in its design. One day soon they would melt and flow together, unified by the sun, their true purpose the mundane equivalent of a vast garden hose. So why the glittering beauty? Was Mother Nature in an exhibitionist mood — flaunting her immeasurable power to create and transform?

Time, Rowe thought. No one second was the same as the

next. Each was a tiny world of possibility. She could seize her life or brush it away. She could fixate on the transient, blind to a wider truth. Or she could accept the fleeting enchantments and distractions of her past for what they were, part of a larger design she could only understand by stepping back. Love was not a solitary crystal of emotion, perfect and discrete. It was an accumulated capacity, a river enriched by dreams and desires and experience. She had loved Marion so she could know better how to love Phoebe. It was that simple.

Her beloved stared down at the handcart with a puzzled frown. "There's something moving in there."

"It's a surprise," Rowe said.

Phoebe lit up. "For me?"

"Have you been good?"

"You tell me." Phoebe giggled and her lips left a warm, damp spot on Rowe's icy cheek. Tucking her arm into Rowe's she walked with her to the laundry and helped clean up the dogs before they moved indoors.

Cara was waiting in the hall, looking like an invitation to sin, in tight black pants and a little butter-yellow angora cardigan with a demure cream lace collar. She took Rowe's coat and said, "You're looking very delectable." Playfully, she patted Rowe's midriff. "No more rolls."

"Amazing what regular exercise can do," Rowe replied blandly.

"You know, it beats me why more people don't just have sex instead of paying a personal trainer." Cara flicked a pointed look from Rowe to Phoebe.

Rowe didn't rise to the bait. "How was L.A.?"

"I worked hard and played hard." Cara's mouth parted in a lazy half-smile. The invitation in her candid gray eyes was unmistakable.

Phoebe touched Rowe's hand. "Come see the tree."

Pulling the hand trolley behind her, Rowe followed the twins into the den, wondering what the hell Cara was playing at. Was she hitting on Rowe to prove something? If so, what? Did she seriously imagine Rowe would flirt with her in front of Phoebe? Was she trying to hurt her twin? Disturbed, she inhaled the fragrance of pine and spice and made an effort to focus her attention on the room.

Phoebe hadn't been kidding when she said she loved decorations. The walls were lavishly garlanded and the tree was decked out in red and gold ornaments. Around its base and hanging from its branches were gifts of all shapes and sizes. Rowe's eyes were drawn past the glittering branches to a portrait on the wall, a pastel of Phoebe holding a sweet-faced spaniel.

She took a couple of paces toward it, captivated. The artist had captured Phoebe in a few deft strokes, revealing her innate sweetness and fascinating contradictions, her innocence and allure. The eyes that stared from her delicate face shone with hope and trust, and something else. Painful knowledge. Rowe caught her breath, her most protective instincts aroused.

Cara materialized at her side. "Isn't it something?"

"Amazing," Rowe agreed.

An arm slipped into hers and her nostrils registered the spicy fragrance she had smelled a moment earlier. It was rich, almost chocolaty, and belonged to Cara, who turned slightly then, her breast brushing Rowe's arm. An accident? Rowe wanted to believe so. She shifted uneasily, putting some air between her body and Cara's.

"Sweetie, did you tell Rowe about meeting Colby?"

Phoebe shook her head, absorbed in rearranging a strand of lights that had dropped from their branch. "I'll tell her later."

"Obviously you've heard of him," Cara was determined to impress. "Colby Boone. Portrait artist to the rich and famous."

Rowe hadn't, but she said, "He's very talented."

"Artists always want to paint Phoebe. Has she shown you her collection of paintings and poems yet?"

Phoebe's head lifted. She cast an imploring look at Cara who responded with a helpless shrug.

"Okay. I put my foot in it. Phoebe would rather you don't know she's been inundated with bad love poems all her life. So, I'll change the subject." She sashayed to the sideboard and set about fixing drinks, asking Rowe, "Is Christmas a big deal in your family?"

Rowe wanted to ignore the question and ask Cara what her problem was, but she could guess. Phoebe must have told her their news. Surmising that it hadn't been greeted with delight, she cast a glance toward her lover who was still hovering in front of the Christmas tree, an edge of strain in her expression. Rowe groaned inwardly. Family dramas—could any Christmas be complete without them?

"When my brother and I were kids, Mom and Dad always went to town for the Santa trip," she said, trying to sound normal. "But these days we don't do anything lavish."

Phoebe turned anxious eyes on her. "I didn't even think when I invited you. Would you normally be with your family?"

"Not this year. I gave my folks a Hawaiian vacation. My dad's almost eighty, and he hasn't been well lately, so it was now or never. The traveling isn't getting any easier. As for my brother..." She grimaced. "He got born again last year and isn't crazy about spending time with the dyke sister."

"My commiserations." Cara handed out glasses of eggnog.

"He'll get over it." Rowe held Phoebe's gaze and gave her a broad smile. "Baby, I have something for you. Is it okay if I give it to you now?"

Phoebe's eyes sparkled at the faint innuendo. "You know how I hate waiting."

Rowe unfastened the heavy canvas that covered her handcart and reached inside. Pulling a squirming little body from the warm cocoon she'd built with blankets and a heating pad, she said, "Merry Christmas."

"Oh, my God!" Phoebe lifted the puppy to her face, beaming. "A pug. I love pugs! She's to die for!"

"How clever of you," Cara directed a semi-sweet remark at Rowe. "Now that she has a puppy, she'll have to stay home to look after it. Won't that be perfect for the two of you?"

Phoebe didn't seem to notice her sister's barb. "Molly...that's what I'll call her." She bestowed a lingering kiss on Rowe. "Thank you, sweetheart. I don't know what to say. She's the best present I've ever had. I mean apart from meeting you."

Rowe knew she had cringed even as she registered Cara's pained expression. It hadn't been her intention to eclipse any gift Phoebe's twin would give. Haplessly, she started to say something self-effacing, but Cara cut her off.

"Listen, why don't I leave you two lovebirds alone for a while, so you can do the personal gift thing without me cramping your style." A brilliant smile. "I need to check on the deer, anyway."

"No. Wait." Phoebe caught at her sister's arm. "I didn't mean it that way."

"Sweetie, you're in love," Cara said in a patient tone. "You were completely tactless all the other times, too." Brushing Phoebe's hand away, she stalked off.

Phoebe promptly burst into tears and wailed, "Why am I so thoughtless?"

"Hush." Rowe wrapped her lover in her arms. "You're not thoughtless, at all. I don't know what your sister's problem is, but don't take it to heart. You're not doing anything wrong."

Cradling her new puppy, Phoebe sobbed against Rowe's chest. "I should have told you," she choked out between hiccups.

"Told me what?"

"About Bev. About everything."

"Who's Bev?"

Phoebe drew back, tears streaming down her face. Thrusting

Molly into Rowe's arms, she blurted, "I was supposed to marry her," and ran from the room.

Dazed, Rowe stared after her, then with slow deliberation, she set her eggnog down, put Molly back in her snug bed in the cart, and headed upstairs. In any soap opera, there was usually an important truth at the bottom of every bizarre plot convolution. The same was true of life's sticky dramas. Refusing to be drawn into the *sturm und drang*, she knocked on Phoebe's door and said, "Baby, let's talk about this."

The door opened and her lover stood in the gap, mouth trembling. "I wanted to tell you, but I thought it would ruin everything."

"Would it help if I said I love you and nothing you say can change that?"

A wobbly smile. "I love you, too. Very much."

"I have an idea," Rowe wiped Phoebe's tears away with both thumbs. "Let's have a nice day. And tonight, after we've made love, you can tell me why you didn't marry Bev. I take it she's history."

Phoebe clasped her hands behind Rowe's neck. "Yes, she's history."

Rowe cupped her chin and kissed her with teasing sensuality. "Another option is we could make love now. But I've never found the smell of burning turkey an aphrodisiac."

Phoebe gave a husky laugh. "Tonight then. Assuming we can move after the dinner I'm cooking."

Rowe guided her down the stairs, an arm around her slender waist.

"What about Cara?" Phoebe asked.

"Somehow I don't see your sister sulking in the feeding barn when she could be opening fabulous Christmas presents. Do you?"

CARA PICKED HAY off her parka and stared down at her Dolce & Gabbana pants. "Shit!" she cursed.

When would she ever learn? All her life she had done stupid things when she lost her temper, then regretted her haste, especially when the consequences involved ruining fine fashion garments.

Why was she allowing Phoebe's latest fling to get under her skin? Did she want Rowe for herself? She gave that a moment's thought. No, absolutely not. True, their neighbor was one of the more attractive women she'd met in her life. Rowe Devlin's knowing blue eyes and lazy smile would have nailed a second glance from Cara any time. The wretched woman positively oozed a controlled sensuality that promised she'd be a whole lot of fun between the sheets.

But Rowe was not the right kind of person for Cara. She was way too traditional for a start, one of those butch types who really just wanted the little woman and the picket fence. No wonder she had fallen for Phoebe with her Martha Stewart home-making skills, coupled with that eternal-virgin thing she had going for her. She had Rowe eating out of her hand, just like all the other schmucks.

Aggravated, Cara kicked a fodder bucket across the feeding barn. It was easy to be innocent and unworldly when you had a twin who dealt with the harsh realities of life so you didn't have to sully your lily white hands. Well, Cara had had enough of that shit. She and Phoebe were twenty-seven years old. That meant she'd been Phoebe's minder and interface with the world for twenty years. *Twenty years!* Enough was enough. She wanted a life of her own. Let Phoebe find out the hard way that the world was not her oyster just because she was sweet and sensitive and beautiful. In fact, the world chewed up women like her and spat them out. And let Rowe find out that Phoebe didn't just have issues, she had a subscription.

Resolved, Cara took her cell phone from her pants pocket and called the United reservations number. She had planned to stay on Islesboro for the next couple of weeks, but the thought of seeing Phoebe and Rowe fawn all over each other the whole time made her nauseous. She was going back to L.A. on the next flight. She would party, shoot some cutaway footage she needed for her next project and select her bedtime companions from the nightclub smorgasbord.

Phoebe and Rowe were welcome to their domestic bliss. She had some advice for them — make the most of it, while it lasts.

Chapter
Twelve

"ARE YOU SURE you want to do this?" Rowe asked, opening the ballroom.

"Of course." Phoebe wandered to the French doors and stared out across the white canvas of the meadow. The ghosthunters were right about this room, she thought, feeling the back of her neck twitch. It was occupied.

She wondered how she could communicate with whoever was here. If she slept in the cottage, would the ghost come to her the way Iris had? She took a few paces into the room. The floorboards creaked. Rowe stared at her with a mixture of trepidation and expectancy.

"I wish I could *make* it happen," Phoebe said, "but I can't."

"Would it help if I left the room? I could go upstairs and check my email."

"We could try that." Phoebe doubted it would make any difference, but she felt self-conscious being watched, so maybe it wasn't a bad idea.

After Rowe had gone, she moved into the center of the dance floor and tried to picture the ballroom in its heyday, softly lit, crowded with the elegant society people who spent their summers in Maine. She imagined women with their hair up and their corsets tight, low necklines revealing pale shoulders. She thought about Juliet, standing at the windows, anxiously awaiting a horse and rider who would never arrive. How humiliating. Had she killed herself over her dashed hopes?

Phoebe paced slowly around the room. She could sense something, a potent sorrow. But that was all. There were no voices, no sudden flashes of awareness. Dismayed, she wandered out into the vestibule, wishing she had more useful information for Rowe. Her lover was barely living in the cottage now, returning only for clothes and dog supplies. Phoebe knew this choice was as much about the ghost as it was about their relationship. For Rowe's sake, she wanted to find a solution.

Chilled, she took refuge in the front parlor where Rowe had built a fire. The room was a little more formal than its counterpart at the Temple's. Floor-length burgundy velvet drapes dressed the windows. These suited the Victorian furniture and ornate plasterwork. The walls were a dark rose shade, with broad mahogany skirting boards and chair rails. Rowe had hung the painting Phoebe gave her above the roll top desk. It was perfect there, just as she had known it would be.

Pleased, she sank down into an armchair near the fire and contemplated the antique artwork. She had the oddest sense that it had hung in that spot before. It was not especially accomplished. The dealer had suggested it was probably painted by a guest. In those days ladies took art lessons and amused themselves by painting amateurish landscapes. It was a change of pace from embroidery and reading.

Dark Harbor Cottage still looked much the same. But instead of sticking with the cheerful summer setting most amateur artists preferred, this painter had rendered a moodier image. The cottage loomed bleak beneath a sullen sky, its windows dark and barren. In the background, the sea was the color of pounded gunmetal. Trees were losing their leaves, and the meadow was no longer lush and green. Somehow the picture embodied the brooding calm before a gale.

Phoebe supposed that was what had struck her when she first saw it—a sense that the painter was waiting for the inevitable and had snatched a few hours to record the gathering of forces that would soon transform her world. For the artist was a woman. Phoebe was certain of that. She stared into the painting and could picture a pale hand holding a brush, a ring on the index finger. Bloodstone and gold. Short nails, neatly filed. The canvas was only half-finished.

A voice. Someone approaching from the cottage. Young. Anxious. A maid in a dark uniform. "Miss Juliet. You must come in now."

A suffocating inability to draw a full breath. "I cannot."

"Mrs. Baker insists. She wants you to read to her."

A sharp, jarring sensation from within her belly. Sick despair. "Oh, God, Becky. What am I to do?"

"Don't cry, Miss." A rough, warm hand encloses hers. A tiny slip of paper is pressed into her palm. Bright blue eyes stare from a pinched childlike face. "We'll take care of this, I promise."

"How?" The paintbrush falls.

Becky picks it up and sets it on the easel. "Don't you worry about that. You must rest and keep up your strength."

"When is my father due back? Is it tomorrow?" Fear clamps

her throat. She places a hand to her belly. The life within responds with another kick.

"Tomorrow evening, Miss."

"He'll know."

"He will not. You're not hardly showing and men are slow to these matters, my Mom says. When you become big, you will take to your bed with a fever. A gentleman does not care to be in the company of sickness."

"Yes. I will become an invalid." She stands. They walk toward the cottage, arm in arm. "And when it is time?"

"You will come to the Carriage House."

"I fear this most terribly, Becky."

"I'll take care of you."

Inside the house, the young maid squeezes her hand and leaves her standing at the bottom of the stairs, exhausted at the very thought of climbing them. She slips into the ballroom and moves along the interior wall, trailing her fingers over the wood paneling until she reaches the count of five. Fearful, she opens the note clenched in her fist.

> *Dear Miss Baker,*
> *My housekeeper has apprised me of your unfortunate predicament. I am willing to assist you. Perhaps you might find a reason to call upon me in the near future that we may discuss several possibilities.*
> *Yours truly,*
> *Verity (Mrs. Henry) Adams*

Hurriedly, she folds the note and jiggles a wood panel until it comes free. She hides the note in the recess and eases the panel back into place. A heady relief makes her head spin and she props herself against the wall, fighting her corset for air. Finally she sinks to the floor, panting, nauseous.

"PHOEBE? ARE YOU okay?" Rowe halted a few yards from her lover, the prospect of another black eye keeping her at a wary distance.

Phoebe stared down at the floorboards. In the waning light, her blood red velvet dress looked even darker against the pale translucence of her skin. "I'm fine." Her voice sounded thin and discordant, but she seemed to know who Rowe was.

Immediately she sprang forward and helped Phoebe to her feet, cradling her close. "Are you going to faint, baby?"

"I think I already did." Phoebe's breathing was shallow and

her skin felt clammy.

"Come on. Let's get out of here." Rowe steered her toward the door, wishing she hadn't asked her to do this. The attempt had obviously distressed her.

"No. Wait." Phoebe stepped back. Fretfully, she moved along the wall, fingering the wood paneling as if searching for something. "That picture I gave you," she said in a distracted tone. "Juliet painted it. She was pregnant."

"Juliet was pregnant?" Rowe was stunned. The thought had never crossed her mind.

"Yes. And keeping it from her family. A maid called Becky was helping her."

"Becky O'Halloran," Rowe murmured, shocked.

Until this instant, she had harbored doubts about Phoebe's "gift." She had rationalized her way to a theory she could live with—that Phoebe was highly sensitive and picked up tiny pieces of information others missed. That she somehow assembled these in her sleep, resulting in unusually lucid and prescient dreams.

But there was simply no way Phoebe could have known about Becky. Rowe had never mentioned the name. She was about to ask another question, when Phoebe gave a small triumphant cry and dislodged one of the wood panels.

"This was where she hid things. Look."

It was hard to see anything in the dark crack. Rowe knelt and slid her hand into the gap, retrieving various objects and placing them on the floor. A wooden cigar box, several knitted baby garments chewed into holes by insects, a gold locket, a small heavy purse and a diary.

"Oh, my God." She grabbed Phoebe and kissed her. "I can't believe this."

Her mind worked overtime. If Juliet had been pregnant that would explain so much. Her despair at being jilted, for a start. Maybe she had walked out into the snow after all. Was she still pregnant when she committed suicide? Rowe knew the answer to that question almost as soon as it crossed her mind. Of course not. The baby had to be Anne Adams, Phoebe's great grandmother.

Juliet had given birth and had somehow managed to get her infant daughter to Verity Adams. Becky must have taken the baby there as soon as it was born. Juliet could not have had the strength. An image flashed into Rowe's mind: Juliet fastening her precious pearl around the neck of her newborn daughter, the one gift she could give, other than life. It made complete sense. And Becky's mom had known the whole story. To preserve reputations, she had taken it to the grave with her.

Rowe wondered what had become of Becky. Had she fled for fear of being found out by Mr. Baker?

"Juliet was so afraid," Phoebe said, fingering the baby garments, her eyes liquid with sorrow. "I wonder what happened to her."

"You don't know?" Somehow Rowe had imagined that if Phoebe saw anything at all, she would automatically know the whole story.

"All I saw was a conversation. Then she came in here and hid a note."

Rowe opened the cigar box. It was crammed with yellowing letters. She and Phoebe went through them, opening each one.

"Here it is." Phoebe handed her a shred of paper.

Rowe scanned the contents that confirmed her guesswork. Verity Adams had known about Juliet's condition and had played a role in covering up the birth. She had adopted the child as her own.

Fascinated, she picked up Juliet's diary and leafed through to the final pages.

> *My time must surely come soon. I am big with child. This confinement is a blessing to the extent that I need no longer appear in morning attire, bursting my corsets.*
>
> *I cannot be sure if my father suspects something is amiss. I have taken to my bed feigning feminine indisposition of a delicate nature. Becky cares for me. Praise God, the snow is too heavy for the doctor to attend upon me...*

The diary entries ceased three weeks before her death. Rowe imagined a desperate young women creeping downstairs in the night to conceal her secrets in the recess behind the wood paneling. Was that why her ghost lingered in this room?

"Did you speak to her?" she asked Phoebe.

"No. That only seems to happen when I'm dreaming. If I connect this way, it's like a vision. I see things through their eyes and feel what they feel."

"That's incredible." If there was a rational explanation for this phenomenon, Rowe couldn't think of one. In fact she was all out of bright ideas to explain anything that went on in Dark Harbor Cottage.

With a sigh, Phoebe placed the letters she'd been reading back in the cigar box. "It's strange. She's my ancestor and all of a sudden, I feel like I know her."

"Well, you sure look like her," Rowe opened the gold locket

and handed it to Phoebe. "I guess that's her Mom."

Phoebe stared down at the tiny sepia portrait. "She looks like one of those silent movie actresses... kind of a Louise Brooks."

"Quite a gene pool." Rowe said.

"What do you think really happened to Juliet?"

"Maybe she had post-partum depression."

It could be that simple, Rowe thought. Maybe Juliet had been stricken with despair after giving away her baby, and had walked out into the snow intent on death. Another possibility presented itself. Perhaps Juliet had set off for her kind neighbor's home bent on seeing her baby, believing she was strong enough to make the distance. She could have fallen, or simply passed out. Perhaps the terrible accident had occurred exactly as the newspapers reported it.

"I hope she comes to me in my dreams," Phoebe said. "There's so much I want to ask her."

"No kidding." Rowe collected Juliet's hidden legacy into a small heap and mused, "Perhaps we've solved this. Perhaps she just wanted you to know who she is. I mean you are her great-great-granddaughter."

Phoebe gave her a hopeful smile. "You think she might be able to move on now?"

"Who knows. I'd love to be able to tell the paranormal crowd that I laid a ghost to rest all by myself. Talk about street cred."

THIS WAS A bad idea, Rowe thought as she watched the second hand tick the night away. It was two a.m. and Phoebe lay sound asleep next to her. She had insisted on staying over at Rowe's cottage, convinced that Juliet would visit her dreams.

In the shadow world of night, her face glowed pale and serene against the pitch black nimbus of her hair. Rowe studied the narrow, delicate features, the dark eyelashes fanned on her cheeks, the fullness of her mouth. Sometimes, in her sleep, Phoebe rolled onto her side, dropping an arm across Rowe's torso and pressing her face into Rowe's shoulder. She never seemed comfortable in that position for long, and invariably abandoned it as if Rowe's body were bumpy furniture taking up space in the bed.

Rowe supposed neither of them was used to sleeping with another person yet. She had no idea what she did in her own sleep. She probably snored and ground her teeth, and Phoebe was too kind to tell her. Taking care not to make the bed bounce, she stretched out, facing away from Phoebe to stare around the moonlit room.

Zoe and Jessie were sprawled on their dog beds, and Molly lay comatose on her back inside her crate, her fat puppy paws flopped over her round belly. Rowe smiled at the sight, happy that Phoebe had fallen in love with the little pug. Rowe had been lucky to find her. There were no puppies at the local pound or the rescue society. It was the wrong time of year. Calling around breeders, she'd chanced on one who had just had a puppy returned after its new owners were posted overseas. Mentioning her name had helped. The guy knew her books and was thrilled to sell one of his dogs to a so-called famous author.

The thought filled Rowe with gloom, and she twisted the heavy signet ring she now wore on her right pinky finger, Phoebe's gift. Her contract discussions were on the brink of collapse and ugly litigation. She had a very simple choice — hand over her pitiful novel or give back half a million bucks. Her publisher was not willing to wait another year for her to write something decent. They wanted a new book now. Period.

"Throw them something," Parker had pleaded on the phone last time they spoke. "Opening chapters and a synopsis. Show them you're getting back on form."

As if. Rowe had fobbed him off with some bullshit about a new idea she was developing. The last thing she needed right now was for her agent to dump her. But she was beginning to doubt she would ever write anything good again.

Lack of sleep was a big help, she chided herself, trying to clear her mind enough to drift off. She felt uneasy, as if something had stirred in the house and was on the prowl. Locking the bedroom door wasn't going to keep the restless presence out, but she'd done so anyway.

Rowe decided she would call Dwayne and Earl the next morning. She was convinced she and Phoebe had uncovered the reason Juliet haunted the ballroom. She must have wanted someone to know the truth about the baby. But what was the presence in the kitchen? Had they unwittingly disturbed it? Was it now patrolling the entire house seeking out sharp objects to hurl?

She closed her eyes and sent a message to whatever was lurking in the ether. *Don't mess with me and I won't mess with you.*

Chapter
Thirteen

ROWE STARED OUT the window of Phoebe's kitchen. "It's landing in the meadow," she said in a tone of disbelief.

Phoebe felt queasy watching a dark helicopter inch through the blizzard beyond the woods. "Maybe they're putting down to get out of the bad weather."

"I think it's a Black Hawk." Rowe crossed to the back door and lifted her barn coat from its hook. "I'm going to go see. They might need help."

"No, don't. It's probably my boss."

Rowe gave her an odd look. "Do they normally send a chopper for you?"

"No, I fly to DC, and they meet me at Dulles airport." Phoebe couldn't believe it. She'd only been home for a few weeks and Vernell hadn't called to let her know about a new case. Something urgent must have come up.

"I guess they couldn't get over here the usual way." Rowe vacillated in the hall. "The ferry's not sailing."

Lying in their usual spot on the rug in front of the wood stove, Molly curled between them, both Jessie and Zoe lifted their heads suddenly and sprang up, hair raised. Alpha to the bone, Jessie ran to the back door, growling and slavering like she had rabies.

Rowe gripped the yellow Lab's collar and tried fruitlessly to calm her down. "This is weird." She craned over her shoulder at Phoebe. "There are guys in the trees."

Phoebe pictured the squads of trainees she saw running around in body armor every day while she was at Quantico. Vernell had probably brought a bunch of them along for a training exercise. With a sense of dread, she moved to Rowe's side. It was hard to make out anything through the steadily falling snow, but she could see shadowy figures converging on the garden. Two men in long overcoats struggled along the pathway Rowe had dug out the day before. It had to be something big to drag Vernell out here when he was supposed to be on vacation, she decided. He didn't look happy about it, either.

An authoritative knock shook the door, and as soon as Rowe had dragged Jessie into the den, Phoebe turned the handle. Vernell and a man she didn't know stood on the back porch. The stranger signaled to some men further back and several advanced toward the house, while others took up positions around the perimeter of the garden. They were not wearing the usual dark blue Quantico clothing, but were in cold weather gear and goggles.

Flinching at the icy wind, Phoebe said, "Quick. Come in," and the two men stepped into the kitchen.

"You can close the door," Vernell said when Phoebe hesitated.

"What about the others?" she asked, concerned to think of anyone standing around outdoors in below freezing weather.

"They're on duty."

"Poor guys. What a day for an exercise."

Vernell made a non-committal sound. He seemed uneasy. "Phoebe, this is Agent Marvin Perry."

"Please to make your acquaintance, Ms. Temple." The agent showed no signs of shaking hands. Instead his cold blue eyes were on Rowe, who was struggling to hang on to the dogs.

"This is my friend, Rowe Devlin." Phoebe tried to say the word "friend" without inflection. She thought she caught a look of surprise on Vernell's face, but nothing shifted in Marvin Perry's expression.

"I'll take the dogs to the front parlor," Rowe said. "Looks like you'll be tied up for a while, so I'll catch up on some reading."

Phoebe thanked her self-consciously, certain the two men had interpreted "friend" and now knew she was a lesbian. She steered them toward the den. "Please have a seat. Would you like some coffee?"

"Good idea." Marvin Perry removed his coat. He was not as tall as Vernell but more solidly built and was casually dressed in black pants and turtleneck. His pants were tucked into snow boots, and he wore a gun in a shoulder holster.

Noting that Vernell had waited for the other agent's cue before removing his own coat and gloves, Phoebe deduced Marvin Perry must be higher ranked. She carried their heavy garments to the laundry and shook them free of snow, starting when a figure passed the window. Wiping the glass free of condensation, she peered out, astounded to see men with guns clearing a path through her garden into the woods. She could hear raised voices from the den but could not make out what was being said.

Both agents fell silent as she returned, but the tension between them hung in the air. Phoebe set cream, sugar and mugs on the coffee table and lifted the coffee pot from the stove.

Before she had a chance to ask his preference, Perry said, "Black, thanks."

He looked like a man who needed to be somewhere else, Phoebe observed. The toes of his boots moved up and down in tiny increments, driven by restless feet. A couple of his fingers tapped a silent Morse code on his thigh. The rest of his body was oddly still, his face impassive. He was handsome in a bland, clean-shaven kind of way, his hair nondescript light brown and cut short. It looked more fashionable than the atypical FBI cut, like it was styled as opposed to barbered.

Wishing Rowe had stayed, Phoebe passed the coffees around and sat down in an armchair. "Well, I can see this isn't a social call," she said in an attempt to lighten the tension.

"I'm afraid not." Vernell stared into his mug. "We need to talk."

Phoebe stifled a sigh. She had been fantasizing about spending the rest of the week with Rowe, continuing their delicious explorations of the past days. Since their night at Dark Harbor Cottage, Rowe had stayed here. Phoebe had never been so happy in her life.

"What did the Assistant Director say about my suggestion?" she asked Vernell.

"Your situation is under review," he said vaguely. "As of today, you've been seconded onto a multi-agency project."

"What does that mean?"

Marvin Perry's eyes locked on her, not so much on her as through her. This surprised Phoebe. Most men stared at her the way zoo animals regarded their keepers at feeding time. "Good coffee," he said.

Phoebe thanked him and yet again yearned for Rowe. It was amazing, she thought, that after such a short time she felt incomplete without her.

Pronouncing the words as if they tasted sour, Vernell said, "Phoebe you need to come with us. You'll be briefed fully later. Right now, we're under some time pressure."

"We can't keep the chopper on the ground too long," Perry elucidated in a silky tone.

"Of course." Phoebe felt bad thinking about the men on the exercise. "Your guys must be freezing out there. They can come inside. Truly, I don't mind."

At this something registered on Perry's face. He seemed amused, although it was impossible to tell. Perhaps he was attempting to channel a human emotion. It probably didn't come easy to him.

Vernell placed his empty mug on the table. "They're fine, Phoebe, but thanks. Do you think you could be ready in fifteen minutes? You'll need to pack clothing for a few days."

"I don't have a choice, right?"

Vernell conceded this with the mild grimace Phoebe recognized from other occasions when there were rules he couldn't bend for her. She stood up, an action quickly echoed by both agents. Not for the first time, it amazed her that men like these, schooled in such old fashioned courtesies, were equally at home blowing someone's head off if the situation called for it.

Before she left, she asked Vernell, "How is June doing?"

"As well as can be expected." His tone softened to the gentle one he used for her. "You saved her life, Phoebe."

"It was a team effort." She touched his arm as she left the room.

In the hall, she stopped for a few seconds and willed herself to calm down. The last thing she wanted to do today was fly off in a helicopter with a bunch of guys carrying guns, then end up eating chocolates in Dr. K.'s chair. She slipped into the parlor, closing the door before the dogs could escape.

"Baby, what's happening?" Rowe asked, setting Molly on the floor.

Phoebe took refuge in her arms. "I have to go."

"Now? Just like that?"

"It sounds important."

"No kidding." Rowe looked disappointed but also proud.

"I'm really sorry," Phoebe mumbled into her chest.

"Don't apologize. It's your job." Rowe dropped a kiss on her cheek. "When will you be back?"

"They said a few days. I have no idea what this is about."

"It's okay. I don't need to know." Rowe kissed her again and said. "Come on. Let's go upstairs and get you packed. I keep thinking any minute a SWAT team is going to break down the door. The place is crawling with guys carrying M-4s."

Phoebe tried not to sound as cranky as she felt. "I guess they had nothing better to do today than play soldiers."

Shutting the dogs in the parlor, they went up to Phoebe's bedroom and fell into each other's arms once more.

"I hate this," Phoebe said. "I just want to stay here with you. I don't care about homeland security."

Rowe brushed her lips across Phoebe's. "How long did you

say we have?"

"Not long enough," Phoebe slid her hand beneath Rowe's sweater, craving warm skin. A knee nudged her thighs apart. The slight pressure against her sex made Phoebe ache. She could almost feel Rowe's fingers parting her.

Something altered in Rowe's face. Eyes glittering wickedly, she said, "We could make them wait. It's only the US government."

Phoebe shivered at the naked desire in her lover's face. "You're so bad."

Rowe reached past her and bolted the door. "You love it."

"I have to pack." Phoebe's protest sounded feeble, even to her.

"No. You have to get me off." Rowe wasn't kidding. She backed Phoebe toward the bed.

"They'll know," Phoebe gasped as she was lifted onto the covers.

"How? Because I'll send you down there looking well fucked?"

Phoebe blushed at the thought. Rowe was already undressing her, warm moist lips following the path bared by her hands. Phoebe squirmed as one nipple then the next was sucked and twisted until it became a tense little stone. Moisture welled, making wet little kisses where her thighs connected. She could hear her own breathing, shallow and fast. She swung her legs over the side of the bed and tried to sit up, but Rowe pushed her firmly down and bent over her.

In her ear, she said, "You know you want this." She took one of Phoebe's hands and drew it down. "Show me how much."

Shivering, Phoebe slid her fingers slowly along the swollen arch of her clit. She could hardly bear her own delicate touch. Knowing she was being watched only intensified her yearning. In a fog of desire, she squeezed her eyes tight shut, blocking out everything but the knowledge of Rowe's presence and the longing this evoked. She registered the hushed tick of her clock, the familiar creaks and whispers of the house, the sound of Rowe undressing. A drawer opening. The muted metallic tease of leather and buckle she had come to recognize over the past few days.

Rowe's hand joined hers, the fingers brushing by to dip into her hot, liquid core. With tantalizing slowness, she teased her apart, stretching her, fingertips gliding and circling a mere tongue's-reach within.

Needing more, Phoebe lifted her hips and begged, "Please."

"Shhh. You don't want those men hearing us, do you?" Rowe

caught her wrist and compelled an end to her self-service, supplanting the familiar strokes with a very different sensation.

Phoebe tensed a little as the smooth, solid head of a cock slid over her clit and between her slippery folds. This time Rowe did not enter by careful degrees. She took Phoebe's hips in her hands, hauled her closer to the edge of the bed, and filled her completely. Before Phoebe's body had a chance to adjust, she withdrew nearly all the way, forcing a cry of protest. Opening her eyes, Phoebe blinked up at her lover then grabbed Rowe's arms, using them to lever herself closer, unable to bear the emptiness.

Rowe laughed softly, "Oh, you want all of me?" She hooked her hands beneath Phoebe's knees, raising her slightly before entering her again, hard and fast.

Phoebe could hardly breathe. The world around her disintegrated into a morass of shapes and colors, and she was aware of nothing but the place where their bodies joined, the bursting, aching pressure within. She could feel Rowe in her belly, so deep inside she could only surrender to the reckless, inescapable ritual of their mating. Blood rushed in her ears. She tightened her legs around Rowe and clenched handfuls of bedcover, unable to control the gasps and whimpers that rose from the back of her throat.

Tension gathered in her limbs and she compressed her thighs harder on either side of Rowe, meeting every thrust with one of her own. She was vaguely aware of Rowe's harsh breathing, her groans, her fierce concentration. Bearing down, anchoring herself, Phoebe couldn't speak or think, her own abandoned cries lost in those of her lover. Sweat broke across her body and a hot, quivering pulse radiated from her clit to her womb as the first waves of orgasm carried her away.

A short while later, in a tangle of flesh and bedding, they stole sated kisses between panting gulps of air. Rowe's breath cooled the damp on Phoebe's cheeks. Her straight, sensual mouth was slightly parted. Phoebe traced its strong line with her index finger then trawled a caressing path down the smooth, definite chin and tanned throat to her breasts. These were very different in shape from her own, firm and fleshy, taut against Rowe's chest. The nipples were small and brown.

Phoebe wished they could spend all day in bed, so she could slowly savor her lover's responsive body. She loved the way Rowe gave herself over to pleasure, gently guiding her so Phoebe never had any doubts about herself. Rowe had no problem expressing her needs and desires, and indulged Phoebe's explorations and curiosity without reservation. Phoebe had never experienced that with any other lover. Rowe made her feel confident in herself as a partner in passion, not simply an object of desire.

With a sigh, she sank back into her pillows, overwhelmed with despair that they would have to be apart for the next few days.

"Baby?" Rowe turned to her. "I didn't hurt you, did I?" A few blonde spikes fell forward, wetly clinging to her brow.

Phoebe pushed them back. "I'll let you know once I've tried walking."

"Oh, God."

Laughing, Phoebe took Rowe's hand and kissed the palm. She felt exquisitely, blissfully happy despite the helicopter waiting in the meadow. "I'm yours," she said. "And I like the way you show me that."

Rowe regarded her gravely. "I'm yours, too, Phoebe."

For a long moment they were silent, then Phoebe said, "We're madly in love, aren't we?"

"Yes." Rowe's voice was husky with emotion. "Madly."

THE WALK TO the chopper was one of the more bizarre experiences of Phoebe's life. Weak with post-orgasmic lethargy, she tried to match the strides of her companions only to find her legs wobbled so much, she almost fell as she crossed the yard. Firing a concerned look at her, Vernell took her arm and adjusted the length of his stride to hers.

A squad of heavily armed men closed into tight formation around them, and they set off along a track carved hastily in the snow. Phoebe could see nothing past the solid shapes that hemmed her in. The men all seemed huge. They were tall to begin with, and in their cold weather clothing, they shuffled along like a herd of linebackers.

As they approached the helicopter, Vernell yelled "Duck!" above the noise of the rotors.

He boarded ahead of her and extended a hand to help her up through the wide door. Perry followed immediately behind.

Vernell handed her a set of earphones, and after thankfully covering her ears, she followed his example, belting herself tightly into the hard troop seat as they waited for the men with machine guns to cram on board. The rotors made a deafening chopping sound until they took off, then the noise abated and they sailed smoothly through the sky as if drifting on the wind.

"Where are we going?" she asked, lifting one earpiece so she could hear his reply.

"We're switching to a plane at Hanscom. That's an air force base."

"What kind of helicopter is this?" One of the trainees eyed her and Phoebe felt silly for asking.

"It's a Black Hawk," Vernell replied.

"Like the one in the film?"

"Yes."

Vernell didn't seem himself today, Phoebe decided. He was probably freezing, and it appeared that this Marvin Perry guy aggravated him. The cramped interior of the Black Hawk was ice cold. Even with heavy clothing on, she could barely feel her feet and hands. She would be glad when they swapped to a real plane.

"Actually the one in the movie was an earlier model," Perry informed her in a patronizing tone. "This is a UH-60M. The refit model. Digital cockpit, increased range and lift capability, et cetera."

"I see." Phoebe tried to sound interested. "I always thought they were black. But they're really a very dark khaki, aren't they?"

This time a couple of the men smirked. They lowered their heads quickly. Apparently they weren't supposed to be looking at her.

"Sometimes for night operations we paint them black," Perry said without expression.

Phoebe gazed out the open door at the winter landscape below and marveled, "You can see so much."

"The Black Hawks have always had superior nap-of-the-earth flight capability." Evidently, Marvin Perry was the kind of guy who couldn't resist flaunting his knowledge. "And they've worked on vulnerability reduction with the refit."

"Does that mean it's harder for these to get shot down now?" Phoebe asked.

"Simplistically speaking, yes." He warmed to his theme. "Mission safety is contingent on so many factors, but the digital avionics improve situational awareness. Coupled with survivability and deployability enhancements, a commander finds he has more options in battlespace."

Phoebe fell short of an intelligent response. "I suppose that's pretty important, since we're invading countries these days."

"For some of us, there have always been wars." A harsh note entered Perry's voice and he shot a sideways glance at Vernell, as if directing the comment to him. "We have to get an edge any way we can. It's win or die."

Chapter
Fourteen

A SHAPELY AUBURN-HAIRED woman in a cream business shirt and navy slacks sat down in the armchair nearest Phoebe's. The lights dimmed, and the screen at the front of the room lit up with the images ingrained into memory on September 11. The first plane plowing into the World Trade Center, then the second. People surging through a haze of dust and debris, screaming and sobbing. The faces of emergency workers, heavy with defeat and exhaustion.

The woman pressed a remote control, freezing the image, and the lights came back on. Turning discreetly made-up hazel eyes on Phoebe, she said, "This is what we're up against." She stuck out her hand. "I'm Eve Kent. I lost my brother that day."

"Oh." Phoebe shook hands with her. Already, she felt morally obliged, no doubt the response they were aiming for. "I'm very sorry."

"Thank you." Eve pushed her wavy auburn hair behind her ears in a gesture of eloquent weariness. "I dedicate every working day to him. That's why I'm talking to you."

"You want me to try and contact your brother?"

For a split-second hope registered in Eve's face before a cooler emotion prevailed. "No. Nothing like that. But it's thoughtful of you to offer." She placed a hand over Phoebe's and stared earnestly into her eyes. Everything about her manner said, *Trust me.* "You're here because we believe you may be able to prevent another 9/11."

"I wish that was true." Phoebe wondered how she was supposed to convince these people that her gift didn't come with multiple choice options. Obviously they thought she was holding out and were trying to soften their approach by sending in a woman with a sad story. Phoebe wasn't stupid. She knew when she was being manipulated. "It's like I told Mr. Perry and those other men—I can't choose what I dream."

"But what if you could do something?" Eve coaxed softly.

"You would want to, wouldn't you?"

Phoebe felt trapped. How could any decent person say no to a question like that? Carefully, she said, "If I ever dream about terrorists, I'll let you folks know right away."

Eve nodded. Phoebe could almost hear her mind working. "I'm curious," she said. "Do you and your sister notice any kind of telepathy? I know many twins do."

Wondering where this was headed, Phoebe replied, "In some ways we do. We can sense things about one another. When I had my accident, Cara knew. She tried calling my cell phone about twenty seconds after it happened."

"I had the same experience with my brother," Eve lowered her voice to a near whisper. "We were fraternal twins. When he died, I just knew. People think you convince yourself of that afterwards, and sometimes I wonder. But I felt like something had crushed my body. I couldn't breathe. It was like dying." Tears drowned her eyes, and she brushed them impatiently away, plainly uncomfortable to have revealed herself.

"Don't listen to other people," Phoebe said. "Part of you died with him. Of course you felt it."

Eve visibly relaxed. "Yes. That's exactly what it was...part of me dying. I hadn't thought of it that way, but you're right."

"You still feel him sometimes, don't you?"

Eve stared down at the beige carpet. Phoebe sensed she wanted to speak but couldn't. It dawned on her then that they were being monitored. This was the CIA. There were probably cameras in the bathrooms. What was Vernell thinking, bringing her here? She stole a cautious glance at her companion and reminded herself that no matter how genuine Eve seemed, she was one of *them*. And right now they were being nice to her because they wanted something. What would happen if she said no?

Phoebe had tried to convince them they were barking up the wrong tree. This was not television. She was not superhuman. Even if she wanted to, she couldn't explain exactly how her powers worked. She fully expected that one day she would wake up and find the gift gone.

"I can tell you something about your brother," she said, ignoring the fact that Eve had an agenda. She was a still a human being and her pain was real. "When you feel him, he's there. No question. If you speak to him, he'll hear you."

"Is it true? What they say about you?"

"That I'm crazy?"

"No." Eve smiled. "That you're the real deal."

"I'm afraid so."

"And you can talk to dead people just like you and I are talking?"

"Kind of. Although they don't always make sense."

"Dr. Karnovich mentioned a woman you were able to summon intentionally. Iris."

"Yes. She was one of Lester Cordwell's victims. She led me to his house."

"Have you had other experiences like that? Where you've been able to initiate a communication yourself?"

"No. Iris came because she's my friend. And I think saving June Feldstein brought her some peace."

Eve latched onto this like a limpet. "Imagine the peace you could offer victims of the attack. Think about the passengers on flight 93. They fought back." Tears welled in her eyes. "Phoebe, please. Give them the chance to do more...to have justice."

It sounded great in theory, but somehow Phoebe could not imagine how she was supposed to achieve this lofty goal. And even supposing she could conjure up a dead victim, what did the CIA think this person could do for them?

She looked squarely at Eve. "What exactly do you want from me?"

"We think there's another plot."

Could one say *Duh!* to the CIA? Phoebe said. "Well, I'm sure Osama Bin Laden isn't sitting around playing scrabble."

"There's some chatter that's raising flags. I can't go into any detail, but let's say we've had information from very credible sources. We're wondering if we can authenticate this information by using your er...contacts."

Phoebe almost laughed. "You want me to ask dead people to go find Osama and see what he's up to?"

Eve drew a sharp breath. "Could you do that?"

"If I could, I would. But it's not that simple. The thing is, the people I talk to seek me out, and they all have something at stake...there's a personal connection. For example, some of them lead me to their bodies, so that their loved ones can have closure. Even if I could contact some of the people who were on that flight, they may not feel any urge to help."

"If that's the case, we'll accept it," Eve said. "But are you willing to give it a try?"

Phoebe sighed. Did she have a choice?

"WHAT DO YOU mean they have Phoebe?" Cara cradled the phone against her shoulder as she dressed.

"Pack up and get out of there, now." Vernell's tone was

unequivocal.

"You're kidding me, right?"

"Just do it."

"Okay, already." Cara dragged her suitcase out and dumped it on the bed. "Are you going to tell me how the fuck you got my sister into this mess?"

"It was out of my hands, Cara. The Director decided we would be up to our neck in shit if the Company found out about Phoebe and we hadn't offered to share."

"Jesus."

"We're not having this conversation, either. And don't use your cell phone to call me. We can only use land lines."

"Are you telling me they're listening in?" Cara needed coffee. She couldn't get her head around what she was hearing. The CIA had Phoebe and weren't letting her go home. They were spying on Vernell, and Cara was about to get a knock on the door. What planet was this?

"Do not go home," Vernell said emphatically. "Draw out a couple of thousand bucks in cash from the ATM. Drive to the airport and hand in your rental car. Take a shuttle to Anaheim. I've made a reservation for you at the Econo Lodge at the Disneyland Maingate under the name Diane Harris. Pay cash for your room and deposit. I'll phone you there tonight."

Cara pulled on a turtleneck and jeans, blown away that Vernell had just laid out a plan for her to disappear. "I don't get it. Why do they want *me*?"

"So far, they're not buying that only one of you is psychic. They have you pegged as a back-up."

"Oh right. These are the same geniuses who said Saddam Hussein had a nuclear arsenal?"

"Actually, most of our friends in Langley weren't convinced of that. But the truth was inconvenient for the Pentagon at that time."

"And now your pals think my sister is going to make them look good by tracking down terrorists? Did you tell them that's ridiculous?"

"To be fair, we can't be certain that it is. We're only starting to find out what Phoebe is capable of."

Shoving clothing into the case, Cara said, "You know something. That's not really the point. If my sister doesn't want to do this, no one can force her to."

"On the contrary," Vernell said silkily. "The CIA can detain Phoebe indefinitely if they think she's not cooperating."

"What are you talking about?"

"The Patriot Act. If the Company decides to play hardball,

they could classify Phoebe as a material witness to an ongoing terrorism plot. They could lock her up in a military prison and throw away the key. That's why you need to be on the outside."

Fear cramped Cara's gut. This couldn't be happening. "My sister doesn't know the first thing about terrorists."

"Unfortunately, the Company can pretend to believe otherwise and that's all it takes."

"You can't be serious. This is America. The government can't just detain a citizen on some phony charge because it suits them!"

"That's not strictly true," Vernell said wearily. "Understand something, Cara. All we have to do is label someone as an enemy combatant and we can detain them indefinitely. It makes no difference whether the basis is true or false. They have no access to legal counsel and no right to a hearing."

Cara's head spun. She had heard about the sweeping powers of the Patriot Act but she had assumed the usual checks and balances must apply. "I thought Congress was planning to amend the Patriot Act so this kind of police-state stuff can't happen," she said.

"Actually, if Congress passes Patriot Two, we'll have even wider powers," Vernell replied. "For example, your sister could be stripped of her citizenship without recourse."

Struggling to take in the enormity of the situation, Cara carried the phone around the apartment as she gathered up the last of her possessions. "How do we get her out of this?" she asked shakily.

"I've told her to cooperate. And I've told them she can't perform under stress. So right now, she's getting kid glove treatment. That could change any time if they think she's withholding."

Cara slumped down on the bed and stared up at the ceiling. "You promised nothing like this was going to happen."

"Back then I didn't know what Phoebe could do. I thought we could keep her under wraps."

"If this goes bad, I'm taking it straight to the media."

"And the White House will kill the story," Vernell said in his calm, lucid way. "In the interests of national security."

"I see." Cara got back onto her feet and closed the suitcase. Her whole body shook with rage. "So what you're telling me is we now live in a fascist state but we just haven't woken up to the fact yet?"

"That's maybe a little strong."

"Oh, really? I'm checking into a cheap hotel under a fake name so I can't be hauled off by a government agency on some bogus pretext. But you're telling me my constitutional rights are still intact?"

Vernell didn't respond. "Diane Harris," he reminded her, and hung up.

Chapter
Fifteen

ROWE JERKED UPRIGHT and groped for the lamp next to her bed, certain she'd heard something break. The sound came from downstairs. As she hit the switch, the bulb blew. Cursing, she slid out from beneath the warm covers and groped her way to the light switch near the door. When nothing happened, she jiggled it up and down a few times and muttered some foul language. Perfect. Yet another home improvement to add to her expensive list — rewiring the house.

She stumbled to her dresser and opened the top drawer, feeling around for her flashlight. The dogs were awake now and Jessie instantly rushed to the door, whining softly.

"It's three in the morning," Rowe said. "You do not need to go out."

At the sound of her voice, Zoe's tail thumped against the floor and Molly woke up, emitting small excited yelps.

Resigning herself to the inevitable, Rowe slid her feet into fleece-lined boots, scooped the puppy from the crate, and opened the bedroom door. The two Labs preceded her down the stairs to the front entrance and she let them out. They never went far from the house during late night bathroom breaks, content to squat in the snow a few feet from the front steps before rushing back indoors.

Rowe put Molly down near them, so she would get the general idea. The little pug caught on immediately and almost buried herself in snow when she scampered back into the house after her role models. Getting colder by the second, Rowe locked the door and tried the downstairs lights. There was no power, and she would probably end up electrocuting herself if she started fiddling with the mains in pitch darkness. The repairs would have to wait until morning. With any luck she could convince Earl and Dwayne to do the job for her if they managed to get over to the island. She had never been much of a butch when it came to electrical problems or car repairs.

She panned her flashlight around the hall, looking for evidence of the breakage. It was probably a light fitting, she decided. She had replaced bulbs in all the chandeliers soon after moving in, but many of the glass shades were broken at the base. A gust of wind would knock them from their brackets. Already a couple had fallen from the decrepit fixture nearest the kitchen. She should have installed new fittings through the entire hall, instead of simply replacing the chandelier in the vestibule.

Rowe took a few paces past the stairs, the dogs at her heels. The dank smell of the kitchen had filtered through the crack beneath the door and drifted along the airless corridor. A soft repetitive thud transformed her irritation to a crawling unease. Unable to identify the sound, she trained her dark-adapted eyes on the kitchen door, and moved toward it. The floorboards were less likely to creak where they met the skirting boards, so Rowe slid her back along the paneled wall. She was creeping and knew this was idiotic. There was no one else in the house. And even if there was, whoever or whatever was hiding in her kitchen already knew she was downstairs.

Reminding herself that she had a couple of big, protective dogs with her, she took a few more steps then glanced back over her shoulder. Jessie and Zoe were pacing the vestibule, waiting for her to get with the program and return to bed. Only Molly seemed unperturbed, nestling hotly against Rowe's throat as they inched into the darkness. Listening intently, she stopped at the kitchen door, turned the handle with excruciating finesse, and peered into the room.

The thudding was coming from one of the cupboards near the sink. As Rowe held the beam on it, the door drifted open then banged shut. Rolling her eyes at her own paranoia, she marched into the kitchen and closed the noisy culprit, fiddling with the antiquated latch to secure it. She turned to leave, but an icy gust of wind cut through the room and the door to the hall slammed violently shut. Rowe jumped with fright and shone the flashlight manically about. One of the cupboard doors below the knife drawer swung back and forth as if an invisible child had hold of it.

"Okay. You win," she said with a show of bravado. "It's all yours. I'm outta here."

She had barely uttered the words when a dining chair crashed to the floor and everything in the room began to shake. She wanted to believe it was an earthquake, but in her gut she knew it was a force infinitely worse on some level. Nothing was as it should be. Crockery began to fall from cupboard shelves, smashing on the tiled counters and the floor. Inside their drawer, the kitchen knives rattled viciously.

Rowe ran for the door and groped for the handle. Something buzzed past her head and smashed into the wood. Shock spurred her into motion and she wrenched the door open and ran into the hall. An object flew after her and landed with a distinctive metallic twang. A long, lethal blade was caught in the beam as her flashlight traveled ahead. Hugging Molly close, she sprinted to the vestibule, yelling for the dogs to come. All she could think of was getting out. Behind her glass smashed and cupboards banged like gunshot fire.

"Have the fucking place," she yelled as she frantically unchained the front door and twisted the deadlock.

Howling, Jessie clawed at the heavy wood. She and Zoe burst out into the night and bolted across the moonwashed meadow. Rowe tried to run through the snow, but it was up to her knees. Grunting from sheer effort, she flailed and stumbled away from her home. Wetness invaded her boots and climbed the brushed cotton of her pyjamas. Her teeth chattered as the bitter cold penetrated her inadequate garments.

Somehow she made it to the birch trees, panting with exertion, sucking musty air through lips so numb she couldn't feel them. She could not afford to rest. A few more minutes and she would be at Phoebe's. Forcing herself to move, she took a short cut through the trees, figuring it would lead more directly to the back of the house. She'd only made it a few yards when she caught her foot in a root mass and she was thrown forward, her flashlight flying from her hand. Instinctively she enfolded the puppy against her chest with both arms and braced herself for the fall.

Instead of finding snow, her head struck a solid mass, and the last thing she knew was warm blood in her mouth and an explosion of light beneath her eyelids.

PHOEBE SAT UP and turned on the lamp next to her bed, blinking in the harsh light. She was supposed to be dreaming of Abu Mus'ab Al-Zarqawi, the terrorist whose photograph was optimistically positioned next to her bed. Instead, she had been lying wide awake, her mind harried. She wanted Rowe. All she could think about was her lover, and her yearnings had finally exploded into urgent agitation. She needed to go home. It had been a mistake to come here. She should have refused.

Distraught, she gazed at her sterile surroundings. The suite the Langley folks had accommodated her in was pretending to be a home away from home. A bunch of spring flowers graced a glass-topped coffee table. Several Van Gogh prints splashed brazen color against the pristine white walls. Books no one had ever opened stood neatly at attention on a white shelf near the bed, and someone had actually rustled up a frilly pink bedcover, gender coding her like a baby in a hospital nursery.

Phoebe stared up at the ceiling trying to see where the cameras were hidden. She knew she was being watched and wondered how long they planned to keep this up before they realized she couldn't summon ghosts at will, or see into the future. She had managed to keep a straight face when one of the interview team asked whether a crystal ball would help her. Someone else had hooked her up to a polygraph and proceeded to ask all kinds of stupid questions, especially about Cara.

With a despondent sigh, Phoebe tried her twin's cell phone again and got the voice mail. She didn't bother to leave yet another message. Maybe Cara had left the phone somewhere by accident. Maybe that's why she wasn't picking up. Phoebe hadn't been able to get hold of her since being spirited away by the CIA. She wasn't worried so much as puzzled. It was the first time her sister had ever let two days pass without communicating.

Cara was fine; she could sense that. But she could also sense something was not quite right. It was as if the invisible cord that joined them had been yanked sharply and the vibrations were still tingling at Phoebe's end. Cara had been in a mood when she left for L.A., and their conversations since then had been tense. Was she still upset about Rowe?

Phoebe called the Isola Bella again, and no one answered. Cara had probably gone out to a late night club, she rationalized. That was nothing unusual, although her twin usually sent a text-message if she wouldn't be picking up her phone for a while. Perhaps she had called Dark Harbor Cottage, expecting to find Phoebe there. Flustered, she dialed Rowe's number. So far she had not been able to get away from her minders long enough to make a private phone call, and she'd hesitated to phone Rowe from her room in case someone was listening in. It seemed like no one had guessed at their relationship, and she wanted to keep it that way.

After a few rings, the phone switched to voicemail. Deflated, Phoebe left a lame *we're-just-good-friends* message and dropped her cell phone back on the bedside table. She felt incredibly alone. Even Vernell was impossible to get hold of. Phoebe could tell he felt guilty about everything that had happened. It made him look bad, she supposed. He had promised to keep the CIA out of the picture, and now, here she was in the upscale version of a padded cell with a tracking device fitted to her wrist like she was a menace to society. While she was here at Langley, she wasn't any use to the FBI either. No doubt there were cases Vernell wanted her to work on, but he would have to sit back and wait for the CIA to figure out that she was never going to be a psychic spy for them.

She studied the self-satisfied face of Al-Zarqawi. If she could only tell them what this depraved individual was planning, she would be able to go home. Marvin Perry had taken her aside after dinner last night and told her she had nothing to worry about.

"Your security is our first priority," he'd said. "It's necessary to house you in a controlled environment while we conduct our preliminary interviews."

"So, I can go home after this?" Phoebe asked.

"If it is ascertained that you cannot provide useful information, you will be free to go."

"How long will that take?"

"We can't put a time frame on it. Of course, if you can assist us, you'll find the Agency very flexible about your location and lifestyle."

"I just want to go home." Phoebe added some emotional weight by mentioning her obligations. "I got a puppy for Christmas. Our neighbor's looking after her, but I can't expect her to do that indefinitely."

"If you wish, we can pick up your pet, and it can be here with you," Perry offered as if he sympathized. But meeting his light blue eyes was like looking into a pair of mirror lenses. Phoebe had no idea what was happening behind them.

"We'll see how it goes," she said. A paranoid fantasy played in her mind. Molly strapped to electrodes, Marvin Perry operating the voltage. *Talk or your puppy suffers.*

"By the way," her minder said, watching her face intently, "have you managed to get in touch with your sister?"

"Not yet." Phoebe faked unconcern.

"If you'd like us to make enquiries, just say the word."

"It's okay." Phoebe could only imagine Cara's reaction if a bunch of scary guys in dark glasses showed up at her apartment, demanding to know why she hadn't picked up her phone in two days.

Glucose seeped into Perry's tone. "I'm sure your sister's fine. But keep me posted."

Their conversation had ended when Eve entered the room, wanting to discuss some of the tests they had done that day. After Perry left, she told Phoebe, "He's a nicer guy when he thinks he's winning."

ROWE HAD NO idea how long she lay in the snow before she forced her eyes open. Slowly, she became aware of feeling strangely compressed. She could smell wet dog, and something warm countered the numbness of her face. As she stirred, so too did a body on either side of her, and she grasped the fact that she was sandwiched tightly between her two Labs. Blinking, she stared into Jessie's face and was greeted with licks and whines. Something moved against her chest and Phoebe's puppy stuck its head up, apparently none the worse for wear.

Galvanized into action, Jessie scrambled to her feet and seized a mouthful of Rowe's pajama jacket, dragging on it until Rowe managed to stand. Pain shot through her right foot the moment she rested her weight on it. She recognized the sensations instantly. That ankle had been sprained before.

Placing her free hand against the nearest tree to prop herself up, she tried to clear the fog in her head. The trunk was slippery with ice and felt even colder than her extremities. Her head pounded, and to make matters worse, she was so dizzy she wondered if she could walk. But Jessie wasn't taking no for an answer. Positioning herself at Rowe's side, the tall yellow Lab urged her into motion. Grasping a handful of scruff to steady herself, Rowe focused on taking one step at a time and somehow they made it through the maze of trees to the house. Foggily, she reached behind a small bird cote mounted to one side of the door and withdrew a spare house key. Thank God, she thought, then corrected that to Thank Dog.

They fell wetly into the hall, and setting Molly on her feet, Rowe immediately pulled off her boots and pajamas. The garments were stiff, the moisture in them having frozen. She wrapped herself in one of the coats hanging on the Temple's antique stand and caught a glimpse of her face in the mirror next to it. She was blue with cold. Blood glued her hair to her lacerated forehead, and red trickles progressed slowly around her eyes and down her nose.

Shivering uncontrollably, she dried off the dogs with a towel from the kitchen, then summoned them upstairs to Phoebe's bathroom. Traces of her lover's perfume lingered, comforting Rowe while at the same time reminding her that she was alone when she needed Phoebe's arms so badly she wanted to cry out her name. She turned on the faucets and the oil heaters around the walls and washed the blood from her face. Then she sank down on the floor, her head in her hands, and sobbed.

CARA POURED HERSELF a second glass of vodka and inspected the black spa tub that was tiled like an afterthought into one corner of her ugly king room. How thoughtful of Vernell to have secured the best accommodations in this downscale tourist inn. And, what luck...she could see the Disneyland fireworks from her balcony, not to mention revel constantly in the happy squeals of small children wearing mouse ears. Thanks a bunch, she thought.

She sprayed bleach all over the tub and collapsed into a pink mock-French Provincial chair while she waited for the germs to die. A tiny spider crossed the beige wall to a chocolate box landscape hanging above the bed. The painting's cobalt blue tones clashed with the dark gray-green carpeting and the busy floral bedspread. Sipping her vodka, Cara watched the spider's progress and wondered how in hell she was going to get herself and her twin out of this jam.

A wave of misery swamped her. Ever since Christmas, she and Phoebe had spoken like strangers, and it was all her fault. She was jealous, she realized. Jealous that Phoebe had found someone who really did seem to love her, who seemed to look past the lovely exterior to the person within and cherish her. The rapport between them was obvious, and very different from anything Cara had observed in her twin's previous relationships. Rowe was the first woman Cara could imagine Phoebe being with long-term, and for some reason the thought had shaken her to the core.

She should have been celebrating, she thought crossly. Didn't she want a life herself? Wouldn't it be wonderful if Phoebe was with a woman who truly understood her and who was willing to take over Cara's protective role? Rowe was the ideal candidate, the kind of woman who wanted a partner she could shield and adore. They were made for each other. What had Cara been thinking? Frustrated with herself, she finished her vodka and turned her thoughts to the business at hand.

Vernell had phoned a few hours earlier. The conversation had been brief. He had ordered her to stay put in this nightmare of cheesy family values for a couple of days.

"Blend in with the crowd," he suggested. "Go see Disneyland so no one notices anything unusual about you."

"Other than the lack of snot-nosed brats and no husband wearing a Pirates of the Caribbean T-shirt?"

"Go tomorrow. Ten a.m. The Enchanted Tiki Room. A man will ask if you're enjoying the show."

"And I'll say it sucks."

"You'll tell him you prefer the Jungle Cruise. He'll ask if you could show him the way. You'll leave together."

Cara felt like pointing out that if he wanted to keep her in the Magic Kingdom for more than five minutes, he would need to send a total goddess, not some newly minted Keanu Reeves look-alike. She jotted down a few notes and said, "So, this guy is going to tell me where to next. Is that the deal?"

"We'll move you to a safe location."

"Vernell, I have a job to do. I can't just vanish off the face of the earth. Tell them they'll never get anywhere with Phoebe if she's pining for home. They have to cut her loose."

"I did. They said they would make her bedroom more feminine."

"Christ."

"I'm sorry about your work."

"Hey, me, too. And I'm sorry I talked Phoebe into spending that week in Quantico."

"She saved a woman's life."

"And just think how many other victims she could help if you got her away from those morons."

"The Director feels she may be able to save thousands of lives if she could see what the terrorists are hatching. I think it's probably worth a try, don't you?"

"Remind me." Frustration made Cara's voice rise. "How much are we borrowing from the Chinese so we can run a war that puts billions of dollars straight into the pockets of companies like Halliburton, while we let Bin Laden get away? This is such bullshit."

"All I can tell you is that everyone working in the field wants Bin Laden and his network brought to justice."

Some of Cara's fury dissipated. "I believe that. And I know a lot of good people in your line of work have been shafted for telling truths no one wants to hear. Tell me honestly...am I just the suspicious type, or does it seem like maybe our leaders prefer to keep Bin Laden at large because it suits their political ends?"

"I can't speak to that." Vernell paused for a few beats. "I'm asking you to trust me, Cara. I won't hang you or your sister out to dry. Okay?"

"Okay. That's good enough for me," Cara was suddenly overcome with weariness. "Thanks for doing this."

"No problem. Get some sleep."

"You, too."

Cara had spent rest of the evening vacillating over whether to call Phoebe. She could go to a pay phone, she thought. But they could trace any inward call to Phoebe's cell. So maybe she would phone Rowe instead and ask her to pass on a message. Whatever she did, she would have to use land lines. They couldn't trace those calls without a wire tap. Maybe she could buy pre-paid cell phones and throw them in the trash after making a call, the way terrorists did.

In the end she hadn't called anyone. Instead, she'd found a liquor store and stocked up on Grey Goose, then sat in a Starbucks feeling sorry for herself. When she returned to the hotel a kid licking an ice cream cone had run right into her, smearing her Gaultier leather jacket with frozen yogurt. No apology of course. She said, *Fuck*, and his parents asked her to mind her language in front of little Johnny. She then congratulated them on doing such a fine job of teaching their kid to be an asshole, because there weren't enough in the world. The husband said he didn't like her attitude. Cara shut her mouth at that point, belatedly remembering she was supposed to be inconspicuous.

All in all, it was a red letter day.

Chapter
Sixteen

"I BROUGHT THIS upon her." Juliet knelt beside a fair-haired girl lying in the snow. "How can I ever forgive myself?"

Phoebe stared down at the inert body. The girl's hands were bound behind her back, and her feet were tied together.

Juliet bent low and asked, "Becky, can you hear me?"

A small-boned face turned toward them. "My mother calls me, but I cannot answer."

Juliet looked up at Phoebe. "Will you help us?"

Phoebe gazed around. They were not far from the cottage. She saw a man's silhouette in the parlor window. "Who is that?" she asked Juliet.

"My father. This is his work." She indicated Becky's bound hands. "He thought she stole my pearl."

"What can I do?" Phoebe asked, stricken.

"He wronged us," Juliet said.

"I can't change that."

"The truth must be told and the great wrong undone."

"It is too late for your father to face justice," Phoebe said gently. "The worms had the last word."

"And we lie lost to our own." Juliet stood and, without a backward glance, she drifted toward the cottage.

"Wait. What do you mean?" Phoebe struggled after her. "Juliet. Wait!"

A strange paralysis claimed her. The air felt like porridge. She could not swim through it. When she looked back, all she could see was an infinite tundra of white, a never-land unblemished by form or memory. Silence seduced her, descending like a curtain between self and emotion. Unmoored from her fears and sorrows and joys, she surrendered to the void, aware only of the muted metronome of her heartbeat and the certainty that she was utterly alone.

Phoebe had no idea how much time passed before a discordant sound punctured the tranquility of her sleep and she was once more present in her skin. She opened her eyes to find a squat man with an Einstein hair-do and a yellow bowtie standing at the end of her bed.

"Good morning, Phoebe," he said. "I trust you dreamt well."

Phoebe had never imagined she would be so thrilled to hear that thick Russian accent. "Dr. K! How wonderful. I'm so happy."

"This joyful reception I did not anticipate," he replied dryly.

"What are you doing here?"

"Let us say they made me an offer I could not refuse." He placed a box of chocolates on her pink bedspread. "And in this regard, I must report an interesting discovery. My own reactions were that of the prisoner who fears his cell but also longs for it. I was relieved. Grateful. This compels me to assume that all it will take to make the experience truly comforting is starvation and the torture of my genitals."

Phoebe gave a small shudder. If Dr. K was making a joke, it wasn't very funny.

He responded to her shock with an apologetic smile. "Forgive an old man's levity, dear Ms. Golden. I spent nine years in Perm 36. It was a gulag for dissidents. Writers, human rights activists and so forth."

"Oh, my God. Why did they do that to you?"

"The official crime was anti-Soviet activities. You understand that could mean anything the Party did not approve of. They incarcerated a friend of mine for translating George Orwell's books."

"Unbelievable."

"My wife was convicted also. She did not survive."

"I'm so very sorry." Phoebe was appalled that anything her own government did could remind this man even remotely of the totalitarian hell he had left behind. A wave of shame swept through her.

The doctor moved close and took her pulse, sliding a sliver of paper into her palm. Discreetly she transferred it beneath the covers, tucking it into the pocket of her nightshirt. Dr. K listened to her chest and tapped her back a few times, making a show of examining her.

After he lowered his stethoscope, Phoebe said, "Please excuse me for a moment, Doctor," and went into the bathroom, hoping the CIA had the decency not have cameras there as well.

She unfurled the note and read: *We must convince them you are seeing something even if you are not.* Phoebe tore the message into pieces and flushed these down the toilet. Vernell had told her more or less the same thing, insisting that she appear to cooperate no matter how ridiculous the tests. No one wanted the

CIA to think she couldn't help. Why? Puzzled, Phoebe returned to the bedroom. She had expected to be sent home in disgrace the minute they discovered she couldn't spy on terrorists through telepathy. Apparently not.

"Are we going to be working together today, Doctor?" she asked.

He nodded. "With your permission, I would like to use hypnosis. We had pleasing outcomes on the last occasion."

"Good idea." Phoebe forced a smile. "I've tried to explain that I have no control over my dreams, but I don't think they understand."

"Do not agitate yourself. We will achieve the desired results using other methods."

"I hope so," Phoebe said with all the sincerity she could muster. "Wouldn't it be wonderful if we could help catch a terrorist?"

"There is no higher calling than one's duty to the mother country," the psychiatrist returned gravely.

"CALM DOWN, BABY," Rowe switched the phone to her other ear as she stirred scrambled eggs. "I'm sorry I wasn't at home."

"Is everything all right? Is Molly okay?"

"She's a pistol and all's well on the home front. When are you coming back?"

"Don't even ask." Phoebe sounded strained. "Have you spoken with Cara?"

"Not since she went to L.A."

Silence. Then, "Please try calling her. She hasn't been picking up."

"You sound worried."

"I can't really talk right now. I was just thinking about...everything."

"I miss you."

A small sound, almost a whimper. "Me, too."

Rowe felt uneasy. Something wasn't right. "Where are you?"

"Langley," Phoebe said in an undertone.

"The CIA headquarters?" Rowe quit stirring the eggs and took them off the heat.

"Uh huh."

"Homeland Security stuff?"

"Yes."

Understanding now why her lover couldn't talk, Rowe asked, "Are you in any trouble?"

"No. I'm working on something important. That's all."

"Well, don't worry about things here. I'm going to be staying at your place for a few days and I'll—"

"Rowe, I have something to tell you," Phoebe cut in. Speaking in a rapid undertone, she said, "The woman who died in the snow was Becky."

"No. It was Juliet," Rowe said, assuming Phoebe had the two women muddled.

"I saw her," Phoebe insisted. "She was left in the snow with her hands and feet tied. Juliet's father did it. He thought she stole the pearl. It's a long story."

"Are you sure it was Becky?" It didn't compute.

"I know what I saw. Juliet showed her to me."

Rowe struggled to process the information. If it was Becky who had died that night, where was Juliet? Whose body was in Juliet's grave? Before she could ask any more questions, Phoebe said she had to go.

"Can I call you later?" Rowe asked.

"It's better if I call you." Phoebe's voice was husky. "I'm sorry about this."

"I know. Me, too. I love you."

"I love you, too," Phoebe whispered.

Rowe held the phone to her ear for several seconds after it clicked into dull silence. The Black Hawk helicopter made more sense now. The men Phoebe had taken for trainees were obviously some type of commando unit. Whatever Phoebe's work was, it must be much more serious than she had let on. Fear rippled along Rowe's spine. Was her lover involved in the kind of operation the government pretended never happened? If something went wrong and Phoebe didn't come back, would anyone tell her next of kin? Rowe had heard about black ops. Was that what Phoebe really did?

Unnerved, she dialed Cara's cell phone and got no answer. Phoebe had sounded worried about her sister. Why? Had something happened to Cara because of Phoebe's job?

Rowe stared down at the semi-cooked eggs, her appetite gone. She felt like she was standing in quicksand. What was she going to do? Combing her mind for something to latch on to before she tied herself in knots, she switched track to Juliet. Phoebe had sounded so certain about what she saw—Becky, murdered by her employer for the sake of a piece of jewelry. Could Thomas Baker have passed off a dead housemaid as his daughter to the police? Why would he have done such a thing? Had he buried Becky in his daughter's grave? Rowe cast her mind back to the inscription on Juliet's gravestone: *Pray you now, forget and forgive.* Was this Baker's weak attempt at an apology for committing a crime? Had he intended to scare the girl, only to kill her by mistake?

Illogical as it seemed, Rowe found it made sense in a horrible kind of way. "I'm a genius," she announced.

Zoe and Jessie gazed at her like she was all that and more.

"Juliet feels responsible for what happened," she informed her admiring audience. "That's why she's hanging around. She can only rest in peace if the truth comes out."

She wondered what had happened to Juliet in the end. Had she severed all ties with her family and made a new life somewhere? In those days the shame of an illegitimate birth could compel desperate measures. Rowe scrolled through her contact list and dialed Dwayne Schottenheimer. "Any chance you guys can get out here?"

"Uh...I think the ferry's sailing tomorrow."

"Good, it's time we had that chat with the Disappointed Dancer. I think I know what happened back then."

"Excellent," Dwayne said. "Would it be okay if we filmed the event? We're making a television documentary."

"Sure. Why not." She heard a voice in the background urge: *For fuck's sake ask her.*

"Yeah. Also, we were wondering if you'd be willing to do an introduction. We have a script."

"Tell me about this documentary."

"It's called *Hell Hath No Fury.* It's about female ghosts. Like...uh...why there are more of them and what it takes to lay them to rest. We've sold it to PBS."

"I'll be on TV talking about ghosts?" her agent would wet himself. Maybe this was a blessing in disguise. Maybe they could sell her publisher the idea that there was a book tie-in and buy a few precious months for Rowe to come up with the requisite bestseller.

"Rowe?"

"I'm here," she said.

"We can pay you," Dwayne assured her.

THE HAPPIEST PLACE on earth was a smile-required zone heaving with the smell of warm churro and the sighs of exhausted parents. Cara got her picture taken with the Little Mermaid. It looked like she was squeezing one of the sea nymphet's clam-covered breasts. She posted it home to Islesboro, figuring the CIA had better things to do than intercept her mail. She then located that kitsch nirvana, the Enchanted Tiki Garden.

She was ten minutes early for her rendezvous and slid into a spot near some grandparents who were getting right in the spirit of things. She couldn't see anyone who looked like an FBI agent.

Island drums beat, and Jose the animatronic parrot performed his shtick. The termite-infested tiki room of yesteryear had been rebuilt since Cara last saw it, the dusty, decrepit birds replaced with sleek new examples of taxidermy. They still squawked out the same alarmingly perky tune, and Cara found herself singing along silently as if the words had been lodged in some deep cavern of the mind, just waiting for the opportunity to tumble out.

A tourist with a Grecian-for-Men tinted comb-over plunked himself down in the chair next to hers, juggling his camera and a Dole pineapple whip. He was in baggy peach shorts, a loud shirt, sandals, and a panama hat that still had the price tag on it. Several tiny pieces of bloody tissue clung to his chin where he had cut himself shaving, all but proclaiming him as newly separated. No self-respecting woman would send her husband out the door in that condition.

Mr. Not So Cool leaned toward her after a short interval and asked if she could take his photo. Picturing her contact sighing over this transitory bummer, Cara fired off a hurried snap and handed the camera back, trying not to be really obvious about scanning the room.

"Enjoying the show?" the tourist asked.

Cara blinked. This scrawny suburbanite couldn't possibly be her contact. Any loser on the make would try and strike up conversation with a lameass question like that one. If Vernell got out more he'd have known that and dreamed up a more original pick-up line.

Just in case, she replied carefully, "I prefer the Jungle Cruise."

To her complete horror, the tourist asked, "Would you mind showing me the way there?"

This could not be happening, Cara thought. Obviously this moron, recently cut loose by his wife, was trying to hook up with a single female for his Disney adventure. Asking her to take him to the cruise was exactly the kind of response a guy like him would make.

She rose from her chair and said, "Listen, I'm not interested. Okay?"

The tourist took her arm. "I'd really like your help finding that Jungle Cruise."

A built guy turned around and intoned in a deep bass. "Hey, pal, the lady said she doesn't want to know."

Wisely, her would-be date dropped her arm. Cara smiled her thanks at the hunk and moved to the back of the room, wondering if her buff defender was the man she was waiting for. Suave, fit, elegantly dressed in Tommy Bahama gear, he looked like he could be an undercover fed. Relieved to have made the connection, she settled into a spare chair and waited for him to make his move. Instead, to her disgust, the tourist got up a few minutes later and beat a path straight for her.

"Christ," she muttered as he slid into the next chair. "Can't you guys ever take no for an answer?"

He picked off one of the bloody dabs of tissue and said, "Vernell sent me."

Cara groaned. "I am such an idiot."

"Shall we take that walk to the Jungle Cruise?"

She smiled feebly. "My pleasure."

MARVIN PERRY WAS a man accustomed to getting what he wanted. Phoebe could tell by the way his glacial eyes narrowed a fraction when she asked to speak to whoever was in charge.

"What is this about, Ms. Temple?" he enquired softly. The nails of his right hand whitened a little. His fingers weren't resting on the table so much as pressing against it.

"My session with Dr. Karnovich went very well, as you know," she said guardedly. "But I told him only some of what I saw." It wasn't exactly a lie. She had written down the gist of it on toilet tissue and Dr. K had suggested she keep the juiciest details off the session tapes so she had some key information to sell.

"What are you saying?" Perry asked with quiet menace.

Phoebe contemplated the variables. She had never been a successful gambler. Cara said the problem was lack of confidence. Somehow hers communicated itself to card dealers and slot machines. A man like Perry would see straight through her attempts to horse trade for what she wanted most—which was to go home. Yet, despite her uncertainty, she had an edge over him, and they both knew it. He wanted what she had, and she could sense he resented the hell out of her for that.

He had expected her to be a fake, Phoebe realized. That would have been easier for him. His breed preferred not to bring certain ideas to their equations. People like Phoebe were inconvenient because they gave rise to doubts, to the awful possibility that reality was not black and white. In Perry's world, psychics were attention-seeking crazies who had never solved a single case. Belief in life after death was the kind of nonsense that clouded the judgment of Joe Average, making him rush off to church each Sunday just in case God was really watching. The Marvin Perry type needed no such reassurance. Their lives were not plagued by humanity's eternal questions: Why am I here? Is there an afterlife? Will my sins be judged?

For a moment Phoebe felt almost sorry for her handler. What a dilemma she must represent. He badly wanted any information she could provide, but he also wanted her to fail so he could be proved right.

Smiling to herself, she proceeded to both thrill and disturb him, announcing, "Mr. Perry, I know where there's a dirty bomb."

"GET ME ON your next flight to Portland, Maine, please," Cara told the ticket agent at the United counter.

Her heart thudded. Vernell wasn't going to be happy, but so what? She had read her new instructions carefully and had followed them to the letter. Except that when she arrived at the Greyhound bus depot, she simply couldn't do it. Taking a bus to Seattle, then crossing to Vancouver, was the diametric opposite of what she really needed to do. She needed to go home. The compulsion was overwhelming. She had no idea what was happening with Phoebe but she knew they were on the same page and that somehow everything was going to be okay.

She had walked out of the bus station and flagged a cab to LAX. Now she was about to spend the next eight hours flying. To get to Portland, she would have a layover in Chicago. Would the CIA track her down and be waiting for her there? She couldn't fly under her Diane Harris alias. Security regulations meant you had to carry a photo ID matching the name on the ticket.

As the agent slid her driver's license back across the counter, Cara wondered if her name had already triggered a series of alarms. She tried to read the ticket agent's face for signs. He looked robotically cheerful as he handed over a couple of boarding passes and thanked her for choosing United.

Cara made it through security without being arrested and vacillated over whether to kill the next eighty minutes in the Red Carpet Lounge or at the gate. She chose the gate, thinking her chances of making a getaway would be better if she was in a crowded public place. She flopped down into a plastic chair and refrained from laughing hysterically. In the space of a few days her life had spun so completely out of control it was almost funny. And now she had wantonly disregarded FBI instructions because she had a feeling she had to get home. She suspected the urge had filtered from Phoebe's unconscious into her own. But what if it was more than that. What if Phoebe was sending a signal intentionally? I'm losing it, she thought.

Only she must have said it out loud because the woman sitting opposite her lifted her dark head and said, "Hey, Cara," like they were old friends.

"Fran!" Cara knew she was blushing. She struggled for something cool to say. This was the first time she'd ever run into a one night stand after the one night.

Fran read her mind. "I know. Weird isn't it?"

"For you too, huh?" She looked good, Cara thought. Hot, actually. And a little older than Cara had thought at Girlbar. Jeans. Button down white shirt. Nice boots. *Really* nice boots. Cara gestured at them. "Valerie Coe?"

"No one ever knows that!" Fran hitched her jeans up her leg a little. Her black boots were inlaid with midnight blue leather in a naturalistic pattern.

"Outstanding." Cara coveted them instantly. "Is she still taking no new customers?"

"She only has one pair of hands, I guess."

"It's just as well. I don't need another excuse to spend money on boots."

"Tell me about it. Lucky I have a career. I could never buy these if I had to wait tables to finish college."

Cara tried to remember what Fran was studying and came up blank. "Remind me. What's your career?"

"Okay. I realize this will be the end of a beautiful friendship, so for the record I just want to say it was great while it lasted." She grinned. "I'm a trial consultant."

"Is that like Gene Hackman in *Runaway Jury?*"

"Kind of, although I think I'm better looking than him."

"I'd testify to that."

A busty woman two seats along from Fran fired off a frown in their direction. She wore heavy make-up and a fish emblem on her lapel. In her spare time she probably wrote letters to the school board insisting they teach teens abstinence instead of birth control.

"I have a suggestion," Cara said. "Why don't we continue this conversation in the comfort and privacy of the United lounge? I have a spare guest pass. Want to use it?"

"Best idea I've heard all day." Fran got to her feet and picked up Cara's cabin bag, dropping it on top of her own larger wheelie.

"Where are you headed today?" Cara asked as they strolled along the walkway.

"Portland, Maine."

"Me, too."

"That's home for you, right?"

"Almost. I live on Islesboro."

"No shit. That's where I'm staying."

"At this time of year? You're brave."

"My grandmother lives there," Fran said. "She hasn't been well lately, so I thought I'd go spend a few days."

"God, I probably know her," Cara said.

"Dotty Prescott," Fran supplied. "She lives in—"

"Ames Cove. My grandmother used to play bridge with them."

"Oh, my God. Are you Elizabeth Temple's granddaughter?"

"One of them."

"This is too bizarre." Fran stopped walking so she could clap her forehead a couple of times. "I can't believe I never made the connection."

"Why would you?" Cara asked. "We didn't do last names."

"I've seen your photo. My Gran's only been trying to fix me up with you for about five years."

"Wait...are you the granddaughter with the pet armadillo?"

"I liberated him a while back."

Cara burst out laughing. "Every time you're in town, I have to dream up some excuse Dottie hasn't heard before so I can avoid coming to dinner."

"I promise I won't let on." Fran resumed walking.

"I have a better idea," Cara said on an impulse she didn't feel like suppressing. "Let's date. You know...just while you're on the island."

Fran's gleaming hazel eyes found hers in a look that said she hadn't forgotten a minute of their night together. "I'd like that."

"ARE YOU SURE I need to be there?" Phoebe belted herself in as they taxied along the tarmac at Langley Air Force Base.

"Those are my orders."

"And I'm going home afterwards?"

"Yes." Marvin's chill blue eyes registered an emotion she could not identify. Grudging respect? In a tone of mordant resignation, he said, "You're a smart woman, Ms. Temple."

"Please call me Phoebe. I mean, we are spending rather a lot of time together."

A few muscles moved in his face, bringing him the closest to a smile Phoebe had ever seen. "Okay, Phoebe. And I'm Marvin."

Their plane stopped, and the engines gathered power for a

few seconds before propelling them along the runway.
Automatically, Phoebe clutched at her seat arms, relaxing only
after their steep climb was over and they had leveled out.

Marvin returned to his topic. "When did you decide to
ransom your information?"

"I didn't. I decided to go home. But I got the impression that
your bosses had other plans."

"You have to see it from our point of view," Marvin said.
"There's only one of you. Given your capabilities, it is imperative
we prevent other parties gaining access to you."

"What other parties? Aren't you guys *it?*"

"Phoebe, there's not an intelligence agency in the world that
wouldn't trade damned near anything for an asset like you. If
you fell into the wrong hands the consequences could be
unthinkable."

"No one knows about me except you people," Phoebe
reminded him. "I think you're being paranoid."

"We found out about you within twenty-four hours. So we
may not be the only ones."

"You knew before the FBI Director told you?"

Marvin made a scornful sound. "Not much happens in
Quantico that we don't know about. And when you and your
sister appeared in that television footage of Cordwell's
arrest...that was all the confirmation we needed."

It occurred to Phoebe then that people who made an art form
of spying on others could probably find out anything they
wanted if they had the power of the government behind them.
The CIA probably knew everything about her. She would never
have a private life again.

"What if I'm wrong about the bomb?" she asked, picturing a
squad of men breaking down a door and terrorizing an innocent
Arab American family on the strength of something she'd seen
under hypnosis.

"You're not." Marvin said. "We authenticated a few details
before we informed the Department of Defense. But even if you
were, the deal stands."

Phoebe contained her relief. One thing she'd learned, being
around Marvin and his henchmen, was that wearing a poker face
helped. "So, what happens now? We have this meeting, then
what?"

"The Attorney General will issue arrest warrants once he's
satisfied that we have reasonable cause."

"But what if the terrorists try to do something?"

"Your friend Agent Jefferson is setting up the surveillance
operation with Eve Kent as we speak. The suspects aren't going

anywhere without us knowing."

Phoebe was happy they'd involved Vernell and she could imagine Eve's satisfaction with finally having the chance to catch some terrorists in the act. She hadn't expected her session with Dr. Karnovich to yield any real information, but to her astonishment, she was visited by a Muslim woman who had died when the twin towers collapsed. Since then, the woman had hung around a Mosque in Nashville where her son prayed. There she had overheard two men who belonged to an al-Quaeda cell. It seemed as if they were involved in something big. She took Phoebe to a place where they hid materials. These were clearly radioactive.

Marvin had been stupefied when she gave him the address and described the canisters. His hands had actually quivered as he took notes. Even now his face gave away something of his disquiet.

Curious about his role, she asked, "Marvin, what exactly is your job?"

"Right now, my job is to deliver you to the meeting in one piece."

"Thanks for sharing."

Phoebe tried to imagine the man next to her going home to a wife, and children who called him Daddy and stretched their arms out so they could be flipped up into the air. No, she decided, there was just him. If he ever went home it would be to a neat apartment devoid of personality. He would have a flat screen TV and a collection of workout DVDs. Instead of houseplants, his few polished surfaces would feature one of those mind puzzles and maybe a wedding photo of his parents in a modern silver frame—or people meant to look like parents so his real ones were protected. Was Marvin Perry even his name?

"Those men in the Black Hawk that day you came to Islesboro—they weren't FBI trainees, were they?" she asked.

"No, they were Marines from a special ops unit we work with sometimes."

Phoebe almost laughed. Only it wasn't really funny. The CIA had sent in a team of military commandos to pick her up. Were they expecting a fight? Would they have marched her to their chopper at gunpoint?

Appalled, she asked, "Was that supposed to scare me?"

"Not at all." Marvin seemed genuinely surprised. "Our assignment was to provide security."

The Gulfstream began a sharp descent, then hit the runway and braked so hard Phoebe had to brace herself so she wouldn't hit the seat in front of her. It had taken slightly less than twenty minutes to arrive at their destination.

"Where are we?" she asked.

"Andrews Air Force Base."

"Wow. Isn't this where the President's plane takes off?"

"Sometimes."

She peered out the tiny round window. Wait 'til Cara heard about this.

"Our meeting is at the Pentagon," Marvin informed her without inflection.

"The Pentagon?" Phoebe croaked. "I didn't think people like me were allowed there?"

"You have a high security clearance, and we're under DOD orders."

Department of Defense. Phoebe was getting used to the weird acronyms and jargon. "Who's the meeting with?"

"You don't need to know at this time."

"UN-FUCKING-BELIEVABLE." Rowe stared around the shambles of her kitchen.

Every cupboard door was wide open, its contents smashed on the floor. Shards of glass and broken crockery extended from the sink counter to the wall cabinets on the far side. A couple of carving knives were buried in the door. The place looked like a tornado had hit it. Surely this was not Juliet's doing.

Livid, she banged her fist on the counter and yelled, "Enough! This is my house, and I am not being driven out by a ghost who has toddler tantrums."

She kicked a path through the remains of her favorite dinner set and wine glasses, shoved open the rotting back door, and stalked across the frozen yard to the Carriage House. There, among her seldom-used tools, she found a crowbar, a sledgehammer, and some heavy suede gloves. She lugged these items back to the kitchen and set them on the counter, then hauled every freestanding piece of furniture outdoors, leaving only her refrigerator in the room. When she was done, she swept the breakage into a heap and wrapped the fragments in newspaper before filling a couple of huge trash bags with them.

"Okay," she announced to the peeling walls, "you've had your turn. Now it's mine."

She pulled on her gloves, picked up the crowbar, and began systematically ripping out the cabinetry. Half of it was worm eaten, so it fell easily from the nails that held it in place. Fueled by rage, she carried the timber outside, hurling it onto a pile in the middle of the yard.

As the day progressed the pile grew higher until all that was left of her kitchen were bare walls and floorboards. Having a blast, she ripped out the back door and took a sledgehammer to the frame. Something about the way the door was recessed had always struck her as odd, but she had assumed poor building design. The wall on one side was a couple of feet deep, but on the other it was flush with the counter. Maybe there had once been a pantry, she mused, and it had been boarded over to provide a wall for a table and chairs. She scratched away some paint and paper and found bricks and mortar. Whoever had wanted to get rid of the pantry had made sure it was permanent.

Curious, she lifted the sledgehammer and took a swing at the bricks around the doorframe, amazed when several easily caved in, revealing a hollow behind. She was about to open the hole up some more when a voice arrested her.

"Jeez, Louise." Dwayne stepped into the room, his sky blue eyes wide below an advancing tide of carrot hair. Apparently his mother had been too busy to give him a trim recently.

"Dude, what's up?" Earl lowered a couple of steel cases to the floor and sized Rowe up like he was mentally taking measurements for a straitjacket.

"I'm taking this wall out," Rowe said. "I can't wait for the builders to come in March. Whatever is in this shitheap of a room tried to kill me the other night."

"Right," Dwayne drawled in a soothing tone. "Let's just stop for a moment and take a breath. Are you feeling okay?"

An excellent question.

"His mom's a shrink." Earl just threw it out there, rubbing his chin with a pudgy knuckle.

Dwayne manufactured a cough. "Uh...here's what I'm thinking. We take some readings in here and maybe we discuss what you've found out about the Dancer and we try talking to her. Then we can tear the place apart if you still want to."

Earl plucked one of the carving knives from the door. "Class Five, my friends. Maybe even demonic." He opened one of his cases and hauled out a bunch of photographs. Flipping through them, he said, "We caught a bunch of globules on film in here. Take a look."

Rowe studied the example he handed over. Weird circular forms floated all over the picture as if light spots had rained on the camera lens. Amazed, she said, "This is the ghost?"

"Not exactly," Earl answered. "It's energy disturbance. When we get this shit on a photo, we know we're onto something."

"So...uh, what have you got on the Dancer?" Dwayne asked her.

"A friend of mine was over here. She's the sensitive type. She found something in the ballroom."

Rowe led the para-nerds down the hallway, sliding her feet sideways to shift broken glass out of the way. She was thankful she'd left the dogs at Phoebe's.

Earl gleefully helped clear their path. "Man, this entity really can't handle being ignored. I've had girlfriends like that."

Doubting it, Rowe opened the ballroom doors and counted the wood panels until she found Juliet's hiding place. "The Dancer is Juliet Baker. She was pregnant." Rowe removed the panel. "She hid some stuff in here. Her diary, some letters, and a few baby garments."

"She was uh...pregnant when she died?" Dwayne was agog.

"No. She had the baby, and her maid must have taken it to the Baker's neighbor. Mrs. Adams adopted the child."

Dwayne could not suppress his excitement. "Man, you've cracked this wide open. I'm guessing the baby is what it's all about."

"There's something else. I don't think it was Juliet who died in the snow. I think it could have been Becky O'Halloran, the maid. I think Mr. Baker killed the girl, and Juliet blamed herself, and that's why her ghost is hanging around."

Her companions stared at her, not quite willing to suspend disbelief.

"I don't have any direct evidence." Rowe avoided mentioning Phoebe. If the local paranormal community got wind of a psychic who was the real thing, they would never leave her alone.

Earl asked, "Why would Baker whack the maid?"

The pearl story would be a problem to explain without revealing Phoebe, so Rowe said, "He found out about the baby and went off. He killed Becky because she was the one covering everything up. Maybe he was trying to find out where the baby was and she wouldn't tell him."

"The bad-tempered type." Dwayne ran with it. "Violent. Drinking, maybe."

"And it turned out to be the perfect solution to his problems," Rowe said. "He claims the body is Juliet's and sends her off in disgrace to start a new life someplace where no one will ask any questions."

"This is what the Dancer's been trying to tell people." Dwayne seemed convinced.

"Becky's mother suspected," Rowe said. "She must have thought her daughter was dead and that Thomas Baker did it. That's why her letters are full of talk about his sin."

"An exhumation," Earl declared. "That's how we can prove it. There are O'Halloran's all along the Midcoast. We could compare DNA with theirs and with your neighbors. That way we'd know for sure who's buried in there."

"Yeah, except how do we uh...get a court order. We need some actual proof that it could be Becky O'Halloran."

"And we can only get that if we trace Juliet." Rowe sighed. She had already thought this through and knew they were at an impasse. If the dead girl was Becky, that meant Juliet had vanished into thin air.

They shared a despondent silence for a few moments.

Eventually Dwayne broke ranks, his expression brooding. "How do we explain the activity in the kitchen? Did he uh...kill Becky there? If he did, there could be blood. That would prove a crime had occurred, and if they matched the blood to O'Halloran DNA, we could have a case."

Rowe pictured the maid as Phoebe had described her, tied up and left to die in the snow. How did that fit with Phoebe's other vision of blood on the kitchen floor and someone chasing her out of the house? Did Baker attack Becky in the kitchen? Did he run outdoors after her and tie her up, leaving her to freeze to death so it would look like an accident? Where was Juliet when all of this happened?

She went through Phoebe's account once more in her mind and was suddenly blinded by the obvious. She turned to Earl. "That recording you made in the kitchen. The voice that yells *Run...* " She got to her feet and the guys hastily followed suit. "I think I know what happened in there."

They hurried along the hall to the kitchen. Rowe pointed at the hole in the brick façade. "There's a cavity behind that wall. Let's open it up."

Her companions gave her strange looks, but who were they to question Rowe Devlin, horror queen? Carefully they tapped out brick after brick until they had opened up a hole large enough to admit their heads.

Rowe shone her flashlight into the cavity and felt the air flee her lungs. A mummified woman lay in a fetal position on the floor, enshrouded in a dusty nightgown. "Juliet," she said.

"SHE PROBABLY LIVED for a few days after she was walled in," the Medical Examiner said. "Actual cause of death is not apparent at this time."

One of the detectives approached Rowe, a compact young woman with sparrow brown hair and bright dark eyes. "We'll need to bring a crime scene team in, Ms. Devlin. I'm sorry for the inconvenience."

"No problem." Rowe was having trouble holding back tears. Surprised by the strength of her emotions, she said, "If you don't mind, I'm going to step outside."

"Go right ahead. Would you like a female officer with you?"

"No. I'll be fine, thanks. I just need some fresh air."

She joined Dwayne and Earl on the front steps. They'd scraped off the ice and had laid out some broken cabinet planks from the kitchen. Rowe sat on one of these a step higher than the ghostbusters. No one said a word. They stared out at the snow, foggy breaths floating in wreaths around their heads.

A murderer had lived in her house, Rowe thought, and his crimes had lived after him. But he had left a loose end. His daughter's baby had survived and had borne children. Now, generations later one of her descendents had unlocked his secret. If there was such a thing as karma, this sure qualified.

She wondered what Phoebe was going to say. She owed her lover an apology, she decided, for ever doubting her. How strange it must be to live with knowledge most people would doubt. Was her gift a blessing or a curse?

A rapid whooping sound invaded her reflections and Rowe lifted her head, certain the sound could mean only one thing. She stood up, joy and hope stealing her breath. Like a giant mechanical wasp, a black helicopter descended onto the meadow, churning the snow into clouds.

"Awesome," Dwayne breathed.

Earl shoved him. "Dude. It's the government. I told you they were watching us."

He and Dwayne got to their feet and gazed slack-jawed as the chopper landed and the rotors slowed to a lethargic whoop.

"The fucking thing is unmarked." Earl declared in a hunted tone. "You know what that means. We're talking black ops. They're gonna close us down."

Dwayne grabbed his pal's arm. "We gotta get out of here."

"No way, man. Shot while trying to flee. Fuck that." He turned to Rowe. "You're a witness. Whatever goes down here, you need to tell the world."

"Settle, guys." Rowe's heart raced. "They're not interested in you." She craned, trying to see into the dark recess beyond the chopper's open door.

Several dark figures jumped out, armed to the teeth like last time. One of them turned to assist a smaller female figure. As they moved away from the dangerous blades, the wind caught at the woman's long raven hair and she reached up to stop her woolen hat from being blown off.

Rowe waved but she wasn't sure if Phoebe saw her, having been hemmed in by her hulking companions. The last man off the chopper was not in commando gear, but an overcoat and dark glasses. He strode out into the open and took a long look around. The cop cars must have attracted his attention because he signaled his men, and one of them set off in a shuffling run across the meadow toward Rowe and her apprehensive buddies.

When he reached the bottom of the steps, he queried, "Which one of you is Rowe Devlin?"

"Guilty." Rowe said.

"Would you come with me please, ma'am?"

Stepping between Rowe and the visitor with the machine gun, Dwayne stammered, "If you...uh...want to take her, you have to get through me first."

"Are you fucking crazy?" Earl hissed.

The commando slowly removed his dark glasses. In a tone that was borderline parental, he informed Dwayne, "This doesn't concern you, son. But since we're having a conversation, have you ever thought about a career in the military?"

Dwayne flushed almost as red as his hair. "Uh...not really."

"Well your country needs young men with courage, such as yourself." Withdrawing a business card from somewhere in his body armor, the commando placed it in Dwayne's hand. "This is the name of a recruiting officer. Tell him Captain Tony Gerhardt sent you."

"Yes, sir." Dwayne seemed overwhelmed.

The captain clapped him on the shoulder. "I once had a verbal affliction myself. Getting rid of it is just another debt I owe this man's army. Think about it, son."

"I will uh...sir. Thank you, sir." Dwayne seemed like a duck in water, a salute right around the corner.

Earl gave him an incredulous look.

"And son..." The captain wasn't quite done. "Less cologne."

The two young males watched with worried expressions as Rowe pulled up her hood and set off toward the chopper with her gun-toting escort. They had barely made it twenty paces when Phoebe broke from the pack and struggled through the snow toward her, arms outstretched.

Rowe swung her off the ground just like in the cheesy commercials and kissed her without regard to the flurry of armed men descending on them. "I love you baby," she said.

"I adore you." Phoebe held her like she would never let go. "Take me home."

Chapter
Seventeen

A SNOWPLOUGH LED the funeral procession, a crushed mailbox clinging to the blade like an oversized tuna can. This struck Rowe as a uniquely Maine touch. Likewise the organ-pipes of ice suspended from the cliffs and the opaline reflections on the pale winter sea. Distant islands and vessels seemed woven of the same liquid material, shimmering mirage-like on the limitless horizon.

A startling number of vehicles joined the cortege as they proceeded along the eighty mile route to the Evergreen cemetery in Portland. Rowe drove her Lexus, with Phoebe in the back seat next to one of the androids the CIA insisted on supplying. His colleague was glued to her back bumper in a black Ford with extremely dark tinted windows. Very funereal. In front of her, the hearse carried Juliet in her elegant blond oak coffin, and trailing behind were Dwayne and Earl, who had tied lavish black bows to the door handles of Dwayne's decrepit car.

Several members of the MPRA had muscled in on the highly publicized proceedings. They were followed by the entire O'Halloran clan, now local celebrities after staging a mock trial for Thomas Baker and hanging him in effigy, complete with the sack over his head, and a preacher reading from Leviticus.

The press had shown up in force for the church service in Camden and already had their cameras set up around the gravesite when the procession arrived. There was nothing else happening on the Midcoast at this time of year, other than motor vehicle accidents and the occasional pothead protest outside the Rockland town hall.

The remarkable weather wouldn't hold, Rowe decided, as they left their cars at the frozen duck pond and straggled along a sloping serpentine path to Juliet's grave. For now, the sky was a limpid blue and the snow glittered crystalline white in the early afternoon sun. It was too soon for spring, and hard to believe there would ever be a summer, but today a hint of thaw lingered in the air. Rowe tightened her grip on Phoebe's hand and wondered how she could have imagined herself alive before this woman upended her world.

As the funeral directors transported the coffin to the grave, she felt strangely moved, as if she had known Juliet and cared for her. After some angst, they had decided to bury her in the existing plot. The headstone had been ripped up when Becky O'Halloran's body was exhumed, and Phoebe had settled on a more fitting monument, which included the names of Juliet's descendents. Cara thought she'd gone a little overboard, with the angel leaning against the side of the tall headstone, a tiny fawn curled at her feet. But Rowe had made no attempt to talk her out of it. Juliet's diary was littered with sketches of deer. Her new epitaph had also been drawn from her personal notes:

When I look out into God's infinity,
and know I am also His work, my soul rejoices.

"I hope she likes it," Phoebe whispered in Rowe's ear.

"I'm sure she will."

"The service was nice. I liked the Emily Dickinson reading you chose."

"I hope Cara wasn't disappointed." Phoebe's twin had suggested some lyrics from a Patty Smith song, but Rowe thought she should run with something more in step with Juliet's period.

"She didn't mind." A wistful note entered Phoebe's voice. "I wish she would talk to me."

"I thought things were better between you."

"They are, but she's...closed me out. I can't explain it. I even wrote that letter to Bev. But she didn't care."

Rowe had sensed Cara's distance, too. Since her return from L.A., she'd been friendly and charming. And she had stopped hitting on Rowe, thankfully. But she seemed to be brooding. Even escalating DVD sales for her work didn't thrill her. The one thing that perked her up was a phone message last week from someone called Fran. This had prompted her immediate departure from the house, and she didn't show up again for several days. Since then, she'd been on her cell phone for hours talking to the mystery woman, but she refused to answer any questions about her.

Phoebe was beside herself with curiosity, and her nose was out of joint. She was convinced Cara had a girlfriend. A real one, not a sex toy like most of them. It bothered her endlessly that the girlfriend must live in the area but Cara had not introduced her.

Rowe cast a glance around the mourners. Cara had brought her own car and had somehow ended up miles back in the procession after they left Camden. Spotting a dark head, Rowe waved and Cara emerged from the O'Halloran throng with an athletic young woman at her side.

Rowe elbowed Phoebe gently. "I have a feeling your sister wants you to meet someone."

She heard a soft, quick breath and Phoebe said, "Wow. She never brings anyone home."

Rowe lowered her gaze to the piled up snow around the yawning grave. "We're not exactly home."

"You know what I mean. I never meet any of them. Oh, God. I hope she likes me."

"Don't stare, baby."

Phoebe tucked her arm into Rowe's and said urgently, "Shall I invite her for dinner?"

"How about we leave that for Cara to do in her own time?"

Phoebe beamed. "If she's met someone local, she won't want to leave."

Rowe sighed. She couldn't blame Cara for wanting to make her own life somewhere else. It seemed inevitable, now that Phoebe was settling down and wouldn't need so much from her.

"She looks friendly," Phoebe murmured.

Rowe waited for Cara's companion to spot Phoebe and react like a fool. Instead the woman broke into a broad, genuine smile.

"Hey, you must be Phoebe," she said. "I'm Fran. Cara says you play mahjong with my grandma, Dotty Prescott."

"You're not the granddaughter who tampers with the cogs of justice?"

"At your service," Fran said.

Cara looked on like butter wouldn't melt. "We're dating," she said. "Nothing serious. Just having some fun while Fran's in town."

Startled that Cara would announce this in front of her girlfriend, Rowe shook Fran's hand and said, "I'm Rowe. Phoebe's partner. How long are here for?"

"Until Cara's done with me, I guess." She seemed good-humored about Cara's admission, even self-satisfied.

Rowe intercepted a disconcerted stare from Phoebe and said, "Well it's great to meet you, Fran. I hope we'll see some more of you."

The priest undid his greatcoat so that everyone could see he was the guy in charge and declared in a voice too squeaky for his impressive robes, "We gather today to say goodbye and to thank God for a life."

Rowe bent her head like everyone else. Only she thanked God she had picked the right twin.

"ARE YOU SERIOUS? They found a dirty bomb exactly where you saw it?"

"I'm not supposed to tell anyone," Phoebe said. "But I don't want to have to hide half my life from you."

Rowe gazed down at the head on her shoulder. "I can keep my mouth shut."

"I know." Phoebe tilted her head and found Rowe's lips, planting a delicate kiss. Her hair spilled in a dark wave across the bedding. Moonlight played across her features. Bright, liquid eyes held Rowe's. "I love you."

"I love you, too. I nearly died without you."

Phoebe was still upset over that incident. She'd been mortified when Rowe told her what had happened that night, and seemed to blame herself for not warning Rowe to stay away from the cottage. Juliet's ghost hadn't meant her any harm. Rowe understood that, now. She had simply wanted to destroy the kitchen so her body would be found and finally laid to rest.

Not wanting Phoebe to dwell on her imagined shortcomings, Rowe changed tack. "Are those CIA gorillas going to hang around here forever?"

"That's the compromise. I get to live at home, and I get to work for Vernell for half my hours, but I have to have 'round the clock security." A note of anxiety entered Phoebe's voice. "Can you stand it?"

"So long as they don't sleep in the bedroom."

"Cara says she's going to talk some sense into Marvin Perry."

Rowe called to mind that serene hired-killer face and said, "I don't think much of her chances."

"She says she might buy that place she saw in L.A." Phoebe's tone was burdened with emotion.

"I have a better idea." Rowe rolled onto her side and took Phoebe's face in her hands, knowing what it meant to her to have her twin close by. "Why don't you move into the cottage with me. Cara can have keep right on living here, and you and she can walk across the meadow whenever you want to see one another."

"Really? You're okay about living there...after everything that happened?"

Rowe thought about it. Somehow it seemed fitting that Juliet's great-great-granddaughter should live in Dark Harbor Cottage. Juliet had reached out to Phoebe, needing to free herself

of guilt and sorrow. There was no escaping that the cottage had
been the scene of terrible suffering. But Rowe had a sense that
bringing happiness to its four walls would be part of setting
Juliet free. Already when she walked through the front door, the
air seemed lighter.

"I want to live there with you, darling," she told Phoebe.

Her lover smiled. "We'll build a beautiful garden where the
kitchen was, so there's nothing left of that...ugliness." A tear
spilled onto her cheek, glistening in the silvery light. "I can't
believe he did that to his own daughter?"

"I know."

Rowe contemplated the horrible facts the forensic
pathologist had reported. Juliet had been stabbed at least three
times but had not died of her wounds. In pain and probably
feverish with infection, she had died of dehydration and cold
after days spent beating and scratching on the walls of her tomb.
Her fingernails were broken and the bones of her hands
damaged. She had bound her wounds by tearing strips from the
nightgown she was wearing. These makeshift bandages were
found with her remains, stained with blood from which her DNA
had been sampled and matched to that of the twins.

From her own research, Rowe had learned that Thomas
Baker returned to New York with his invalid wife as soon as the
snow melted. He had kept the cottage closed up for almost
twenty years. It was sold when he lost most of his money in the
crash of 1929. None of the subsequent owners lived there very
long, and eventually the cottage was rented out as a summer
home for many years. Its resident ghost was considered a
drawcard by the leasing agents.

"Poor Juliet," Phoebe toyed with the pearl at her throat. She
wore it to bed of late, telling Rowe she wanted Juliet to know she
was remembered. "She told me what happened."

Rowe had suspected as much, but she'd figured Phoebe
would tell her when she was ready. "Was that what woke you up
a few nights ago?"

"Yes. It was horrible."

"I'm sorry, baby. We don't have to talk about it—"

"No. I want to. She heard them in the kitchen and came
downstairs. Her father was beating Becky. He caught her
burning the sheets from the birth. The cook's husband told on
them after Becky rejected his advances."

Rowe could just imagine how that played out. A senior
servant foolishly tells her husband the girls' secret. This asshole
sees an opportunity for himself and when he's knocked back, he
takes his revenge, at the same time currying favor with the

master of the house. The same story must have played itself out time and again in those days, and it was always the woman who bore the consequences.

Becky loved Juliet, Rowe decided — maybe she was even *in love* with her mistress. She had tried to protect her in every way she could. With increasing sorrow, she listened as Phoebe described the way the murders went down. Juliet, weak from childbirth, had tried to drag her father off Becky. She located a carving knife and ordered him to leave the maid alone.

"Becky told the cook about the pearl, you see," Phoebe said. "She didn't want anyone thinking Juliet abandoned her baby with nothing."

"Don't tell me." It was all falling into place — another story of men's greed, lust and amorality. "The cook's husband told Baker a different story."

"Juliet said her father had a foul temper. Mrs. Baker was an invalid because he threw her down a flight of stairs one day."

Rowe sighed. "No wonder she was terrified of him finding out she was pregnant."

"He wrestled with her," Phoebe said. "That was when Juliet screamed for Becky to run."

The scream Phoebe had heard the day she ran from the kitchen and gave Rowe her black eye. It all made sense now.

"In the end he got a hold of the knife and stabbed her. Then he left her bleeding on the kitchen floor and went after Becky." Phoebe wiped a hand across her eyes. Shoulders shaking, she said, "Juliet dragged herself into the pantry to hide and after a while he came back. He was raving about how Becky would tell him what he wanted to know. He emptied the provisions from the pantry and nailed boards over it. By the time he was done, it was almost dawn, and Becky was dead."

"So he went out and untied her hands and feet," Rowe said numbly. She knew the rest. "He made it look like an accident."

"He actually had the presence of mind to dress her in one of Juliet's gowns and tie a lace cap over her head." Phoebe's voice dripped bitter contempt. "When the doctor arrived he played the grieving father. He sent the servants home, supposedly for a day of mourning, and personally bricked up the pantry."

Rowe could hardly bear to imagine. "I hope he rots in hell."

"I'm not sure if there is a hell," Phoebe whispered.

"Don't go looking, okay?"

She felt Phoebe smile. "Okay."

"Thank you for telling me what happened."

Phoebe cuddled closer, her wet eyelashes painting Rowe's cheek. After some time had passed, she murmured, "Juliet's still here. I'm not sure why."

"The banishment didn't work?" Rowe was dismayed. After the funeral, they'd performed cleansing rituals and summoned Juliet. They invited her to let go and rest in peace, the CIA guys impassively looking on like they saw the paranormal every day.

"Don't worry," Phoebe said drowsily. "If she gets antsy, I'll talk to her. I think she likes me."

My lover has friends on the other side, Rowe thought. And she's a top secret CIA asset with security guards who have instructions to kill anyone who lays a hand on her. At least, that's how it seemed from the paranoid way they behaved. Then there was Marvin Perry. They didn't come any scarier than that guy. And he and Vernell were having some kind of pissing contest over who would get to play with Phoebe next. It was stranger than fiction.

Rowe stroked Phoebe's hair and kissed her forehead, feeling her limbs grow heavy as she sank into sleep. "I love you, baby," she whispered, overwhelmed with her good fortune.

Life had taken a very odd turn, but Rowe knew in her bones she was finally on the right track again. Maybe Phoebe was right—maybe she had never left it and everything had happened for a reason. It had taken a lot of disappointment and disillusion to drive her from Manhattan to Maine. Had she stayed where she was, licking her self-inflicted wounds, she would never have met Phoebe.

She listened to the soft sounds of the house and discerned that one of them was the sound of whichever CIA man had pulled the graveyard shift. He was standing at the bedroom door, she realized, disconcerted. Muffled voices penetrated the solid wood, then a female figure entered the room.

"Cara." Rowe whispered in surprise.

Phoebe's twin crept over to the bed. "Is she asleep?"

"I think so. Is something wrong?"

She dawdled around the bed to Rowe. "I couldn't sleep. There's something I want to say." She hesitated. "If you'd prefer, we can talk tomorrow."

Rowe felt awkward, detecting an uncharacteristic vulnerability in Cara. Taking a guess at what was troubling her, she said. "Cara, I can't ever take your place and I'm not trying to."

Cara wrapped her robe more firmly around her, and hugged herself against the cold. "Am I that obvious?"

"I know this isn't easy for either of you. Phoebe's terrified you're going to leave."

She glanced down at her lover, concerned they might have

woken her. But Phoebe was serenely unawares. It always amazed Rowe how quickly and deeply sleep claimed her. Phoebe had said it was like leaving one world and entering another and that sometimes she was afraid she wouldn't find her way back.

"I don't want to leave," Cara said. "But I want to be fair to the two of you. If I'm here, I think things could get kind of crowded. Don't you?" She reached across Rowe and stroked her sister's hair. "It's hard to explain...sometimes I feel like we can never be completely ourselves. It's like I don't know where she begins and I end."

"I'm not sure you can fight that," Rowe said. "Please don't try on my account."

Cara tilted her head slightly to one side and stroked her bottom lip with a finger. The unconscious gesture jolted Rowe. Phoebe did exactly the same thing when she was struggling with a thought.

"You're a rarity," Cara said. "Most women would be jealous. Christ, I would."

Rowe took careful measure of herself. Was she being honest with herself suggesting Cara stay? Or was she being noble, trying to give Phoebe what she wanted without regard to her own feelings? She couldn't afford to kid herself about this important issue, only to be filled with resentment after the fact.

"I feel incredibly lucky to have found Phoebe," she said with increasing confidence in her own perspective. "I love her. I love who she is. And you are so profoundly a part of her, that to deny it — to try and carve you away — would harm her. It would change her, and I couldn't bear that. Do you see?"

"Yes. I see exactly." Cara smiled gravely and padded across to the window. She drew the curtains back and gazed out into the night. Cast in silhouette by the silver radiance of the moon, she stood still as a sylph watching her own reflection in a pool.

That's how it was for them, Rowe mused. The Temple twins were mirror images. In order to see herself, each would have to find some way to look beyond her twin. Denying their bond was not the answer.

"Cara," she called softly. "Come sleep with your sister."

For a few fraught seconds Cara stared at Rowe, then, without a word, she closed the curtains and crossed to Phoebe's side of the bed, slipping beneath the covers to lie next to her. Phoebe stirred slightly and Rowe felt one of her arms wrap around her twin's middle.

It struck her then that love is a tree with complex roots and boughs broad enough to shelter many. Its fruit is diverse, yet each draws its nourishment from the same source. None steals from another. Phoebe's love for Rowe did not demand the sacrifice of her love for Cara, and Rowe would never ask it. She kissed the top of her darling's head and smiled to herself.

A few months ago she would have found this situation very weird. Even now, if she really thought about it... Yep. It was weird all right. She was in bed with twins, and was madly in love with one of them, having occasionally lusted after the other. Since moving to Maine, most of her fondly-held beliefs about life, love and the universe had gone right out the door. If all this could happen in a matter of weeks who knew what the future might hold? Anything seemed possible.

Rowe made herself a promise. Tomorrow, she would wake up and begin a new life and a new novel. It was time.

THE END

The Heartstoppers Series

Jennifer Fulton's new Heartstoppers Series are hybrid thriller romances with a strong mystery or paranormal component. You can read the series in any order as each is a stand alone story. Tightly woven plots, engaging romance, and delicious sex scenes make these some of the most compelling page-turners in lesbian fiction.

Dark Valentine
(Book II in the Heartstoppers Series)
by Jennifer Fulton

Rhianna Lamb avoided one night stands. But who could resist sexy, charming Jules. They hooked up in a bar, first names only, not exactly Rhianna's style but she needed to escape her life for a few hours. Come tomorrow, she would take the witness stand against Werner Brigham, the man who had stalked and kidnapped her a year earlier. She can't believe it when she walks into the courtroom the next morning and finds herself staring at the woman she just slept with – none other than Julia Valiant, Brigham's hotshot defense attorney. Worse still, the woman whose touch she remembers so well, brutally cross-examines her and demolishes the prosecution's case.

Jules didn't earn her attack dog reputation by soft-peddling witnesses, but she suffers pangs over Rhianna. She is oddly drawn to this woman, a rare occurrence in her life, and by the time the jury returns its verdict, she is determined to see her again. Her chances don't look good when Werner Brigham is acquitted. Worse still, her client seems to think he can return to his old habits, this time with deadly intent. Danger and desire fuel a high stakes cat and mouse game, Jules has to win. But even if she does, will Rhianna ever forgive her?

Available Spring 2007

FORTHCOMING TITLES

published by
Yellow Rose Books

Snow Moon Rising

by Lori L. Lake

Mischka Gallo, a proud Roma woman, knows horses, dancing, and travel. Every day since her birth, she and her extended family have been on the road in their *vardo* wagons meandering mostly through Poland and eastern Germany. She learned early to ignore the taunts and insults of all those who call her people "Gypsies" and do not understand their close-knit society and way of life.

Pauline "Pippi" Stanek has lived a settled life in a small German town along the eastern border of Poland and Germany. In her mid-teens, she meets Mischka and her family through her brother, Emil Stanek, a World War I soldier who went AWOL and was adopted by Mischka's troupe. Mischka and Pippi become fast friends, and they keep in touch over the years. But then the Second World War heats up, and all of Europe is in turmoil. Men are conscripted into the Axis or the Allied armies, "undesirables" are turned over to slave labor camps, and with every day that passes, the danger for Mischka, Emil, and their families increases. The Nazi forces will not stop until they've rounded up and destroyed every Gypsy, Jew, dissident, and homosexual.

On the run and separated from her family, Mischka can hardly comprehend the obstacles that face her. When she is captured, she must use all her wits just to stay alive. Can Mischka survive through the hell of the war in Europe and find her family?

In a world beset by war, two women on either side of the conflagration breach the divide — and save one another. *Snow Moon Rising* is a stunning novel of two women's enduring love and friendship across family, clan, and cultural barriers. It's a novel of desperation and honor, hope and fear at a time when the world was split into a million pieces.

OTHER JENNIFER FULTON TITLES

published by
Yellow Rose Books

MOON ISLAND SERIES

Passion Bay – Two women from opposite ends of the earth meet in paradise. The best-selling love story of Cody Stanton and Annabel Worth, the owners of Moon Island.

Saving Grace – In this steamy second title in the series, Scientist Grace Ramsay seduces novice, Dawn Beaumont with unexpected consequences. Meantime Cody and Annabel face a live-changing catastrophe.

The Sacred Shore – Olivia Pearce promised herself never to love again, but Merris Randall thinks she can change her mind about that. Themes of love, loss, hope and renewal drive one of Fulton's most emotional stories.

A Guarded Heart – Burned out FBI Agent, Pat Roussel takes a private security gig guarding soap star Lauren Douglas. It's meant to be easy money, but Lauren is not at all what she was expecting.

Other YELLOW ROSE Publications

Georgia Beers	Turning The Page	1-930928-51-3	$ 16.99
Georgia Beers	Thy Neighbor's Wife	1-932300-15-5	$ 13.95
Carrie Brennan	Curve	1-932300-41-4	$ 16.95
Carrie Carr	Destiny's Bridge	1-932300-11-2	$ 13.95
Carrie Carr	Faith's Crossing	1-932300-12-0	$ 13.95
Carrie Carr	Hope's Path	1-932300-40-6	$ 17.95
Carrie Carr	Love's Journey	1-930928-67-X	$ 18.99
Carrie Carr	Strength of the Heart	1-930928-75-0	$17.95
Jessica Casavant	Twist of Fate	1-932300-07-4	$ 12.95
Jessica Casavant	Walking Wounded	1-932300-20-1	$ 13.95
Jessica Casavant	Imperfect Past	1-932300-34-1	$ 16.95
Jennifer Fulton	Passion Bay	1-932300-25-2	$ 14.95
Jennifer Fulton	Saving Grace	1-932300-26-0	$ 15.95
Jennifer Fulton	The Sacred Shore	1-932300-35-X	$ 15.95
Jennifer Fulton	A Guarded Heart	1-932300-37-6	$ 16.95
Anna Furtado	The Heart's Desire	1-932300-32-5	$ 15.95
Gabrielle Goldsby	The Caretaker's Daughter	1-932300-18-X	$ 15.95
Melissa Good	Terrors of the High Seas	1-932300-45-7	$ 21.95
Maya Indigal	Until Soon	1-932300-31-7	$ 19.95
Lori L. Lake	Different Dress	1-932300-08-2	$ 19.95
Lori L. Lake	Ricochet In Time	1-932300-17-1	$ 18.95
Meghan O'Brien	Infinite Loop	1-932300-42-2	$ 18.95
Sharon Smith	Into The Dark	1-932300-38-4	$ 17.95
Cate Swannell	Heart's Passage	1-932300-09-0	$ 17.95
Cate Swannell	No Ocean Deep	1-932300-36-8	$ 18.95
L. A. Tucker	The Light Fantastic	1-932300-14-7	$ 24.95

About the Author:

Jennifer Fulton lives in the shadow of the Rocky Mountains with her partner and animal companions. Her vice of choice is writing, however she is also devoted to her wonderful daughter, and her hobbies — fly fishing, cinema, and fine cooking. Jennifer started writing stories almost as soon as she could read them, and never stopped. Under pen names Jennifer Fulton and Rose Beecham, she has published eleven lesbian novels and a handful of short stories.

Printed in the United States
51323LVS00003B/237